MW01103401

A Touch of Strange

AMAZING TALES OF THE COAST

Dick Hammond

ILLUSTRATED BY
Alistair Anderson

Harbour Publishing

Published by
HARBOUR PUBLISHING
P.O. Box 219
Madeira Park, BC
Canada V0N 2H0
www.harbourpublishing.com

Cover, page design and composition by Arifin A. Graham, Alaris Design
Front cover and author photos by Jo Hammond. Sunset photo was taken in
the Pasley Island group in Howe Sound superimposed on the lightning photo
which was taken during a storm off Soames Point, near Gibsons.

Printed in Canada

Harbour Publishing acknowledges the financial support of the Government of
Canada through the Book Publishing Industry Development Program (BPIDP)
and the Canada Council for the Arts, and the Province of British Columbia
through the British Columbia Arts Council, for its publishing activities.

THE CANADA COUNCIL | LE CONSEIL DES ARTS
FOR THE ARTS | DU CANADA
SINCE 1957 | DEPUIS 1957

NATIONAL LIBRARY OF CANADA
CATALOGUING IN PUBLICATION DATA

Hammond, Dick, 1929–
    A touch of strange
    ISBN 1-55017-270-0

    1. Tales—British Columbia—Pacific Coast. I. Title.
PS8565.A5645T68 2001   398.2'09711'1   C2001-910909-1
PR9199.3.H3244T68 2001

This book was printed using vegetable-based inks on acid-free paper containing
100% recycled, post-consumer fibre and was processed without using chlorine.
This 100% old-growth-free paper was provided by New Leaf Papers.

To my wife Josephine, who took time from her own writing
to transcribe mine. Without her ~~nagging~~ encouragement,
this book would have been longer in the making.
Her suggestions were always useful.

And to son Erik and daughter Patricia,
whose comments, while few, were trenchant.

"...for it is difficult to say neither too little or too much; and even moderation is apt not to give the impression of truthfulness.

The friend of the dead who knows the facts is likely to think that the words of the speaker fall short of his knowledge... Another who is not so well informed, when he hears of anything which surpasses his own powers, will be envious and will suspect exaggeration. Mankind are tolerant of the praises of others so long as each hearer thinks that he can do as well or nearly as well himself; but when the speaker rises above him, jealousy is aroused and he begins to be incredulous."

—PERICLES
(from the Oration over the Athenian dead of the first campaign)

Contents

Preface

This is the last book in the trilogy of my father's stories.

I heard these stories many times over a span of forty years. Some of them he told many times, but a few of them only to me, and then somewhat reluctantly. Toward the end of his life he went over most of them with me, very carefully and in great detail.

I'm afraid I forgot much of the detail, especially names, dates and places, but the events are as he told them, with one notable exception: I couldn't hope to reproduce in print the way in which he told them. For Father, like other good tale-spinners I've heard, lived his stories. He acted them out, complete with gesticulations, laughter, explanations, depictions of characters, and such running comments as occurred to him. He imitated the ways his characters spoke, and made valiant if inaccurate attempts at their accents, be they English, Irish, French or German. I couldn't reproduce this, nor do I think it would be appropriate in print.

On the other hand, it would be most inappropriate to subject his stories to the constraints of conventional short story form. Therefore, I've added some brief comments and explanations when I felt the need. I've also used such devices as varying the point of view and ranging somewhat freely between the first, second and third person. Most especially, I've let Father comment on his own stories, in his own way, when memory allows, for these instances are direct quotes. I am sure he would have approved, for he well knew the difference between books and speech.

And finally, it is my sincere wish, as it would have been his, that the stories give you pleasure.

—DICK HAMMOND

The Man Himself

The reader may wish to know something of this man who will be their guide through most of these stories. Here he is, as I knew him.

In appearance, rather unimpressive. Weight about one-sixty, lighter as he grew older. Height, five feet, ten and a half inches. Blue eyes, fair hair, alert gaze. Moved without apparent effort. Heavy forearms, thick wrists, large fingers. Very strange fingernails: thick, curved on backs, seemingly halfway between nails and claws.

Sincerely courteous, especially to women (much appreciated in that time and place!). Not patient with any sort of pretension. Perhaps most notable, a puckish sense of humour, often a cause of distress to his wife. For example:

It was common in those days to have guests at supper. They might be friends of friends, seldom-seen relatives, even strangers passing by. Various sorts, some of them a bit stuffy, or trying—perhaps too hard—to be polite. He had a favourite story for this sort of guest. At the first convenient moment, he would trot it out.

"Say, did you ever happen to hear the story about the Irishman and the English waiter?"

Of course they never had, and would in any case be too polite to say so.

At this point my mother, for whom propriety was a form of religion, would protest, "Hal! You're not going to tell that story? Not at the dinner table!"

It was for form's sake. She knew he would not be stopped.

"What's wrong with it?" (innocently). "It's a good story."

I

"Well, I don't think it's a good story, and certainly not while we're eating."

By now the guests would be curious; they would attempt to placate her—not possible, and coax him—not necessary.

"Well, it seems that Paddy" (generic name in those days for Irishmen in jokes) "has come into a bit of money. The first thing he decides to do is to have a meal in a posh restaurant. So he asks a cab driver to take him to the fanciest restaurant in town, and in he goes. And, it's posh, all right—there's more forks and spoons on the table than Paddy has in his whole kitchen. So he sits down and picks up the menu. After a while, the waiter comes over to the table. He's English, and he's as high-nosed as only a waiter in an expensive eating place can be." (Father's "English" accent is not something I can convey. Just imagine to yourself a supremely haughty English waiter, who strongly disapproves of his client.)

"He stares at a spot about a foot above Paddy's head, and asks, 'Do you wish to order, sir?' Now, the only word on the menu that Paddy knows is 'oysters,' so he says, 'I'll just start off with a plate of these *oysters in the shell*, my good man.' You see, it takes more than a snooty waiter to bother an Irishman like Paddy.

"So off the waiter goes, and back he comes with a plate of raw oysters on their shell, and he leaves Paddy to go to it. After a while, he comes back again, but the oysters are all still there, and Paddy is frowning a bit. So he asks, 'Is there something wrong, sir?'

"'Well,' says Paddy, 'it's just that I can't figure out how to eat these things.'

"The waiter can't believe what he's hearing. 'Cawn't eat a raw oyster? Why, there's nothing easier in the world.'

"'Show me,' says Paddy.

"So the waiter picks up a shell from the plate, sucks the oyster out, swallows, puts down the shell. 'See,' he says, 'nothing easier.'

"'Hm,' says Paddy. 'Do it again.'

"So the waiter does, but Paddy's still not satisfied, and pretty soon, all the oysters are gone. The waiter says, grinning a little at getting a free meal of oysters from this hayseed, 'I don't see what your problem is. They slide down with no trouble at all.'

"'Oh,' says Paddy, 'they slide down fine. I've had them down two or three times. What I want to know is, how do you keep them down?'"

(Well, I thought it was funny when I was young!)

This story usually had one of two quite different effects. There would be a strained silence, and an obvious attempt to change the subject by either my mother or the guests. The ensuing evening was likely to be short, and chilly. Or the ice would be broken, never to re-form, as the guests relaxed and tried to top the story with something even grosser. This might end in Father recounting the one about the dog vomit—which, I assure you, you don't want to hear—and the evening would be long and full of laughter.

Always, laughter. And music. Father played that "orchestra-in-a-box," the button accordion, which places more note combinations at

the fingertips than any other instrument. (If you haven't heard it, don't knock it!) Also, the harmonica, or mouth organ, as well as I've heard it played. They sang. Everyone sang, whether they had a talent for it or not. People were tolerant. Father had a pleasant tenor voice, very flexible and expressive. Old songs, mostly. Irish songs: "Molly Malone," "My Wild Irish Rose." Or English: some very old, with strange words that I wish I could remember. "The Twa Corbies," "Unquiet Grave," "Three Loving Brothers"—my favourite when young, for the story it told, and the delicious violence!

"Oh no, oh no," said Captain Sir John Howard,
"That it never can be,
For I'll take your ship, and your treasure too,
And your bodies I'll give to the sea, the sea,
Your bodies I'll give to the sea."

Great stuff!

And always, of course, the stories. Sometimes Father alone, sometimes matched story for story by the guest or guests. Sometimes well told, often not. Some true, some not so true, some obviously "stretchers." No matter, if they entertained. Most of the last seemed to me to be hunting stories, often concerning marvellous triumphs of marksmanship. And for these, Father was not so tolerant as for the others. He was so good with a rifle, that for him to tell the truth seemed to be shameless boasting, so perhaps he resented being the only one compelled to be truthful! As the evening wore on, the shooting stories would grow more unlikely and he would begin to goad the guests to account to ever more incredible shooting feats. At last, he would tell the story of the geese, which I always looked forward to. It went something like this:

"That reminds me," he would begin, "of the time I came across the flock of geese. I'd hunted all afternoon and never saw a thing. It was starting to get dark, so I headed back to the boat. I came out on a little rocky point at one end of a long pebble beach, and stopped there for a look around. The deer sometimes come down on the beach in the evenings, you know, so I didn't make any noise. And there, on the far end of the beach, was a flock of geese!"

The guest would be listening politely, waiting more or less patiently for his turn. Mentally rehearsing his next story so that it would outdo the one he was hearing; obviously to be some account of a difficult shot accomplished against odds.

"Like I said, it was getting dark, and they didn't see me. They were a long ways off, I'd say a hundred yards, at least. I really wanted to take home a goose, but if I tried to get any closer, they'd spook, so I decided I'd have to shoot from where I was. Now, I suddenly realized that the only bullets I had were the big two-fifty grain 'brush cutters.' If I hit a goose with one of those, there wouldn't be much meat left, so it would have to be a head shot."

The other's expression would change at this. Unlikely was permitted, even welcomed. But impossible was regarded as an insult to the hearer's experience and/or intelligence, and Father was nearing that line.

"So I raised the gun and took a good bead, when I got to thinking, two geese would be a lot better than one. But I knew I'd only have time for one shot before they flew. They were bunched pretty close together, so I thought, I'll just wait 'til two of their necks cross, and with any luck I'll get two geese with one shot!"

About now he would sneak a sly glance at his target, to see the effect of his story so far. He was seldom disappointed. The other would usually be squirming as if his chair were cushioned with rocks. Father would prolong the torture.

"It was probably more like a hundred and fifty yards. My gun was sighted in at a hundred, so I'd have to aim about three inches high, maybe four. I decided to make it four. There was a bit of a wind blowing off the water. Fifteen, maybe twenty miles an hour. That meant allowing about four inches to the right. Gusty, too. I'd have to pick the time right."

At this point in the story, one guest I remember was in such a fury that his face was red, his eyes bulged, and he was making unconscious pushing-off motions with his hands! But at last, perhaps not without a couple of final stings.

"It was so dusky now I could just barely make them out, when I saw two of them together. Their necks crossed, and I fired . . ." Pause, glance at tormented guest, who couldn't possibly top this, then, quickly, "And the geese all jumped up and flew away!"

He was amazingly strong for a man of his size. I didn't realize this until I had left home for a few years, and then came back to go handlogging with him. I'd done a lot of axe and hammer work, and my last job before joining him was using the big broadaxe—sixteen inches on the edge—to square eighty-foot fir trees for bridge timbers. I weighed one-seventy, and was unjustifiably vain about my strength and my skill with an axe. He was fifty-five years old, weighed one-fifty, and I discovered immediately that I was no match for him.

Handlogging—done the old way, with hand tools—can be unbelievably hard work. It requires constant use of axe, saw or logging jacks, each one—if you'll pardon the Irishism—harder than the other. There is no part of the work where you can ease off a bit, let the muscles catch up a bit. And Father believed in eight-hour days; more, if necessary to finish getting a tree out. I had my fair share of youthful male vanity. I would match him blow for blow or die in the attempt!

At the end of a day's work, I was so tired that, on the way home in the boat, I would fall asleep sitting upright, propped in a corner by the window, hands so stiff half an hour after quitting work that they wouldn't close. In the first few weeks I lost ten pounds, then gained twelve. I began to feel I could hold my own—almost. Yet try as I would—ah, how I tried!—this man more than twice my age and twenty pounds lighter was the better axeman. He was quite aware of and amused by my efforts, and encouraged them.

One day, when we had finished eating lunch (half an hour, part of it spent honing axes), he said, "If you're going to be an axeman, you should be able to do this trick."

Taking his match case from his pocket, he selected a match and placed it on the stump of the tree we had just felled, and put one of the iron wedges on the stem of the match. Then he picked up his long-handled falling axe and, with an easy, full-armed swing, buried the blade in the stump by the match head, and lit the match. (On a full-circle swing, the axe head travels about fourteen feet.) I tried, and chopped the match head off.

He laughed, and told me, "There's a trick to it. You have to hit about an eighth of an inch from the match. As the axe goes in the wood, the taper of the blade will bring it against the head of the match."

Nothing to it, indeed, if you can guide an axe that accurately. I wasted a lot of matches!

I survived, and toughened. In two or three months, instead of falling asleep on the way home, I began to take my turn at steering.

At last the time came when I felt ready to mount my challenge. I felt sorry for the old man. It might come as quite a shock to him that his son could beat him at his own specialty. Perhaps, I consoled myself, it would make him proud!

Our target for that day was a fir tree of above-average size: about five feet in diameter. The chopping-out of the "undercut," the wedge-shaped notch that would guide the direction of the tree's fall, would be the occasion. This notch has a dual purpose. It guides the direction of fall to within an arm's length of accuracy, thus preventing possible damage to young trees (handlogging is selective logging: when done properly, the logged area appears almost untouched), and the angled top of the wedge gives the falling tree a forward nudge as it slides off the stump. Given a good slope, and a bit of luck, the tree might continue to move, shedding branches as it goes, until it thunders into the water, all ready to be cut into logs. To do this effectively, the notch must be made quite large—from one-quarter to one-third of the diameter of the tree. This was work for the axes, one man to each side of the cut. These double-bitted axes are very specialized tools, meant for that job and no other. If one was to be found in a modern logging camp, it would likely be hung on a wall as the antique it is. Its forty-two-inch handle comes level with the average man's belt. The long, narrow heads—three and a half to four inches wide—measure fourteen inches from edge to edge. Unlike the heavy single-blade competition axe, designed to be used for a brief time in soft wood, these axes are made to cut deeply into hard fir butts. In softer wood they can only be used with great care, for too hard a blow will bury the blade to where the handle will break before it can be wihdrawn. A cut done by competent fallers can be almost as smooth as if it had been planed. Axe marks mean inefficiency. Oh, a smooth cut is easy enough, but one with no waste blows, not at all easy. Two men using these axes to fell a tree is perhaps the ultimate test of axemanship. The cuts overlap at the centre of the notch. There can be no mistake, no hesitation. Your axe must be gone from there when your partner's arrives. The conditions are equal for both men. Even on flat ground, springboards are always used. The rhythmic swaying of this six-foot-long, six-inch-wide board, one end locked in a small hole cut in the tree, reinforces the rhythm of the axe swing, and adds power to the blow.

Here it was, on equal footing, that I would make my stand. For I had not been working with him long before I noticed that at the end of each cut, Father would be finished a few seconds before me, standing there leaning on his axe, watching my last few strokes with a critical eye. After a few (totally ineffective) attempts at reversing this picture, I ceased to try. But I had not given up. I knew it would take time. Now I was ready.

My axe was honed to a razor edge. (Literally. I tested it on the hair of my forearm.) It was heavier than his, the largest of its kind the Sager company made. He preferred the next size down, a three and a half-inch blade instead of my four-inch. But then I outweighed him by twenty pounds!

We set the boards. (If you have a taste for antique trivia: seven strokes to set a springboard, if you waste none. Less in softer wood.) We stepped on the boards, tested their spring, took our stances. Father, as the head faller, took the first cut. I felt a surge of adrenalin as I slammed the axe home into the tough fir. I thought he looked a trifle surprised, but he speeded his strokes to take out equal wood. I leaned into the axe, feeling the power of that special twist of waist and shoulders that gives extra force to the blow; increased the speed of the rhythm. (Either axeman can do this.) He matched me, blow for blow. The chips flew like leaves in the fall winds, as the wood seemed to melt under the axes.

And then, he was leaning on his axe, breathing deeply but steadily, as I took three more strokes to finish my side! I was trying desperately not to gasp for breath like a beached trout, and not succeeding too well.

"That's not bad," he mused thoughtfully. "Not bad at all. You've the makings of a good axeman, with a bit of practice!"

Later, much later, I suspected it was said with tongue in cheek, but at the time I was painfully certain he meant it!

(To give the reader some idea of the fitness level involved, it was about a month after this that I achieved a one-hand chin-up, a long-cherished ambition.)

Writing this account, remembering, I am as amazed as ever—at the unfairness of it. I exercised, he didn't, yet he was, pound for pound, stronger.

I bought cases of ammunition for target practice. He never fired except for a purpose, and yet was the better shot. His good nature robbed this sort of thing of any sting it might have had. But what was that again, about everyone being born equal?

Oh yes, one thing more. I never tried that stunt again!

There have been readers who objected that in these stories I've made Father out to be some sort of paragon, a man without faults. If that was my intent, he'd have scorned me for it, and rightly so. He could be short-tempered, unreasonable and stubborn to the point of obstinacy. (How fortunate that such qualities aren't hereditary!)

For example, he believed in spontaneous generation, the outmoded concept of a more innocent age. Foolish, you might say, and I'd not dispute you, but his reasons may be of interest.

When the logging camp at Vancouver Bay shut down one October, there remained the usual mess of debris where the beach camp had been. But the camp boss was a tidy man, and he had no intention of leaving it that way.

"Clear this mess up and burn it," he ordered. "I want this place looking like a park when we pull out." So they raised a spar tree in a suitable place, and rigged it. Then they hauled in all the culled logs, roots, downed trees, brush, old buildings—all the discarded junk of years of logging—and heaped it around the tree. In its midst they dumped barrels of used oil and grease, and the hundreds of old tires that littered the ground. When they were done, the pile was the size of a five-storey house. Then they set fire to it.

It burned for a month, and at its peak the glow could be seen thirty miles away, reflected from the clouds. In the end there remained only a circle of ash a hundred feet across, for the intensity of the heat burned even the earth to a depth of several feet.

A year passed, and nature began to heal the scar. But in the centre, where the heat had been fiercest, nothing grew. For what could have grown in that sterile ash?

In the spring, a year and half another after the blaze, Father took a friend there to fish the valley. They tied the boat at the camp dock, which had been left in place. Their way led by where the fire had been, and a sight that startled them. In the centre of a strip of ash, a circle the size of a small house was covered by a moss-like carpet of intense green! They walked out over the hardened ash and examined it closely. It proved to be not moss, but millions of tiny green plants so close-packed that, a few feet off, they closely resembled it.

Father dug into the ash with his belt-knife. From each plant a single thread-like white root disappeared into the depths, tapering off to near invisibility at the bottom of his excavation. No wiser, the men continued on their way.

Whether the fishing was good or bad I don't remember, if I ever knew. but on the way back, Father dug up a clump of plants, taking out a cylinder of ash as deep as he could manage, and carried it carefully to the boat. He took it to his garden at Selma Park, separated the clump into five parts, and planted them. The tiny plants survived, and as they grew larger, he pinched out the weakest until there were only five left. Under his care they prospered, and soon they were recognizable as ... baby arbutus trees!

He pulled out all but the strongest, which had grown to about three feet high, when he sold the house and moved to Wilson Creek. He saw it once more, several years later: a fine, healthy young arbutus. For all I know it is growing there yet.

Now, in the crabapple flats of Vancouver Bay, there were no arbutus trees. The nearest were a quarter-mile away on the slopes that border the valley. To think that birds had dropped the seeds was absurd. That seeds could survive such heat, in such quantity, seemed equally absurd. To Father the answer was obvious.

In Jack Hammond's books were many debates on spontaneous generation. Though rejected even then by Science, without a grounding in science, many of the arguments for it were persuasive. So he decided that arbutus trees might not only grow from seeds, but under the right conditions could generate spontaneously, and that the fire somehow produced those conditions.

After all, didn't intelligent people once believe that mice, far more complex than trees, could so generate?

I tried to argue that the seeds, concentrated there by water or some other agency, had lain dormant, possibly for centuries, and that the heat had made potent the life they held. But not all my book learning, nor arguments therefrom, could convince him.

I find this more admirable than otherwise. Far better to hold to one's convictions than be a weathervane reflecting the crowd.

He made enemies. Hating hypocrisy and detesting deception, he seldom resisted the temptation to expose them. Had he been content with that, the resentment of his victims might not have been so bitter. But he had a peculiar skill at making the subject of his shafts look ridiculous, and this people will never forgive.

"Chicken Ernie," so-called because of a "misunderstanding" concerning his neighbour's laying hens, lived on an ill-kept homestead somewhere in the outskirts of Sechelt. When I was very young, I overheard him described as a "low-down, shiftless weasel of a man" and wondered thereafter what a man-weasel would look like. It was a great disappointment to discover eventually that he looked much like other men. But "weasel" seemed to fit him. Not because he was small, for he was of rather more than average size. In fact, people joked that it was marvellous how someone who worked so seldom managed to find so much to eat! But his pudgy face wore a sly and vicious look. It was said of him that he beat his wife, his children, his pig and his cow with indiscriminate brutality. He poached from other men's traps, pit-lamped deer in and out of season and boasted quite untruthfully of his prowess as a hunter.

At that time, Father had a trapline at Northwest (Sargeant) Bay. Returning home along a different way than usual, he came upon marks indicating that something heavy had been dragged along the ground. Always curious, he backtracked the trail to its source. What had taken place there was as plain to read as if he had seen it happen, and he carried a foul temper with him as he resumed his journey.

Back in Sechelt, he hadn't gone far before he was hailed by a man he knew.

"Did you hear about Chicken Ernie's cougar? Shot it himself. No dog, just tracked it down. Didn't think he had it in him!"

"He doesn't," rejoined Father shortly.

"Well, he's got it over at the store. Nice cat, too. Not old or starved. You should go over and have a look at it."

"I will," said Father, and he did.

On the store steps, Chicken Ernie was holding forth to his audience. "I got it first shot. Hard shot it was, too. He was up in a tree, and I had to get up close under him to get a bead on him. I could see he was getting ready to jump down on me but I got him first. One shot, and no dog!" Then, catching sight of Father, "Guess even you'd have a hard time tracking a cougar down with no dog, eh, Hammond?"

Father went over to the big cat and, to verify what he knew he'd see, examined it for a moment.

"You're not saying much," taunted Chicken Ernie. "What's the matter, cat got your tongue?" He roared with merriment at his own humour, and there were a few chuckles from the group of men.

"Hard thing to do all right, track a cougar with no dog," agreed Father.

"You're damn right it is, but I can do it," boasted Chicken Ernie. "So what do you say now, Hammond? You look kind of sour. Something bothering you?"

"Well," mused Father, "there's a couple of things that puzzle me a bit."

"Trot 'em out. I'll put you straight."

"Just how far did you say he was up that tree?"

"Oh, twenty feet, maybe thirty. Yeah, more like thirty. Close enough to jump at me, though."

"That must have been some cat," admired Father, "to climb that far with a bear trap on its front leg." Chicken Ernie's face, normally florid, turned fiery red. "And you must be a pretty good climber yourself to go forty feet up a tree with a gun so you could shoot down through his head!"

One of the men went over to the cougar, and the rest crowded after. They rolled it on its back.

"By God," said one. "Hal's right. The bone's broken, and that's got to be a bear trap mark that high on the leg. And the shot *did* go through the top of his head." All eyes turned on Chicken Ernie. Gone now were the attitudes of amused tolerance, replaced by expressions of contempt. Though the big cats were eagerly hunted, they were respected. Catching them in traps was a thing not done.

Caught in a trap of his own making, he stammered incoherently, "I didn't...I mean, I never...God damn you, Hammond, you bastard. I got it, didn't I, no matter what you..."

Father had noticed Major Sutherland, chief constable for Sechelt and area, watching from the veranda. "Isn't there a law about setting a bear trap on a trail?" he asked innocently to no one in particular. "You'd better hope the Major doesn't hear about it." (Knowing that individual was listening.) "And if he finds out the deer guts you used for bait came from a doe, I wouldn't like to be in your shoes!"

Satisfied, and with his good temper restored, he went about his business.

Runaway!

Grandfather Jack taught his sons by example and by precept that when necessary, they must be able to make quick decisions and be willing to act on them as quickly, regardless of what others said or did. His lessons fell on fertile ground.

It took Father some years to settle on the sort of work that suited him best. Being an engineer on a steam donkey held much attraction for him at first, and in fact, through his twenties he even studied for his steam ticket, an onerous course if ever there was one! So it was quite natural that when he first went to work in the woods, he spent every spare moment hanging around the steam engine, wheedling instruction from the engineer.

He learned quickly, and in a surprisingly short time (for he was very young, but there were no rules about such things then) he became competent enough to be offered the job part-time in a small A-frame operation on Agamemnon Channel.

The elderly engineer had come to value his comfort. He preferred to coddle his old bones in the warmth of the engine shed on the A-frame float, and was more than willing to let a young apprentice cope with the perils and discomforts of the steep sidehills.

The operation was somewhat unusual in that the machine on the A-frame also served as the yarder. The timber grew on a flattish "bench" high above the channel, and the logs must be dragged from where the trees were felled to a place where they could be reached from the A-frame. This meant taking the big machine—which was on log skids—off the float, up the steep hillside to collect a pile of logs, then back again to the float, where it would haul them into the water.

For such work there should have been two machines. But this was what used to be known as a "poverty show": the owner was mortgaged down to his bootlaces and couldn't afford another. However, the timber was good, and with a bit of luck he might hold on long enough to pay his debts, or even make a profit.

The first swing, as such are called, went smoothly. The second was also proceeding well; a pile or "deck" of logs had been gathered and the machine was being readied for the trip back to the water. This posed no problems. Yarding the logs down the same track had made a wide, smooth path, so slippery in places that walking was difficult. The method chosen may seem strange, but it was practical, for loggers are the most practical of men. To wear out the brake on the line-drum by using it for that purpose was out of the question. A steam engine under compression is a good brake itself, but again, there is the matter of unnecessary wear and tear on the machinery. But there remains a third method, as efficient and easy on the equipment as one could wish.

The machine is bought to the brink of the hill under its own power, then turned end for end so that it's facing uphill. The strawline, the smallest of the three lines, is fastened to a stump. It won't need to take much strain, only keep the machine from sliding. The haulback, second largest of the three, will be led under the machine and down the hill, moving the machine just far enough that the sled will slide by itself when the strawline is slacked. The haulback line is then run twice around a good strong stump, and joined to the mainline, forming a loop twice as strong as the haulback alone. The machine is then lowered on the doubled lines, which allows for a degree of control otherwise unattainable.

But in a camp this poor (though not only in this sort of camp), the big wire cables, up to half a mile long, are—next to the donkey itself—the most expensive pieces of equipment on the claim. They are not lightly replaced. They are spliced, and patched, and spliced again until they can be used no more. Of course, the more this is done, the more often they break. And on this occasion, on a last hefty pull over some rough ground, the mainline had not only snapped, but had stranded itself so badly it wasn't worth repairing. It was wound in and would be left on the drum until a new piece could be obtained and spliced in.

There was no real problem. Loggers were resourceful then; they had to be. With the haulback, the strawline and a couple of blocks (pulleys), they managed to bring the machine to where it could lower itself by the haulback. So they hooked the line to a big stump and Father began to put tension on it.

But the woods boss, a careful man, had been thinking. "Pull all the line off the drum. I want to have a look at it. And lay it out nice and neat. We'll snub her down." This is an ancient method of lowering heavy objects. They were familiar with it and knew what to do. As Father rolled the drum slowly in reverse, the men laid out the line in long zigzags along the hillside, taking care that it wouldn't foul. The boss examined every inch of it with a critical eye and finally pronounced, "It's a piece of junk, but it'll have to do." When Father engaged the drum, intending to rewind the first portion of it, "Under tension lad, under tension." And to the two men standing waiting, "Three turns now, and hold her steady." They would control the machine's rate of descent by letting the coils slip around the stump. There used to be a logger's saying, "Two turns will do. Three will hold the devil!" I don't suppose it's used much any more. To Father he called, "Slack the strawline." When this was done, they loosed it, ran it through a snatchblock and back to the machine. It would be used to bring the end of the repaired mainline back up the hill. The line was left slack; there was no point now in tightening it. Now it was the men's task to ease the machine to the water while the engine idled, steam up, in case it was needed. As expected, all went smoothly at first. but then disaster struck with startling speed.

The haulback wasn't in much better shape than the mainline. They had swapped ends on it several times, so that the better part was where the work was hardest. This had been done recently, and the section nearest the drum spool was whiskered with "jaggers," broken single strands of steel, sharp as needles, sticking out half an inch or more.

The men were used to watching warily for these, for should they become careless, even their heavy leather gloves could easily be pierced. And there is a way of easing your grip onto the line, checking by feel if it's safe to apply pressure. But no precautions will keep you safe if mischance dictates otherwise.

The constant pressure on the wire nearest the core had caused it to deform, to retain some of the circular shape of the drum. It wasn't easy to feed it smoothly into the stump. Loggers are used to coping with difficulties such as these, and they were managing. But then a quick twisting motion of the uncoiling line drove a sharp jagger into one man's wrist just as the other was shifting his grip. The slack that resulted allowed the line to kink as it came to the stump, which made it impossible to keep the constant pressure needed for control.

The weight of the big machine ripped the line from the men's hands. They fought to grab it again; with luck they might have brought it under control, but as the kinked part slid around the stump, the upper coil flipped off the top of it and the Devil was loose!

There was nothing they could do now but leap frantically out of the way of the flailing wire as the machine gathered speed on the slippery ground.

As all this was happening, everyone stopped what they were doing and gazed helplessly, unable to do anything but watch, first with shock and then with horror.

The fireman, with nothing much to do but see that the pressure in the boiler stayed up, was the first to react. "Jump, Hal, jump!" he shouted, as he leaped from the sled to land sprawling on the ground.

"Jump!" hollered the foreman and, when Father stayed seated, "Jump, you damned fool!"

But thoughts were flashing through Father's mind like flickers of lightning. The machine would end up on the rocky sea-floor in three hundred feet of water. Even if the line stayed on and it could be salvaged, the Old Man—as loggers always called the owner—couldn't afford to have it fixed. He'd be bankrupt. No one would get their already deferred paycheques...But while he was thinking, his hands went through their practised motions as if they'd a mind of their own. They put a bit of friction on the strawline brake, for the drum was already starting to spin too fast. The line was far too light to stop him, and if it tangled and snapped, someone—probably himself—could get hurt. Then he threw the line drum into drive and jammed the throttle lever to full open.

Steam responds instantly. The drive chain rattled noisily and the big gears screamed as they meshed faster than they'd ever done before, for you never give an empty drum full throttle on no load. With nothing more to be done than to hope his instincts were right, Father settled himself firmly in his seat and gave the whistle signal for "Danger below."

Down on the A-frame float there was consternation as the steam whistle shrieked its warning and the big sled plummeted upon them. It wouldn't actually hit them, for the float was held about forty feet from shore by log stiff-legs. But it must have been an awesome sight, for all of that. And of course they could have had no idea that someone was riding it down.

"I never had a ride like that in all my life," remembered Father when he told the story. "Not even when the logging truck got away from us at Clear Cedar. The machine was going down that slope so fast that I began to think what I was trying to do hadn't a chance. Either the line would break when it came tight, or the drum would rip out of its bearings, or the line wouldn't come in fast enough, and the boiler would crack in the cold water . . . I'd be all right, of course. The worst that could happen if it went under was that I'd get wet." Father was always the optimist. That was far from the worst that could have happened, and he knew it!

Dimly, he heard shouting over the noise of the gears. The line began to tighten; he cut the power, rammed the big counterweighted brake lever home and braced himself. The cable came tight and the iron seat hit him in the back with the force of a sledgehammer blow. But it could have been worse. As he'd hoped, the quarter mile of cable had spring enough in it to cushion the shock. The machine held together, and though the end of the sled splashed into the water as the wire stretched, tension drew it almost out again. He'd feared for the big iron boiler, but it was securely fastened with guy wires, and they held. But everything loose—wood, tools, containers, rigging—all catapulted off the deck and peppered the water in front of the float like giant bird-shot.

The big sheet-iron roof was held up on four sturdy posts. They snapped where they were fastened at the base, and the roof somersaulted into the air, hit the water on its curved back with a mighty splash, and slid up onto the float's deck like some grotesque monster attacking from the sea. It came to rest in the middle of the big shed, its posts sticking up like ungainly legs!

No one was hurt. They'd gathered for safety on the farthest end of the float. Imagine their shock as they saw the young engineer rise from his seat, leap lightly to the ground and sit watching from a convenient stump. Making, I'm certain, what was probably a good attempt to appear nonchalant, as everyone rushed to the near end of the float, all talking at once.

Father noted with interest that it was the first time he'd seen the

Old Man speechless, if only for moments; but recovering quickly, he made up for the lapse with volume of profanity.

When an opportunity to break in came, Father said apologetically, "Sorry about the roof. Next time I guess we'll have to make the posts stronger."

His words, and the story that prompted them, was retold—though not always accurately—for many years by those who had been there, and some who hadn't. His reputation was made.

• • •

This sort of bravery, of heedless disregard for personal safety was commonplace in those days. Everyone had seen or heard of similar incidents. Most went unrecorded. Such as, for instance, the escapade involving my uncle Henry and his younger brother Warren, young men just out of their teens . . . Harum-scarum, their elders were wont to call them: bound to come to no good. (They were right, but not for that reason.)

The brothers were working at that time for Neemei's logging camp at Halfmoon Bay, and it must be said that they didn't rate high on the boss's list of most desirable employees. It was in the early thirties; times were hard. In spite of that they'd somehow saved enough money between them to buy a car. Not a new car: cheap as cars were then, that would have been out of the question. But a car it was, and they were handy with tools. They learned how to strip it down and put it back together again, with improvements.

Gleaming in new paint, it was the envy of the young—and many of their elders. One of the modifications the brothers made was to install a new set of brakes from a heavier vehicle, for the roads on the hills behind Halfmoon Bay were steep, brakes were often a weak point, and bragging rights went to those who could stop most quickly on certain of the hills. You can imagine how proud they were of it!

The public road was too tame for them. They liked to drive the logging roads. It didn't bother them if they met a loaded truck coming down. Though there were few places to pass, or even pull out of the way, they delighted in driving downhill backwards just ahead of the truck descending, even though in some stretches the truck drivers went down without using their brakes, to conserve them.

Behind the little community of Halfmoon Bay, the logging road went straight back into the hills, the grade so steep that most cars had to gear well down to negotiate it. (How high a gear you could conquer that hill in was also a matter of pride. It was, after all, a long time ago, the machine age still novel.)

One day, their work done, the two decided it was a good day for a drive. The last load of logs had yet to come in; they'd go to meet it. Away they went, bouncing the old car ruthlessly through the ruts. Almost to the top of the steepest part, and there came the logging truck with its load, yellow paint shining in the sun, red bark glowing.

Warren, the reckless one, was driving. "He's coming down pretty fast," he said. "Wants to get home for supper, I guess." He laughed as he shifted gears to gain more speed. "Let's give him a scare!" Henry had been trying to see which driver it was, and when he answered, his voice was pitched high. "There's no one behind the wheel. The brakes must've gone, he's jumped. She's a runaway!"

"The curve at the dump," answered his brother tersely as he slammed the car to a stop, then took off backwards down the hill. "We've got to warn them," grunted Henry as they speeded through the ruts.

"No time," answered Warren. Though irresponsible (or perhaps because of it), they were sharp. Both had known in that first instant what danger threatened. The road in that section was seldom graded, the ruts so deep only those cars that sat high off the ground could traverse them. The saying in camp was that you could take your hands off the wheel and read a book, you'd still get safely to the beach. Driverless or not, the truck would stay on the road, and reach camp still carrying its load of logs. But the road curved as it reached the log dump, on the outside of the curve; two houses. Their occupants would be there, getting ready for the evening meal. The truck would never make the curve; truck and logs would overturn. The houses and those inside would be crushed.

"What can we do?" asked Henry. They'd reached a wide spot in the road. "Watch me," said his brother. He braked strongly as he swung the steering wheel. The car tilted alarmingly as it climbed out of the ruts and the wheels on the uphill side lifted high off the ground. But Henry was used to this sort of thing when his brother was driving, and he had a firm grip on the door frame. With deft motions Warren changed gears and skidded the car into a wild turn. Now they faced downhill, as they must if what he had in mind was to work. For he was going to try to use the car to slow the truck, and he'd need both brake and gears for that. Reverse gear was too low; if he tried to use it the engine would explode. His brother had caught on by now. He laughed gleefully as he shouted, "Go to it!"

The truck was bearing down on them. It wasn't as big as trucks became later, and the driver had left it in the lowest gear he could reach before he jumped, so it wasn't going as fast as it might have, but the grade was steepening. Warren chose second gear, and slowed until their bumpers touched. Then he began to apply the car's oversized brakes.

It was a near thing. The truck slowed a bit, gained speed on the steep part, slowed again as the grade flattened. Their engine screamed and the brakes gushed smoke. The car was narrower than the truck track; the wheels tried constantly to ride the edges. If one had caught for an instant, the car would have slewed sideways and the relentless load behind would have crushed them. But luck—or skill—was with them that day. They made it safely down the steep part, and as the road neared the water, it flattened. When they reached the curve the truck was under control.

As they drew near the beach, Henry reached over and held the horn button down. They'd found a big brass klaxon with a raucous bleat and it held pride of place on the left front fender. The noise brought everyone out to see what was happening. It didn't take much effort to read the signs—the car, smoke pouring from its overheated brakes, the driverless truck—especially as thoughts of just such an event were a constant source of worry to those who lived in the houses on the bend.

In an instant, the two youths were surrounded by admirers. The camp boss pushed through. He walked over to the truck and inspected it. Then he looked at the houses. "Hm-m...could have been nasty," was all his comment. Then to one of his men, "Take the crummy and pick Mike up. You know how he hates to walk." And finally, to the brothers, "I suppose you went up to play games with the trucks again, eh? Serve you right if you'd got run over!" Not a word of praise; he was a dour man. But he told them to go to the shop and have the mechanic install a new set of brakes. They refused. They liked to do that sort of work themselves. But he paid for the parts.

The Mountain Men

I've mentioned the Johnstone brothers of Jervis Inlet in various of my father's tales. I regret not having been able to do it more often, but there are too few stories, too dimly remembered. Father knew of the family long before he met them, for their fame—or notoriety—had spread throughout that part of the coast.

Incomparable men! As wild and free as the unexplored mountains that surrounded their home. Even then, you would have had to go far to find their match. Their exploits should have been the stuff of legend, and had they stayed in Kentucky where they came from, this may well have been the case. But their patriarch chose, for whatever reasons, to come to this country and homestead near the head of Jervis Inlet. Here there was no call for heroes, no opportunity for them to display their prowess in a mainly law-abiding land. Where there was no one to sing of such things had they happened, in any case. If there had been no Homer, we would know nothing of Odysseus and his travels, nor aught about the heroes of the siege of Troy. And here at Jervis Inlet there was no immortal struggle, and sad to say, we have produced no Homer. Thus it is that our adventurers have died—for the most part—unsung and unremembered.

The Johnstones loved exploring the rugged lands behind their home, the jumbled terrain from which spring, among others, the Eliho, Bute and Toba rivers. They did much of this exploring in winter, on homemade snowshoes. Their preferred way-bread was the sweet fat that lines the body cavity of a mountain goat—it turns hard in the cold, and by all accounts is remarkably palatable. They called it belly-fat, and said it gave them strength; certainly their fortitude and endurance were legendary in those parts, especially that of Frank and his brother Forrest, or Jud. They were relentless hunters, magnificent marksmen, and if they feared anything, mention of it has escaped me. But it must be admitted that their humour was, at times, somewhat primitive.

These were the men that Father grew up wishing to emulate, and though he hadn't their physical stature, he made a pretty fair try at it, to my mind.

One of the first things he did when he bought his boat was to begin to explore Jervis Inlet, and to strike up acquaintance with the Johnstones. They seem to have been first amused, and then intrigued, by this eager young man who so obviously admired them. But when they found that good as they were with their guns, he was better, they treated him as one of their own sort. This meant making him the butt of the same kind of humour to which they subjected each other.

Once, when the Granite Island quarry was temporarily shut down for some forgotten reason, Father went up the inlet to stay with them for a few days. They welcomed him boisterously and, as was the custom, invited him in for the evening meal.

This was in early fall, and naturally the talk turned to hunting. (In fact, the talk always turned to hunting, but sooner at that time of year.) After a bit, amidst the jests and talk of what they'd done and were going to do, Frank asked, "Say, Hal, did we ever tell you how brother Steve here went for a ride on a bear?"

"No, you never, but I'd sure like to hear it."

"Well, it happened up one of the slides over yonder," pointing across the inlet. "It was about this time last fall. We'd gone to get a bear for winter meat. Nothing like a good fat fall bear to keep your belly warm in winter. Steve drew the lot for the first shot, and danged if he didn't drop the bear just like . . . " Snap of the fingers. "So he runs over to bleed it. Now, you know that the best way to do that is to stand over top of it, grab it by an ear to lift its head up, and cut its throat. But what he didn't know when he made that head-shot was this: that old gun of his didn't have pop enough to go through a bear's skull bone. He should have gone for a heart shot at that range, but then, he didn't want to spoil any meat.

"So anyhow, what had happened was he'd just cold-cocked the critter, and when it felt the knife, why, up it rose and made off down the slope with him astride its back!"

"How far did they go?" asked his young listener, enthralled.

"Depends on who he's telling the story to," said Frank, amidst laughter. Then, casually, "Come to think of it, it's 'bout time for some more bear meat. How'd you like to come out with us tomorrow and help us pick out a nice fat one?"

Father shook his head morosely. "My gun's too light for bear. But I'd sure like to." (This was before he owned the powerful 38:55 Winchester.)

"Don't worry. You can use mine. It's shot so many bear you don't hardly have to aim it!" Frank assured him. "I'll take Paw's gun; he don't hunt much any more."

The evening went quickly, full of talk and laughter, and stories of their forays into the surrounding mountains. Father mostly listened. He was too young to have many stories of his own. It didn't matter. A good and appreciative listener can make an evening memorable.

Early next morning they set off into the foothills of Princess Louisa Inlet, working their way along the edge of a slide the hunters thought might produce a bear worth having. And sure enough, about halfway up, a bear there was, digging out avalanche lily roots and washing them down with blueberries.

"There you are, Hal," whispered Frank. "Guest gets first shot. Don't spoil the meat. Hit him behind the ear."

Remembered Father, "It was an easy shot. I upped with the gun, drew a bead behind the bear's ear, and fired. The bear jumped up and looked around to see where the noise came from. Frank said, 'Must be the morning light. Give it another go.' This time I saw a bit of rock dust fly up off to one side, and I heard a couple of snickers of laughter. I could feel my ears burning. The bear was scrambling off across the rocks, and I squeezed off a shot that I *knew* was on the mark. But the bear kept right on going."

He handed the gun to the grinning Frank. "Here, it's your turn. I can't hit it."

The bear was by this time almost into the bush on the other side of the rock slide.

"Oh, I think I'll pass," said Frank.

Brother Jud spoke up. "Didn't you tell Hal about the gun?"

"No, I thought a hot shot like him wouldn't need telling." And to shouts of laughter at Father's baffled look, "Couldn't you tell when you hefted it? That gun shoots four inches high at that range, and seven inches to the left."

It had all been a set-up, an elaborate practical joke. It was too early to bring in the winter's meat, the weather too warm. Father didn't mind. He told me once, "I'd never had such a compliment in all my life, that they'd gone to that much effort to play a joke on me."

But what impresses me the most is that these men were so familiar with their guns they never bothered to sight them in. They simply knew where to aim at any given distance!

Not long after that came another outing in which Jud and Frank Johnstone would play a small part. Father had a best friend, a young man named Archie, whom he'd known for several years. They'd hunted and fished together, had similar outlooks, and thoroughly enjoyed each other's company.

Archie lived at that time in Gillies Bay on Texada Island, which was near enough to Granite Island that they saw each other frequently. One day when they met, Archie opened with, "Hal, I've got a problem."

"Name it," said Father.

"Well, there's this fellow from England. He's a relative of some kind. Not close, but close enough my family wants me to give him a good time. It seems he likes to climb mountains; he's always asking where there's a good one he can climb."

"He's come to a good place to find mountains," offered Father.

"Yes, but I'm working, and so are you. We haven't time to go up Jervis or anywhere like that. I thought we might take him up the west face of Shepherd." (On Texada.)

"Good place to climb," approved Father.

"Yeah, but he wants to meet some of the 'back-country men' he's heard about. Who do you know that's wild enough for him to go home and talk about?"

Father considered this carefully. "Well, there's Martin Warnock. He's working at Lang Bay. And I think Steve and Jud Johnstone have their boat up on the ways at Lund; they should be wild enough for him!"

So it was decided, and so it happened one sunny September morning. Father took Jud and Steve and Martin Warnock to Gillies Bay, where they picked up Archie and his guest. The place they'd chosen to climb was only a few miles farther south, and they anchored there in a little cove partway down Sabine Channel.

The trip didn't begin well. Archie's guest, a well-built man only a bit older than Jud, the eldest of the group, was determined to impress them with his prowess as a mountain climber. Father found it difficult to decide which he found more offensive—the man's boasting about mountains he'd climbed, or his derogatory comments about the one they'd chosen to ascend. "Call this a mountain? It'd just be called an outcrop in the Alps!" and so on, and on...

Father was fairly tolerant about such things, but poor Archie was acutely embarrassed, and the others almost openly hostile. But that face of Texada Island is steep, and soon they must save their breath for climbing. Certainly the man was competent at that. He'd obviously climbed before, and there was no need to wait for him.

Partway up the sheer rise of Mt. Shepherd, a ledge slopes up to the south, and partway along that they came upon an oddity. Sometime, perhaps a hundred years before, a young fir tree about fifty feet tall had uprooted, and fallen across the ledge. The lower half of the roots, bent but not broken, had stayed in the ground, and the tree continued growing, its leading shoot still straining for the sky. The result was a tree, now almost four feet through at the root, that ran out over the abyss, then turned at a right angle, where the new growth had itself become a fair-sized fir a couple of feet in diameter. A dropped stone might have come to rest about eight hundred feet below it. They stopped to look at the strange sight.

"Sure would make a good ship's keel and bow," suggested Jud.

"Kind of hard to get it down in one piece," judged his brother.

Some imp of mischief invaded Father's mind. "Bet none of you can walk out there, touch the tree and walk back again."

Confident in their abilities, the brothers felt they had nothing to prove, to others or to themselves.

"Too easy," scoffed Steve. "Anyone could do that."

"Yeah," seconded Jud. "I guess even Mr. Mountain Man here could do it.'"

All eyes focussed on the visitor, for it hadn't escaped their sharp gaze that he'd spent very little time looking down to admire the view. He looked a bit uncomfortable, but what could he do in such company, under those challenging eyes?

"Of course I could do it," he blustered. "But these leather boots aren't right for it."

"Take them off," suggested Martin. "Can't beat sock feet for that sort of thing."

Cornered, the reluctant aerialist removed his boots, climbed up on the trunk and advanced gingerly out upon it. His extreme caution brought laughter from the three "wild men," for one of the things such men hate is hypocrisy, pretending a skill you don't possess. Bragging is all right, even admired, but you must be able to back up your brag.

The reluctant venturer had gone about halfway to his goal. At that point there was a knob, or burl, across its girth, where the tree had healed a wound most likely caused by falling rock, and the trunk sloped down a bit from there. He stopped, and his distress was evident. Father felt the stirrings of pity. Not far beneath his exterior beat a soft and sympathetic heart.

"Come back," he called. "You've gone far enough." The laughter turned to jeers.

"Yeah, come back. We don't want to have to climb down there and pick what's left of you out of the rocks."

But to come back meant to turn around, and that's much harder than walking. He couldn't manage it. He tried a tentative step or two backwards but couldn't do that either. He sank to his knees and crouched there, not knowing what to do next. Finally, agonizingly, he began to shift his position, an inch at a time, until he was facing the ledge again. But then he made the mistake he'd been so careful to avoid: he looked down through the gulf of air to the cruel rocks below.

He froze, then uttering a little whimpering sound, leaned forward, dropped to his chest and hugged the tree trunk with his arms and legs.

"Now what do we do?" asked Archie.

"Leave him there. He'll come down when he's hungry enough," offered one of the Johnstones.

"Tell him he's in the Alps," suggested the other. "That's where he did all that great climbing."

"We can't leave him there like that," protested Father.

"I can," said Martin Warnock, cruelly.

Father jumped up on the log, walked out to where the hapless man still clutched it. "Come on," he urged. "It's not so bad." And, squatting down, "Hold onto me and don't look down," and he tried to take the other's hand.

Thinking back on it, he told me, "His arm was as stiff as an iron bar, and he was shaking all over like a dog in a wet sack. I've never seen anyone in such a funk."

He knew then he'd need help. Leaping lightly over the hunched man onto the burl, he faced around and looked at the others. Archie would be of no use. He made no secret of the fact that he needed good solid rock to hold onto when he climbed. Jud and Steve were enjoying the situation too much to end it. That left Martin, hugely grinning, but who just might help.

"Come on, Martin, lend us a hand," he called. "We don't want to stand around here all day."

Martin Warnock considered the matter, but made no move.

Father had an idea. "Just think about how he'll feel when we drag him up the log," he suggested.

That did it. Martin walked out, and they pulled and pried and tugged until they got the obstinate mountaineer to within a yard of the ledge. Whereupon he sprang up with such force that he almost knocked Martin off the tree!

Father noticed the man's hands were dripping blood. "Let me look at your hands."

He told me, "I've never seen anything to beat it. He'd torn the nails off most of the fingers of both hands, dragging them against the rough fir bark when we moved him. I felt awful over that, but then, what else could we have done?"

And there was nothing else to do but to go home. There was much talk and laughter on the return trip, but the mountaineer from across the sea was very, very quiet.

• • •

Several years later, after he became a guide, Father had an oddly similar experience. His client wanted to hunt mountain goat. He

scarcely needed a guide for this. Mountain goats could be seen on virtually every rocky height on the coast, white specks that showed plainly against the dark rock. However, it didn't seem to Father that he had an obligation to inform his clients of this.

He was working out of Lund at that time, and on the date duly arranged he was waiting on the dock when the SS *Cardero* arrived, right on schedule. There was only one passenger, an athletic-looking man not much older than Father, carrying gun cases and a packsack. Father introduced himself and led the way to his boat.

He usually took his goat-seeking clients to one of the more accessible hills in the area. But this one had made it clear from the start that his hobby was climbing mountains, and that the steeper the climb, the better he'd enjoy it. After checking him over, Father decided to take him into Toba Inlet, to a place a couple of miles above Brem River that he thought would be steep enough for anyone.

That part of Toba Inlet is an impressive sight. Though only a few thousand feet high, the black basalt crags plunge precipitously into the bright green glacial water flowing to the gulf. At first or even second glance, few would be foolish enough to try to hunt there. But those black rock cliffs were home to many goats, some of them trophy animals of remarkable dimensions. To inexperienced eyes they would seem to be beyond the reach of human endeavour, but Father had explored there and knew it could be done.

Strips of green lace many of those forbidding slopes, inconsequential save to the keenest eye. Basalt cracks as it cools, and into these cracks, some of them only a few inches wide, the tiny flakes of cypress, or yellow cedar trees, have blown and taken root. Thus what might have only been climbed by experienced mountaineers with suitable equipment, now provided a fairly plausible ladder of tough, stringy branches, strong as a rope—if you had the strength and nerve to use it. Father thought it might offer a new experience to his client.

In September the water is usually calm in Toba Inlet. Father went to a spot that he knew wasn't too deep for a stern anchor, but as they were preparing to go ashore he noticed the fine leather boots his client was wearing. He pointed to them. "You can't wear those where we're going."

"Why not? They're the best climbing boots you can buy."

"Not for here they're not. If you're going to wear them we'll have to go somewhere else."

But the man had seen the white shapes of goats on the black rocks far above them. This was what he'd come for, and he wasn't about to go and leave them. "What should I wear?"

"These," Father answered, gesturing toward his ankle-high canvas running shoes with their yellow gum-rubber soles. "You can have my spare pair."

So the change was made, and off they went with a shore line and their guns.

Father had hunted the area before, and led the way by a steep but easy route to where a ledge angled sharply up to their left. The rock of the ledge was scarcely visible, so thickly was it covered with ropy-branched yellow cedar, somehow finding nourishment to grow out of seemingly solid rock. As they made their way up this odd pathway by stepping on the branches near where they emerged from the rock, his companion admitted ruefully, "You were right, leather wouldn't be much use on this stuff."

The higher they climbed, the more their footing depended on the grip of the soft rubber on the stringy little trees and their sloping branches. Father was relieved. The man appeared to have no fear of height, and handled himself well. In fact, he seemed to be enjoying the experience.

Imperceptibly the ledge grew narrower, until at last there was no ledge at all. Only a narrow crack, out of which thrust a dense line of tough little trees, growing so close together that their branches obscured the view below. That was of no concern to Father. He knew that he could safely hang from a single branch not much thicker than a pencil. The little trees were deceptive. Small as they were, they were very old, their dense wood strengthened by snow and wind.

A startled exclamation from behind caused him to turn abruptly to see what was the matter. His companion was looking down through a rare gap in the tangle of dark green foliage.

"There's no ledge," he gasped.

"No," said Father. "We don't need one."

"You don't mean you expect me to traverse this face on a line of tree branches!"

"Why not?" asked Father reasonably.

But this wasn't the same man who had set out so confidently just a short while before. For some strange reason, without solid rock beneath his feet, or at least to hold to, he completely lost his nerve. The easy motions with which he'd climbed this far became stiff and clumsy as he pressed himself against the rock face and tried to find non-existent handgrips on the smooth basalt. Slowly and awkwardly he progressed in this way for a few dozen feet; then, with a cry of terror, he slipped between the branches and hung there by his hands over the black rocks three hundred feet below. "Help me!" he gasped.

Father couldn't believe what he was hearing. This man had climbed the Matterhorn, and the sheer peaks of Mont Blanc. What terrors could this pleasant afternoon's outing hold for such a one? He went quickly back, crouched, and held the man's wrist reassuringly. "It's all right," he said. "There's no danger. These trees will hold ten of you."

But again: "Help me," came the answer.

The stricken man's gun hung askew from its shoulder sling, blocking his attempts to pull himself up. It should have posed no problem, but he seemed incapable of dealing with it. Father slipped out of his own sling and hung his gun on a branch. "Here, let me take your gun," he said, reaching for the sling.

"Damn the gun! Pull me up!" All this time, the man's feet had been scrabbling futilely against the rock wall.

"You may wonder," Father used to say, "why a man like that, who climbed mountains for fun, didn't just pull himself back up. Especially with the strength you get when you're scared. But I've seen the same thing happen other times since then. Panic throws your mind out of kilter. All his strength went into hanging on. His grip probably bruised the wood, but the rest of him didn't get the right orders. Except his feet. He was kicking them like a panicked pig on ice!"

But in a few tries, with Father's help, the thoroughly disorganized climber heaved himself back to the safety of the cushioning branches.

Once there, he recovered quickly, and even seemed to feel a bit sheepish about the way he'd acted. But he made no objection to Father's suggestion that they try a more ordinary route.

The way back went smoothly enough, but Father's sharp eyes noted drops and smears of blood along the way. When they reached solid rock and could walk almost normally, he saw that his companion was limping. "What did you do to your foot?" he asked.

The other seemed surprised. "I don't know, but now you ask, my toes hurt quite a bit."

"Let's have a look at them."

At this point in the story he would shake his head in awe at the memory. "I guess they did hurt a bit," he'd say. "When he was kicking against the rock, he'd torn off most of his toenails, and he hadn't noticed a thing at the time!"

When they got back to the boat, Father put some salve on the injured toes and bandaged them as best he could. He tried to apologize for insisting on the soft-toed shoes, but the other would have none of it.

"You were right," he argued. "It was the thing to do. I don't know what got into me. You must think I'm an awful fool. But my brain just stopped working. I've always climbed above the treeline, with rope and rock crampons, and solid rock to grip to. To see air under my feet like that took me by surprise, I guess. I think I could get used to it pretty quickly. It's a great way to climb and I'd like to try it again. But I don't think my feet are up to it just now. And I don't suppose you'd want to give me another chance anyhow, acting the way I did." All this completely won Father over, and he assured the other he'd be most happy to try again next year.

The man was obviously in much pain by then, and Father decided he'd do what he could to make amends. He cruised the boat slowly along below the bluffs. Chance is notoriously fickle: now it made easy for them what it had made hard before. They spied about a dozen goats strung out across one of the rock faces—a long shot, but not too long.

"There you are," said Father. "Do you want a trophy, or one you can eat?"

"I'll try for that big brute off to the left there, and I'll eat him too if I get him," said the other, readying for his shot.

"That old billy will be as tough as boot leather, and taste worse," cautioned Father.

"Never mind about that. The cook I've got could make a shoebox taste good. We'll eat him." And so saying, he fired. It was a good shot. The stricken goat dropped from its perch, bounced off the rocks a few times and landed in a strip of shrubby trees not more than a hundred feet from the water.

"Nice shot," approved Father. "That will tenderize it some." He knew that goat meat will take a fall that would bruise other meats into inedibility. When he retrieved it, they were glad to see that the excellent set of horns was unbroken.

It hadn't been much of a hunt by Father's standards, but he thought his client would remember it.

Snakes

Father hated snakes. Perhaps "hate" is too strong a word; disgust and loathing may be more accurate. The reason is interesting, for it shows how easily and quickly a child's brain may be programmed for the rest of its life.

It happened when he was about three years old, on a day in late summer on the farm at Texada Island. His father was turning the hay so that it would dry more quickly, and his brother Cliff was helping him. Hal was wandering about the field playing with snakes, for he was much taken with these big "worms," as he called them.

When he found one, he would run after it, put his foot on its tail and shout, "Look at this big worm, Daddy! Look at this big worm I've got!"

He was wearing an old pair of Cliff's canvas shoes to protect his feet from the sharp stubble. They were well worn, and his big toes stuck out through holes in the cloth. He chased down a good-sized snake and put his foot on it, shouting gleefully, "Look Daddy..."

But this snake didn't thrash helplessly. It coiled back and sank its fangs deep into his big toe! He gave a kick to shake it off, but the curved teeth stuck in the flesh, and the snake flopped and twisted sickeningly as he kicked. The happy shouts turned instantly to screams of terror.

His father and brother came running to see what was the matter. By the time they got there, the screams had turned to yells of rage, and he was kicking to destroy, not escape.

Telling the family about it afterwards, his father said, "His leg was just a blur. He was kicking more like a trapped animal than a human."

The snake was still firmly attached to his toe, but it was dead. Jack had to hold his son down and pry the jaws off with his fingers. He held the snake up, and it swayed even more limply than a dead snake usually does. Every joint in its backbone had been dislocated!

And so, for more than seventy years, though he tolerated all forms of life, and though he well knew the snake was only defending itself, Father refused to touch, and hated even to see, a snake.

• • •

This phobia may have changed the course of his life. When he was about twenty-one years old or thereabouts, he made a bit of extra money taking groups of people out in his boat for guided tours. From his base in Pender Harbour, all the islands in and around the mouth of Jervis Inlet were within easy reach.

One of the charters was by a group who wanted to explore Nelson Island, so he anchored in Hidden Bay and took them along some of the old logging roads, and over some of the bridges his father had built. It was, from the beginning, a very special trip, one to be remembered to the end of his life, in spite of the outcome. For among his charges was the most beautiful, interesting and altogether the most desirable young woman he had ever seen! And not only that, she appeared to be unattached, loved the outdoors and seemed very much taken with this young man who was so competent in it.

By the time they had reached the centre of the island, they felt they had known each other for years instead of hours.

On Nelson Island there used to be—perhaps still are—some of what must be the largest garter snakes along the lower mainland of BC. I have seen one nearly four feet long, and Father said this was in no way exceptional. I don't know if they are a special strain, or if it is simply that conditions are unusually favourable. These are not big snakes as snakes grow, of course, but they were quite big enough for Father!

Their way led over a series of step-like ledges between two masses of rock, and there, in the dry grass about halfway up, was one of these big snakes. Distracted by his companion, Father was almost on top of it before he saw it. He stepped back quickly and held out a warning hand.

"Stay back," he cautioned. "Snake! Just wait there a moment. I'll kill it," he said bravely, as he looked around for a suitable weapon.

The young woman had moved up alongside him, and was looking down at the snake with great interest. He turned to shepherd her back out of danger.

"Oh," she breathed. "Isn't he beautiful?" (It was one of those striped with black, yellow and red. They are beautiful.) "You surely aren't going to hurt it, are you? They're quite harmless, you know."

To his horror, she stepped around him and, stooping over, picked the snake up gently in her hands. She turned around and held it out to him. Father took three steps back in one bound. He turned to make certain he was far enough away, and couldn't believe what he saw. She had put the snake across her shoulders, and around the back of her neck. Its head was partway down her upper arm, its tongue darting out to taste the strange air, and she was crooning to it and stroking its neck!

He told me, "That was enough for me. From then on she was just another person in the bunch. Every time I looked at her, I thought of that snake crawling over her skin and I felt sick, and the thought of touching that skin myself...Ugh! I'd always smell snake on it."

She put the snake down gently by the side of the trail and they continued on their tour. The day was half over, and Father led them by a different route back to Hidden Bay, and then to Pender Harbour.

The poor girl! I wonder what she thought. Why did the attentive young swain of the way in become the coolly efficient and polite tour guide on the return journey? She gave him her address, but he never used it.

If it had not been for a snake and a young boy's toe, I would probably not exist to write these stories. But on the other hand, someone else might have done it sooner, and better!

The Well

Of his various encounters with snakes, he told the one about the well most often. Perhaps for the same reason people go to horror movies.

He and his brother Cliff were coming back down the Gulf of Georgia from Stuart Island one nice fall day. When they came to Redonda Island, they decided to stop at an abandoned apple orchard that they knew of, to see if they could find any unusual apples.

Old orchards were a common sight along the coast. Even now, you may find places where hundreds of dead and dying fruit trees have lost the struggle for light to the native evergreens.

It seemed like such a great way to make money in the early days. Just clear the land, plant a few hundred trees, and in only four or five years transport the apples cheaply by boat or barge to the fast-growing fruit-hungry cities around the gulf. It wasn't such a bad idea. Apple trees grow well on the lower coast: the soil is suitable, the winters are mild and there is ample water. But so many orchards sprang up that their fruit became a serious competitor to the big farms in the BC interior, and some of those were owned by people with money and influence, who went into action.

Apples grown on the coast sometimes develop small round black spots, caused by a variety of spore that settles on them in wet weather. It is harmless, and won't spread among apples in storage or from picked apples to apple trees. In fact, it had already spread everywhere that it could. Somehow (no one had any doubt how!) the government was persuaded that this was a disease that would spread all over the country if it wasn't checked. The government acted. That year, the loads of apples were met at the docks by inspectors. Zealous men all, determined to stop the blight in its tracks.

Embittered farmers, their hopes dashed, told Father how, if only one apple in a load was found with a spot, the whole load was ordered dumped. There was no appeal.

It didn't seem to bother anyone that the rule seemed to apply only to apples from the shores and islands of certain parts of the coast. And that, according to Father, is the reason for the hundreds of deserted orchards.

• • •

(I do not vouch for this story, but only repeat it as it was told to me. D.H.)

It was at one of these farms that Father and Cliff decided to stop. They anchored the boat, went ashore and wandered around for a while sampling apples. It was quite a big farm, and long rows of apple trees stretched off into the encroaching forest. The land sloped gently up from the beach, and where the woods began, there was a house with broken windows and a collapsed roof. Father decided to investigate, while his brother stayed, strolling through the trees, looking for the perfect apple.

Father walked up to the house and looked in the windows. The floor was rotten, and strips of torn paper hung from the walls. Nothing of interest was visible. Seeing no reason to go inside, he walked around the side of the house. Ivy was thick on the ground. He should have known better, but he walked across a patch of it to inspect an outbuilding. Without warning, the ground gave way under his feet and he felt himself dropping. Like a cat, he twisted and flung his arms out, catching at the tough ivy strands with both hands. They held, and he lay sprawled there with his chest on the ground and his feet dangling. There was the sound of debris falling into water. Untangling his feet from the clinging vines, he flipped himself back onto solid ground and turned to see what he had fallen into. It was a well, about five feet square, which had been covered with planks, now rotted and fallen away; a common enough hazard around old farms. He walked around it, pulling back the ivy so that the whole opening was exposed. He was very conscientious about that sort of thing, and would mark it so that others might be warned.

There is something fascinating about wells. One always has to look into them. He knelt at one corner and, bracing his hands on the edges, leaned as far down as he could so that his eyes would adapt to the gloom. But it was only about ten feet deep and not as dark as he had expected, for the rays of the noon sun lit the bottom quite clearly.

The first thing he saw was a human skeleton in the corner across from him, sitting in water up to its ribs. The skull was at an angle, supported by the corner, and seemed to be peering up at him in amusement. There were a few tatters of shirt hanging on the bones.

He stared down, frozen with shock and horror. Not at the bones. Father was quite nonchalant about bones when the owner had finished with them. What held his horrified gaze were the snakes. The well was full of snakes! The whole surface of the water seemed to be slowly moving. The water was full of snakes, the floating pieces of plank were covered with snakes, and the walls for the length of a man's arm were festooned with snakes, for their constant efforts to escape had worn grooves in the soft clay, until they came to a harder material in which they could make no mark.

"Thousands of snakes," he told me. "More snakes than I ever dreamed about in my worst nightmares." (Hundreds? I think we can safely drop a zero in this instance.)

The skull moved a little. A snake oozed out from behind it and undulated down the ladder of the ribs. Father felt his hand sliding, very slowly, in the loose earth on the edge of the well, but only with a part of his mind where it didn't really register. What mattered were the snakes, coiling and coiling, and the whispering sound of their moving. The sunlight made their eyes glisten like points of gold...

He thought he might have yelled. Cliff said afterwards that he did. It must have been quite a yell, because Cliff was not one to be deflected from his purpose until he was quite ready. Walking more quickly than usual, he came to where his brother was kneeling and peered into the well. He glanced at his brother's hands, now almost on the slippery clay below the edge, and said comfortingly, as he reached down and pulled Father away from the well, "You silly fool, you can't drink out of there, your neck's not long enough!"

"As soon as my eyes left those snakes," Father told me, "I was all right again. But I couldn't have looked away to save my soul!"

Cliff went to the well edge and looked in. He threw a few chunks at the snakes, one of which managed to knock the skull from the shoulder it rested on. They speculated on who it might be, and how long it had been there. Perhaps it was the owner of the orchard, made hopeless by the collapse of his dreams, but they decided he would probably have found an easier way to kill himself. More likely, they thought, a solitary wanderer.

Before they left, they found a chunk of fallen tree and threw it into the well as a sort of ladder. Cliff scoffed but Father thought that even a snake should have its chance.

On the way back, they reported their find to the police at Powell River, but they never heard whether the bones had been identified.

I asked Father what he thought would have happened if he had fallen in the well. He said promptly, "There would have been a trail up the side of that well. I'd have clawed it out with my fingernails!"

The Hermit of Hotham Sound

On fine weekends Father often took friends for a cruise in his boat on the waters around Pender Harbour. So it was that one Sunday he and three couples were in the boat, gliding across the calm water of Jervis Inlet under the warm fall sun. There were picnic lunches, and time to enjoy them. There was conversation, and laughter, and magnificent scenery.

But sometimes after two or three hours on a small boat in calm weather, the chugging engine sound becomes monotonous. The scenery is just as magnificent, but it changes little. Talk lags. One begins to look for diversion, any diversion.

Thus, when they came to a little cove on the shore of Hotham Sound with a ramshackle float leading to shore and a weathered old shack on the slope behind, everyone was interested.

"An old man lives there," said Father, in answer to their questions. "Has lived there as long as anyone can remember."

One of the girls said impulsively, "Let's go ashore and pay him a visit."

"Oh yes, let's," chorused everyone.

He was doubtful. The old man had a reputation for not receiving visitors kindly.

"Well," someone said, "surely he won't shoot us if we go ashore. If he's not friendly, we can just leave."

So he swung the boat inshore, and made it fast to the old float. And there came the owner, trotting briskly down the path to meet them, accompanied by a large dog.

"Here he comes," said one of the men, "the Hermit of Hotham Sound."

And what a hermit!

"He was," said Father, "the dirtiest man I have ever seen. His clothes were held together with greasy pieces of cord. There seemed to be bits of every meal he had eaten for months in his matted beard and torn shirt, and everything was stained brown with tobacco juice."

He wore no shoes, only grey wool socks, with toes sticking out one end and heels at the other.

But to everyone's relief, he was friendly. Effusively friendly, and so was his dog. On being introduced, the old man shook hands all around.

"It was funny," said Father, "to see everyone trying to wipe their hands on something as soon as possible, without seeming to do so."

The hermit begged them to come up to his house, and as everyone was filled with curiosity about it, they were soon standing in the main room, admiring the view out over the sound. And what a room it was! In it were the stove, a kitchen table with a wash basin full of greyish water, and a bed. And there were the chickens. They occupied most of the surfaces whenever they cared to, to judge from the state of those surfaces.

The floor was of wood, but in most places not distinguishable from the mud of the yard. There was a trail to the stove, and a trail to the table. Dog hair was everywhere.

Would they, inquired their host, have some wine? "If I do say so myself, I make the finest wine you have ever tasted."

As he talked he bustled about, bringing out cracked glasses and cups without handles. He rinsed them in a water bucket, and to the relief of his guests—and Father's amazement—found a not-too-repulsive cloth to wipe them with. Then, with great ceremony, he produced a bottle of wine and filled eveyone's glass or cup.

Father declined, and would not be swayed.

But the wine *was* good, or so everyone exclaimed. They even had samples from another bottle or two.

"Come on, Hal, you don't know what you're missing."

"No, thank you just the same. I'm not much of a wine drinker," he answered quite truthfully.

The old man was so pleased with the praise that now he must show them how it was made. Down they went, cups and glasses in hand, to the space under the house. It was a veritable wine cellar! Everywhere basins and tubs with varying amounts of liquid in them. And over each container hung a grey sock, dripping slowly.

"The secret," the old man was saying, "is not to squeeze it, but let it drip for as long as it takes. That way you get the clearest wine, the pure juice."

Father spoke without thinking—although I wonder about that claim. "I hope you washed them first."

There was a deathly silence. Everyone regarded the grey socks.

One of the women gasped—"Ahhh," and vomited all over the woman standing in front of her. That one looked at her dress, and did the same. The fumes, the sounds, the situation were too much for one of the men. He made it almost to the door before he could hold back no longer.

Father faded quietly back to the boat. Soon his passengers arrived, pale-faced and apologizing to the old man. He, in turn, was expostulating on the disinfectant quality of wine. It didn't seem to help much.

So they took their leave of the Hermit of Hotham Sound.

But he, while the lines were being loosed, put his shaggy head in the cabin window by the steering wheel.

"Young fella," he said slowly. "Next time you come by here, you'd best be beyond shooting range!"

After they had been on their way a while, Father's best friend came into the cabin.

"Hal, that was an awful thing to do."

"It wasn't very nice, was it?"

"No." A pause. "But it sure as hell was funny!"

The Skull

Most people in those days took their religion pretty seriously, and it has often been observed that where religion is strong, the supernatural is never far away. But Father was not superstitious. Indeed, he could often be heard to say, "Now I am not a superstitious man..." but neither was he a complete skeptic. He liked to illustrate his attitude with the story of the man who spilled some salt.

The man looks at the salt on the floor and scoffs, "People think that spilling salt means bad luck, and that the only way to avoid it is to throw some over your left shoulder. Of course that is superstitious nonsense and I don't believe a word of it." He looks around uneasily. "But on the other hand, it can't possibly do any harm." And he throws a bit of salt over his shoulder!

• • •

And then Father might tell the story of

THE SKULL.

He had been to Vancouver and was chugging back to Jervis Inlet in his old gas boat with a rising southeast wind behind him. It took him about five hours to reach Trail Islands, roughly halfway to his destination. By then the seas were rough enough that he decided to anchor in the shelter of one of the islands for a while until the weather improved. He ate lunch and then, launching his skiff, went ashore to walk along the beaches.

Now at this time (early twenties) there was a sort of fad for having a human skull as a parlour ornament. One of his friends made quite

a bit of money cleaning, varnishing and mounting them in one way or another. Unfortunately, he had run out of material. Knowing that Father trapped and hunted and that he knew the location of many old graveyards, he had asked him if he would find some more skulls to mount. He offered quite a handsome sum.

Father laughed at him. "If you want any graves robbed, you'll have to do it yourself."

But when he came to a part of the beach where a bit of bank had caved in and saw a very nice skull there on the gravel, all washed and cleaned by the rain, he picked it up. As the next high tide would surely destroy it, he felt no compunction about taking it home to his friend.

Back on the boat, he stored his find carefully in a drawer in the after-cabin. His boat had two cabins, with a passage between, so that you could go from one side to the other without having to go all the way around. Steering and stove in the forward cabin, sleeping quarters aft. Quite a common design in those days.

He ate supper, still waiting to see what the weather would do. About an hour after dark, the wind dropped, and the sky cleared enough that a bit of moon showed now and again through the slowly moving clouds. Though there was still quite a swell rolling, he decided to continue on in the dark. All went well enough at first, but about half an hour from the islands, the swells changed direction. Instead of coming from directly astern, they now hit the boat from the stern quarter, causing it to pitch in an uncomfortable corkscrewing sort of motion.

Soon afterwards, he began to hear the thumping. Thump thump thump thump *thump* it would go, then again, and again. Obviously, he thought, something loose in the stern cabin—but what? Father kept a neat boat. He prided himself on being able to travel in any weather, should he choose to do so. No loose objects. Everything had its place, and was fastened or stowed securely.

At last he could stand it no longer. He tied down the wheel, turned up the shielded lantern and went out on deck. He listened. There it came again, thump thump thump *thump*. He opened the door of the after-cabin. There was the skull on the floor. He looked at the drawer he had put it in. It was closed. He picked up the skull, went over to the drawer, opened it. It was made so that it had to be lifted and then slid out, so that it wouldn't open in rough weather. However, the boat had been lurching rather oddly: the drawer must have opened, the skull bounced out and the drawer slid closed again.

He replaced the skull, well to the rear of the drawer, and slid it closed. He heard the latch click. Tested it. He watched it suspiciously for a moment or two. The boat's motion showed no sign of moving it. Finally satisfied, he went back to the steering wheel. Another half hour passed.

Now, you should realize that the coast waters were lonely in those days. One seldom saw another boat, especially at night. There were few lights on shore, no city lights in the distance. No radiophones, for marine radio was only used on large boats. Just yourself, on the sea, alone in the dark.

And, once again, thump thump thump *thump*.

He tied the wheel, picked up the lantern, went on deck, opened the door. There in the dim yellow light of the lantern came the skull, rolling down the floor toward him. It stopped about a yard from the door as the boat lurched again. Right side up it sat there, the shadowed eye hollows, the grinning teeth.

And Father would say, "You know, I'm not a superstitious man, but I picked up that skull and I looked at it. It was thin, brittle bone. Why hadn't it smashed when it hit the floor? I looked over at the drawer. It was closed. I said, 'Old fellow, if you don't want to stay in that drawer, fine. But you're not going to roam around in this ship behind my back.' So I flung it overboard."

The Englishman

One of Father's youthful ambitions was to be a guide. To get paid for doing what you most enjoyed seemed almost too good to be true. But when he realized his dream and became a licensed guide, he discovered one unforeseen drawback. Not everyone who wants to hunt should be allowed out with a gun.

"Actually," he would say, "most of the men I took out were pretty good people. Even the ones who didn't know anything about hunting were willing to listen to what they were told, and tried to learn how to handle themselves in the woods."

Some of his clients became his friends, and remained so for many years. But then there were the other sort. Of these, the most memorable was the Englishman.

Now, the English aroused mixed feelings here in the West. The "remittance men" in general had left a bad impression, but in Father's time their day had mostly passed. English ignorance of things practical was a byword, and jokes about their naïveté and general incompetence at the basic skills required in their new home were told with considerable glee. But they also had a reputation for persistence in the face of obstacles, contempt for their own suffering, and bravery that amounted at times to foolhardiness. All qualities that were admired by the westerner.

For Father's part, as half his ancestry was English, he was rather inclined in their favour. So when he received a letter from England saying that he had been highly recommended as a guide for that area and asking if he would take the writer on a hunt for a trophy grizzly bear, he accepted with considerable enthusiasm. Especially as the terms were generous and included a nice bonus for a successful hunt.

At last the stipulated day arrived, and he met his client for the first time on the wharf at Campbell River, from where they would head up-coast to the area that he'd chosen to hunt.

The man was so English! A caricature of an Englishman, in fact, nothing lacking in any way. Heavy-set, red-complexioned, moustachioed and tweeded. A retired army major, complete with polished leather high boots and a pair of lavishly engraved double-barrelled rifles in leather cases.

He was also, to Father's surprise, a good client. An ideal client, in fact. Impervious to bad weather, he was always cheerful. He was intelligent and took direction promptly and well. He sighted his guns in at the first opportunity, and proved to be an excellent shot. Not least in Father's estimation, he not only enjoyed a good story and listened well, he himself had a large fund of hunting stories which he recounted skilfully. A paragon among clients!

He had shot tigers in India, jaguars in South America and—of course—all the noted game animals of Africa. His stories were often thrilling: of guides being saved from tigers; of lions among the bearers, killed with a native in their jaws; of charging elephants brought down over the trampled bodies of native hunters.

"In fact," said Father, "after hearing his stories for a couple of evenings I began to think he was going to find a grizzly bear hunt pretty tame stuff."

At first, they had no luck. There were lots of bears, but no grizzly. Father knew that there was an exceptional trophy animal in the valley, but it was a big valley.

At last, on the evening of the third day, he found its tracks. His client had time for only one more day of hunting, so instead of going back to their base at the river mouth, they made camp right where they were. Father was good at throwing up a quick campsite, and he carried enough food in his small knapsack to make supper and breakfast.

They began the final hunt at daybreak. The huge tracks led along a small stream coming from a rock slide. Father thought the grizzly would be on the slide eating roots or berries, but before they came within sight of the slide, they heard the unmistakable sound of a bear tearing a log apart.

"That will be him," whispered Father. "There won't be another bear near the brute that made these tracks."

He led the way to a big fallen tree, for he always liked to be out of the brush where he could see around him when he was near a grizzly. They both climbed onto the tree near the upturned roots, and there, about seventy yards away, was the bear, ripping open a rotten log for the ants and grubs in it. A really magnificent silver-tip, as big as any Father had ever seen.

"There's your bear, go to it," he said quietly.

The Englishman raised his gun, aimed carefully, fired. The bear flinched, but instead of falling, began licking furiously at its left front paw, evidently the place where it had been hit. Father wasn't particularly surprised. He'd seen many good shots fire wildly off target when excited, though he hadn't expected it of this man.

"Go on, shoot," he urged. As if it had heard, the bear wheeled and stared in their direction. Then the long hair on its back raised up in a ridge, and it charged straight for them. An enraged grizzly covers ground faster than you would believe, and the wounded paw didn't seem to slow it down at all.

Father glanced around at his client. Instead of shooting, he was loading another shell in the breech of his rifle. Then he raised the gun to his shoulder. Then he lowered it again and began to adjust the sight! The bear was very close.

"Shoot!" yelled Father.

Up came the gun, then down again. The man stepped back and down onto a fork that had grown off the main tree, rested his gun in front of him and calmly began to adjust his sight again. Father couldn't believe what was happening, but could spare no time for wondering. The grizzly had arrived at the tree. It stopped, raised its front feet off the ground a bit and peered up at them as if wondering what they were. Then it reared swiftly to its full height and reached.

Though the tree was six feet through, the head of the bear was level with the man's.

Father never carried a rifle when guiding but relied instead on a double-barrelled twelve- gauge shotgun. It was loaded that day with shells containing the extra heavy pellets they used to call goose shot. It was intended only for extreme emergency at the closest range.

"As the bear reached out to grab me, " he said, "it opened its jaws wide. I stuck the muzzle of the gun in its mouth and pulled both triggers. I'd never fired both barrels at once in my life, and the kick must have been tremendous, but I never felt a thing. That double charge of shot split the bear's head wide open, just a little skin left on the front of the skull. It never knew what happened."

He drew a long breath of relief as he looked around at his client. He felt that he had handled himself well. He'd not retreated an inch and had waited until the last possible moment. He thought a word or two of praise would be well deserved.

"What happened," he asked. "Something go wrong with your gun?"

The Englishman was looking at him most strangely. He appeared to be about to explode from some sort of inner pressure. He began to speak.

"You blundering fool!" he roared. "You've ruined my trophy. I've come ten thousand miles to get that grizzly. It may be the last chance I'll ever have, and some blithering bloody incompetent spoils it! Look at it," he commanded. "What good is that to me?"

He lowered his voice a bit, but it was vibrant with passion. "I'll tell you what I'm going to do, sir. I'm going to report you for incompetence. You'll never get another job guiding again."

He was about to continue, but Father had heard enough. He had expected praise and had gotten abuse, and he had gone through surprise, disbelief, shock and anger in approximately that order. Now he began to speak, and when he spoke in anger, people listened.

"Now let me tell you something. I know exactly what you were up to. You didn't just want a bear. Oh no! You wanted another good story to tell at your club. How you saved your guide when he was being mauled by a grizzly. There isn't anything wrong with your gun or your shooting. You shot him in the paw to make him mad, then waited, thinking I'd hold off too long, expecting you to shoot. That's how you got all those other stories, isn't it? I suppose those poor natives in Africa and India didn't have any way to defend themselves. They were counting on you and you 'saved' them at last, didn't you? Or most of them! Well, let me tell you something more. This isn't Africa. Here, we look after our own skins, and if you don't like it, don't come back." Then he had an inspiration. "And as for reporting me, we'll see who plays that game best. When I let the organization of guides know about you, you'll never get a guide to so much as take you out to shoot squirrels!"

If there was such an organization, Father had never heard of it, but the threat apparently struck deeply. The Englishman began to stammer denials, then apologies.

Father cooled down a bit. They examined the bear. With sufficient skill, the head might be repaired. It would make a splendid rug. They skinned it out and carried the hide and head back to the boat.

Their manner to one another was courteous but not cordial. On parting, his client paid the full fee, plus bonus as specified.

Somewhere in England there is probably—even now—a rug made from the hide of a large grizzly. There will be a patched spot on its head.

Though he never stopped taking people hunting, that was Father's last trip as a guide. As he explained to me, "I thought it would be the best job in the world, getting paid to hunt. Instead, it turned what I did for fun into a job. That took all the fun out of it."

The Iron Horse

In my first book of Father's stories, *Tales from Hidden Basin*, I described how Father moved his mother and sisters from the farm in Hidden Basin and brought them to the store at Selma Park. With his mother's lifelong ambition satisfied, he began the restless journeying that would eventually produce these stories.

The three occupations most readily available to him were fishing, farming and logging. Fishing at that time wasn't very profitable, and he didn't care for the smell of aged fish that was inseparable from that work. (They said that you very soon ceased to notice it, but he never cared to test the claim.) He liked farming, but good land was expensive even then, and he wasn't ready to settle down. That left logging. He soon found that work in the woods didn't appeal to him. Work on the water did, and he discovered that he had a real talent for handling logs in the water. But times were hard. Many of the smaller camps, and some bigger ones, paid late or sometimes not at all. He would stay a while, perhaps reorganize the log booming, then move on. It was good experience.

• • •

In this story there is mention of a Chinese cook, and the reader is apt to exclaim "What? Not another Chinese cook!" So I include a few words on the genus Camp Cook, as of fifty to a hundred years ago, and why so many of them were Chinese.

One reason is that they were willing to do it. Cooking has been an honourable profession in China for a very long time; it was held no

60

disgrace to be a cook. And it was one of the few jobs a lone Chinese could have in a logging camp, for there was prejudice against them because they were different, a reason common to most parts of the world. The day of the all-Chinese crew was fading; this was often the only job left. And they made wonderful cooks. Usually sober, always clean and dependable, they were the preferred employees for what was arguably the most important job in a camp. Not that there weren't European cooks, some of them excellent, men and women both. But one woman in a camp full of men can be trouble; they tended to marry, get pregnant, and quit their jobs, not necessarily in that order. Male Europeans also tended to be flawed. Far too often they were drunk, dirty or both, and their level of skill varied enormously. And both sexes tended to get bored with the repetitive menu and begin to experiment. Loggers hated experiments. Any change from the routine of steaks, chops, roasts, etc., was viewed with suspicion and hostility. The Chinese never got bored, never experimented.

After his initial experience with a Chinese cook when he was a boy in Hidden Basin, Father was a bit wary of them at first. But he soon discovered that they were worth getting to know, and once they found you weren't buttering them up to get after-hours snacks, they responded gratefully to friendly advances.

It is quite likely that the Chinese cook was responsible for bringing more pleasure to more people in the camps of the coast than any other thing except liquor, and unlike it, they had no down side.

This story takes place in another of the many small camps that Father worked in for a while when he was young, no later than 1929. In this case I regret the inability to be certain of the time or the place, for there could perhaps be a slight historical interest. Perhaps not. The camp was situated somewhere on the Sechelt Peninsula between Halfmoon Bay and Agamemnon Channel, or so I believe, and was owned by a man named Pete Mien. (Father's pronunciation. Might have been Meaghan or Meehan.) It was a horse logging operation, and there had been a run of bad luck with the animals—lameness, strange illnesses, that sort of thing—and Pete was getting short-tempered. Then one day when he and Father were working on the beach, a man came striding down the road from the woods to where they were standing waiting, for his appearance at that time meant there was bad news of some kind. The men in the woods were competent and wouldn't come to bother the boss with any ordinary problem.

When he was near enough, the man said dramatically, "The big bay dropped dead, halfway down with a load, and somehow lamed his partner Spots when he did it!"

Pete flung down the hammer he was holding and cursed all horses, living or dead, in tones of real sincerity.

"Haul him off in the brush for the crows," he ordered. "Real far, I don't want to smell dead horse when I go up the road. You'll have to work just one team for now. I'll go out and see what I can find."

When the other had gone, he turned to Father. "I wish I could go back to ground-yarding, or maybe A-frame. Anything but horses!" and he stomped off, muttering unkind words about horses. He was gone for three days, and came back with no horses, but he was smiling.

"Have I got a surprise for this camp!" were his first words. But when Father questioned him, he would just grin and shake his head mysteriously. "Nope. You'll just have to wait and see."

Two days more, and see they did. Early in the morning—before breakfast—there was a loud whistle from off shore, heralding the approach of a tug towing a scow. On the scow's deck was a single object draped in a big tarpaulin. The tug stopped a hundred feet or so from shore, and Pete, on the beach, beckoned and pointed to a spot free of rocks. The captain waved, the scow was hauled in and the lines removed. Then the tug went around behind the scow and began to push it toward shore. A man jumped off the bow of the tug, walked over to the draped object and began to unfasten the tarp. The front of the scow hit the beach and, with no load to weigh it down, slid several yards up the gravel. And then the man on the scow pulled the tarp away, revealing a strange red machine such as most of the men there had never seen. Instead of wheels it had cleated tracks. There

was a big metal blade in front, supported by hinged arms, with a system of wires and pulleys to raise or lower it. It looked immensely powerful.

"There you are, boys," announced Pete, his face beaming smiles. "The first logging tractor on the coast!" (Just how much of the coast he meant, I have no idea.) "No more horses," he went on happily. "I've got an iron horse now! And it'll outpull any team you've ever seen, and make its own roads to boot. Now maybe we'll get some logging done!"

The man on the scow came walking up, stood there looking down at them. He was very young, perhaps still in his teens, and very skinny. A mop of blondish hair like a sheepdog's hung over his forehead. He was either trying to grow a beard and moustache or was too lazy to shave: straggly blond hair obscured his lip and fuzzed his receding chin. He looked at them with an expression of amused interest as if he hadn't seen anything quite like them before.

Pete looked up at him. "Tell the skipper we'll have a ramp up in a couple of hours."

"What do you want a ramp for, Dad?" inquired the youth, as earnestly as if he really didn't know.

Pete snorted in disgust. "I'd think," he said, as if to the air, "that even a wet-behind-the-ears townie would know what a ramp is for." Looking up once more, "How do you expect us to get it down? Does it fly?"

The young man grinned down at him insolently. "Oh, you mean you want to get it down there on the ground. Why didn't you say so? I'll get it down for you."

Pete shook his head in mock amazement. "I knew townies were a few inches short of a yard, but I didn't think they were that crazy. He really thinks that thing will fly!" He looked up, but his victim had disappeared. In a changed voice he commanded his crew, "All right. Let's get some logs down here—they'd better be about two feet thick. That thing cost me a pile of money, most of which I haven't got, so I want this done right. Get a ladder so we can get up there and hang a block."

He looked at the scow, measuring the height with his eyes. It was a fair-sized scow, and slanted as it was on the beach, the deck was about four feet above his head. The front was angled in like the bow of a ship. He started to say something, when there came the sound of some kind of motor and then the ferocious blatting of a large and poorly muffled engine. They all scrambled up on the shore to get a look on deck. There was blue smoke coming from the exhaust pipe of the machine. The scrawny young man was at the controls, only he somehow didn't seem so scrawny now. His stance and his look were those of someone who controlled great power. Like a king on his throne he sat there, arms out, hands on the levers.

Said Father, "I think we were all impressed. I know I was. We had a feeling that something unusual was going to happen. What we didn't know was just how unusual. We were about to see a master at his craft; someone born with a skill that most people wouldn't even dream was possible."

(I might add, something like his own strange skill with a rifle!)

The youth saw them watching and waved gaily. He moved levers, and the thing came to life. The sound of the engine became a roar as the gleaming red machine shot down the middle of the deck straight toward them, moving much faster than anyone had expected. It came to the edge, to the ten-foot drop over the edge, and never slowed. The driver had a sort of dreamy look on his narrow face: a rapt look, almost of exaltation. Pete yelled in shock and horror, "Look out, he's gone crazy! My machine!..."

Halfway over the edge, more than halfway; then a quick movement of hands and it stopped even more quckly than it had started. But it was more than halfway over, and the nose of the machine began its plunge to the hard ground below. Another quick move and the tracks reversed, the sharp cleats cut into the wood and pulled it back before it could overbalance, and it hung there on the edge, swaying up and down like a teeter-totter, its driver laughing like a madman at the shocked faces below him.

"Stand back, Dad!" he called. "You ain't seen nothing yet!"

Pete shouted, "You crazy bastard. Get out of my machine!" But the other shook his head mockingly.

"Now, now, Dad. Don't bother the driver. He might drop your toy and break it!" He laughed again, revved the engine, and began to do the impossible.

His hands moved and the machine shot forward about three feet, began to fall. Moved again, back about two feet, and the nose bounced skyward as the cleats gripped. Forward and back, forward and back, and each time the nose dipped forward until the machine was almost vertical, and almost touching the ground. He never for a moment lost the rhythm. But the next time, the watchers knew it would be past vertical, and must fall over backwards. Pete cursed bitterly. The nose dropped, the cleats lost their grip, but as it fell, the operator swung the blade down, and the machine came to rest with scarcely a jolt, the blade supporting it and keeping it from falling over. But now it was standing on end, with the in-sloping bow of the scow slanting away behind it.

"Now what are we supposed to do?" asked Pete furiously. "We'll never get it down from there."

But all he got for an answer was, "Keep your shirt on, Dad, keep your shirt on. Maybe you'll learn something yet."

The engine roared, the blade pulled, then lifted, and the tracks touched the ground. They were moving as they touched, pulling the machine forward until the back of the tracks were even with the edge of the scow. Then they were below the edge, almost falling...He reversed and the cleats cut into the underside of the scow. The tracks started to slip on the ground with the pressure, but he jammed the blade down and held them solid. And then, with infinitely precise movements, he walked the machine down under the sloping bow, until it came to rest on the level ground.

Said Father, "Pete had tears running down his cheeks, and he was cursing like a mule-skinner. Everyone was talking, and no one was listening."

Suddenly the engine roared, and the machine began to move up the beach toward them with that abrupt acceleration no one was used to. Everyone scattered as it charged over the spot where they had been standing. There was a maniac cackle from its driver as he tore full speed up into the camp and into a flock of chickens that the cook kept for their eggs. With outraged squawks the chickens fled, but now he spotted the camp dog sleeping in the sun and chased it, yelping, into the woods. He put the machine into reverse, then sat with his hands folded as it idled slowly back toward the beach. The Chinese cook was standing in the cookhouse doorway, his face one big delighted grin as he watched. One track stopped, and as the other turned, the red monster swung toward the doorway. For a moment it was still. Then it darted forward, clanking, roaring, a creature out of legend. The astonished cook stood paralyzed; at the last moment threw himself backward with a terrified scream. When only inches from the doorway, when the cookhouse seemed doomed, it stopped, with that startling abruptness. The tracks slid a few inches on the soil, and the blade touched the door frame. They heard the crash of dishes falling. Again it idled back, back.

There was a small tree growing in the clearing, six or eight inches thick. The driver gave a cowboy yell and the machine shot forward once more. They thought he would skin by the tree, but he hit it with one track, the cleats cut in, and he climbed the machine up the tree until it was almost vertical again. But the uneven weight made the tree slip from the cleats, and it lodged between track and body. He revved the engine a couple of times, the tracks churned, but the tree was jammed and the machine didn't move. He killed the engine, and climbed down. The whole camp, except for the cook, was standing around. The youth looked at Pete, said blandly, "There you are, Dad. She's all yours."

Pete looked at him, looked at his tractor. "How am I going to get it down out of that tree?" he asked in bafflement.

The young man looked around in surprise, as if wondering how the machine had got up the tree when he wasn't looking. "I don't know, Dad. Cut the tree down, I guess."

"I'm not your dad," snapped Pete, "and how are we going to cut the tree down? We'll have to rig guy lines to lower it. Something might break if we just let it drop."

"Guess so, Dad," indifferently. "That's your problem."

"I'm not your dad!" yelled the infuriated logger. "Thank God for that!"

The youth grinned. "Amen, Pops," he returned mockingly. And then, "I wonder if cookee's got anything to eat. I'm starving." And he sauntered off toward the cookhouse. But after taking only a few steps, he stopped and turned. "When you get her down, Pops, send someone in and I'll show him how to run her. But no greybeards need apply. Give me the youngest man in the camp." And he turned away.

"Cook will kill him," guessed Father.

"Good," said Pete savagely.

However, much to their surprise and Pete's disappointment, Cook not only didn't kill the brash youth but fed him lavishly on the best his cupboards held!

Father was the man Pete thought would be best suited to the job of driving the tractor, but he refused it, after taking a ride. "Too noisy," he said, "and too hard. A man would need arms like a gorilla to pull those levers all day. But way too noisy."

The iron horse, though not without its faults, worked out even better than Pete hoped. It was the end of an era. Word spread. Soon, horses for logging would be the oddity, and the forests would be filled with the roar and stink of engines. Many would come to regret it.

Revenge is Sweet

Working his way from camp to camp, Father arrived eventually at Myrtle Point near Powell River, where he hired on as a boom man. Myrtle Point was the largest camp on that part of the coast. It was a train camp, like all the other big camps of the time. The logs were brought to water by train and rail cars. The high volume of wood meant that the logs must be handled efficiently, so that there was always room in the water at the log dump for the logs on the next string of loaded cars. As the area of sheltered water was limited at Myrtle Point, this wasn't always managed, which often led to costly delays.

In an earlier book I've told how, when the water was jammed with logs and the camp at a standstill, Father offered a plan to solve the present crisis and prevent future ones. The conditions were that he would do the work on contract, with a crew that he would hand-pick himself.

The camp boss, desperate by then and ready to try anything, liked what he heard and accepted the young man's proposal. True to his word, Father reorganized the sorting grounds, hired a crew of top men at a good wage, and there were no further holdups at the log dump.

The time was a couple of years after the first World War, and men were coming home, looking for jobs. Most of them slipped back into civilian life without too much trouble, but not all. Among the exceptions were many of the higher ranking officers, mainly of the army. Most of them only had one skill, that of commanding men.

Or if they were not skilled at it, it was their profession. Although some of them were careful of the welfare of the troops they commanded, to many of them, men were but a means to an end. They were expendable.

These officers arrived back on the coast just when the logging camps were getting bigger, and when many of the old-time camp owners and bosses were either dying off or looking for someone to take over the actual running of the operations. And here were these men, trained to command and ready to go into action. It seemed an ideal solution.

Up until this time, the owners and bosses were mainly men who had been loggers first. There were good ones and bad ones, but they knew what the men faced, what they felt. Men could talk to the boss, on a first-name basis, about their problems.

"But next thing we knew," remembered Father, "here were these new fellows sent out by the head office in Vancouver or Victoria—which was another new thing—and now it was Major this, and Colonel that, and all they were good for was to give orders. They caused a lot of trouble."

The operation at Myrtle Point was one of the larger ones, and perhaps one of the first to receive the benefit of the new order. A new supervisor arrived. He was known as the Colonel. And he was out to make his mark. Except for a few of the returned soldiers, no one had seen boots that high, that tight or that highly polished. Nor the funny little stick he slapped them with when he was in a temper. The boots had slick leather soles, which meant he couldn't walk on logs with them, and thus Father was spared his attentions for a while. But it wasn't long before he was handed a note that requested his presence at the office at a certain time. Having heard something of the Colonel and his methods, Father wasn't eager to know more, but he duly presented himself, and was introduced.

That over, "Hammond, we've got a problem with your operation."

"Not that I know of. Things are going nice and smoothly."

The Colonel shook his head. "That may be so, but you're down on the books as costing us a half cent a thousand more than the operation at Fanny Bay. Why is that?"

"We're sorting the wood eleven ways, they're only doing seven," explained Father. "And besides that, they're in more sheltered water than we are."

"Well, I don't care about that," came the retort. "But it doesn't look good, and it'll have to be changed. After all, it's only half a cent. You and your crew will still be making good wages."

Father had disliked the Colonel and his autocratic manner from the first, and liked him less the longer he was exposed to him. His decision came instantly.

"Well," he drawled, "you can talk that over with the new man."

"What new man?"

"The one you'll have to get to take my place."

"What do you mean—take your place?"

"I mean I've just quit. I don't like the working conditions here any more."

"I suppose you think I'll change my mind, do you? Well, you look to me like a troublemaker. We'll be better off without you." And with a slap of the stick on the polished boots, he was off to reform the rest of the camp. "Looking," as Father recalled, "like he had a broomstick for a backbone."

When he told his crew, they were all for joining him. They'd show "Highboots" this wasn't the army. But he'd have none of it. "Any one of you can run the show now. It's a good job, stick with it. My feet were getting itchy anyhow. Things were getting boring."

So they decided to wait and see how it would go, and he went to work on Vancouver Island for P.B. Anderson, one of the old-type logger bosses. He was a patriarchal despot, but a good man, and fair. Father liked him, although there was a clash of sorts at one time. He had been working there about a month when P.B. approached him. After a few minutes spent discussing Father's work, P.B. changed the subject abruptly. "I've noticed you spend quite a bit of time hunting, and when you're not hunting, you're tramping all over the country on one excuse or another."

"I like to get to know any place I'm at," agreed Father.

"I'm not blaming you, mind. It's quite okay by me. But I thought you might be the man to help me with something."

"I'll do what I can."

"Fine. Good man. Now you know I don't allow liquor to be sold here. Bad thing around a camp. But the men are getting it somewhere. They're coming to work Monday morning so hungover they're no use to anyone for most of the day. I figure that old loafer down along the shore has a still around here someplace, and I'd like to know where it is. I've prowled around a bit, but I can't find it. I know you don't drink, so you're just the man to help me out."

Father knew where the still was, all right. It was hidden not a quarter of a mile from camp. He had found it by the unmistakable smell of the mash. It was cunningly placed near a little creek, less than a hundred yards from the train trestle that crossed the creek valley. No one else walked those tracks, and by using them, the old man would leave no sign to be picked up, and the air stirred up by passage of the train would dissipate any smell of mash that might linger in the little valley.

He shook his head regretfully. "Sorry, P.B., but I'm afraid you've got me figured wrong. You'll have to find someone else. It's not my sort of job."

"What do you mean, it's not your sort of job? What's wrong with it?"

"It's spying, is what's wrong with it. And besides, I don't think you've any right to tell a man what he can do on his time off. If you don't like his work, you can fire him. But you can't tell him what he can or can't do."

"Oh, I can't, eh? Well, I've been doing just that for a long time, and I don't plan on quitting now." He frowned at Father, storm-faced. "As for firing, maybe I should fire you!"

"You could do that."

P.B. stomped off, but the next time they met, he seemed more friendly than before.

Father had been working there for two or three months when one day P.B. stopped him at the cookhouse door. "Say, Hal, you came here from Myrtle Point, didn't you?"

"That's right. Why?"

"Do you know anything about the equipment over there?"

"A bit," said Father cautiously.

"Well, they've got a locie [locomotive] there they want to sell, so I thought you might run me over in your boat and we'll have a look at it."

"Sure thing," said Father, and off they went.

The first thing Father noticed as they pulled into the floating dock was the logs. There were logs everywhere. There were logs stacked on the beaches, the pockets were full, and there was a trainload waiting to be dumped. He counted twenty-two men working but could see none of his old crew.

They went up to the office and found the Colonel. He was effusive in his welcome to the prodigal.

Father said, "Quite a bunch of wood you've got down in the grounds."

"We've got a bit of problem just now," admitted the Colonel. "Say, how would you like to come back to work, Hal? At five cents a thousand more than before," he added when he saw Father's expression.

But the answer was, "No thanks. I like it where I am. We've come to look at the locie you're selling." And he introduced his companion.

On hearing that legendary name and the reason for their visit, the Colonel forgot Father, saying only, "We'll talk about the job later." He was evidently a hard man to discourage!

Off they went to see the locie, parked down by the dump. All along the way there the Colonel sang its praises, and when they approached it he flung his arms wide. "There, isn't she a beauty?"

It's not easy to examine a stationary locomotive for flaws. This one had been polished and painted, and did indeed appear fairly impressive.

"She's a real workhorse," the colonel enthused. "Hal knows her. Tell him what you think, Hal." He looked at Father for confirmation of its virtues.

Father inspected the machine critically. He said finally, "Yes, I know her all right. That's the old Climax that ran off the track last

year. Frame's warped. When you see her coming down the track with a load, she looks like all her wheels are different sizes."

P.B. Anderson laughed. "Well, I guess I'll give this one a pass. She's a bit older than I want anyway."

Revenge is sweet!

The Stove

Father liked the native people. He was predisposed to, of course, having had Charlie, the old Indian, as his mentor. But there was more to it than that. There was a basic similarity, if not an obvious one. Though he worked hard all his life, or perhaps because of it, he always felt that he could have lived as they did, hunting and fishing, knowing the land. He liked their honesty, though most people thought of them as thieves because their sense of property was different. Their sense of humour was similar to his, which is always a bond of sorts, and they shared a certain shrewdness. For the natives could be devious if deviousness was required, though they would not initiate it, and that also described Father's nature.

He was working for a while at a smallish camp on one of the islands above Powell River. Not long, for the owner-boss turned out to be a nasty sort of article.

The camp was in a deep and sheltered bay. Around the point and a ways up the shore lived a couple of Indian families. They had an old fish boat, and for that reason needed money occasionally for fuel and engine parts. Thus, every once in a while they would come chugging around the point with one or two logs in tow, which they would sell to the camp owner. Of course, being what he was, he cheated them. And then he would call them stupid, often within their hearing, because they took what he gave them. As if they had a choice: there was no other camp nearby.

"Stupid Siwashes," he'd sneer. "A white man wouldn't let himself be taken like that."

Father made the mistake of suggesting that "It wouldn't hurt to pay them a fair price," and got a half-hour lecture on looking after one's own interest, and the folly of charity.

One day, the puff-puff of the old boat could be heard as it rounded the point with a tow. This time it was a single big fir log. The boss had seen them coming and was there to meet them. At sight of the big log, free of flaw or knots, he looked like a miser who'd been offered a pot of gold in exchange for coppers. He even rubbed his hands together in the classic, though unconscious, sign of satisfaction.

He said to the Indians, "Good log. Good log. Bring more like it." He counted out some money, as if it were a large and generous sum.

As they left, and while they were yet in earshot, he said to Father, who was there to take it up to the log pocket: "Stupid Siwashes. If they had any brains, they'd hold out for three times what I gave them!" Off he went back to the camp.

Father poled the log along. He came to the "gap" which led to where the logs were kept. As was the usual practice, there was a forty-foot railway track underwater, held on each end by a six-foot boomchain. This holds the shape of the pocket, while leaving an open space to move logs through. As he pushed the big log in, it stopped and wouldn't go any farther.

He told me, "I thought there was a big branch or two under it, so I tried to roll it over with the peavey, but it wouldn't roll. So I pushed it back out and over to the beach so it would ground. The tide was dropping, and I figured I'd cut the branches off when it had gone down enough. In a couple of hours, I took the axe and went over for a look. I just had to laugh. I couldn't help it! The log was just a shell. One side had caught fire a long time ago, and the whole heart had burned out of it. The tree had lived, and the butt and top were solid, but the log was worthless. There was a piece of old wire stapled to it with a big staple, and on the other end was a huge old cast-iron stove, must have weighed about five hundred pounds, to keep the burnt side floating down. I thought, 'stupid Siwashes', are they?'"

He looked at the setup, and thought a bit. About the cheating boss, whom he disliked, and the Indians, whom he liked. Then he went back to work, and when the tide was in again, he unfastened the cross-rail and took the log around to the boom.

A week or so later, he was at the little store on the other side of the island. The Indians were there on their old boat. Father gave his usual cordial greeting, and they talked for a few minutes, about fishing, and other matters of mutual interest. Finally Father said, "Say, I've been meaning to call up your way sometime."

"Ayuh. Sure. Come visit, any time."

Another asked, "Just visit?"

"Well, I was curious, really. I wanted to see the place where stoves grow on trees. Could use a new one for the boat if I could find a young one."

Smiles vanished. Impassive faces regarded him silently. Finally the oldest of them asked, "You tell Boss?"

Father shrugged his shoulders eloquently. "Why tell Boss? Boss always know everything already."

There was a moment of silence. Then they all started laughing.

The elder chuckled. "Ho, that good. Boss always know everything all right."

They were still grinning when Father went up to the store.

A few days later, he was working on the boom when he noticed a canoe with two men in it coming from the point beyond which lived the Indians. They paddled in, and pulled alongside his boat, which was anchored farther out in the bay. He was curious, but not worried. He knew they would steal nothing. But when he went out to his boat after quitting time, he glanced around.

"And there," he told me, "was the nicest slab of smoked salmon you'd ever want to see!" He paused; then, "Unlike a lot of other people I could mention, those folk never forgot a favour."

Home is ...?

Men and women are different. Have you noticed? No, no. I don't mean that difference. In little ways, sometimes in odd ways. Such as the methods by which they locate themselves, or find their way. Women have an excellent means of accomplishing this. It relies on memory and landmarks; using it, directions can be transmitted very accurately. The method can be learned by men, although many of us do not adapt well to it. (I knew a fireman who appeared to have a map of the city of Seattle in his head.) Men, however, have another means, though in most of us it is much less reliable, and certainly less useful on the streets and lanes of cities. It is innate and—I think—cannot be learned. In exceptional cases it can be astonishingly accurate, but that is so rare as to be a matter of disbelief.

The reason for this difference seems to be obvious. For a million years or two, humans have had a home base of some sort: a cave, a sheltering tree, something from which they left to forage for food, and to which they must return. From physiological necessity, women nourished and cared for the children. (With no birth control, there were always children.) Their foraging was done fairly close to the protection of home, and the way to find your way about a relatively small area most efficiently is to memorize landmarks. This also allows you to transmit directions without having to go back there yourself.

Men, being free of the immediate consequences of children, could be most useful foraging farther afield. By hunting. This made greater bulk and strength an advantage. And it also meant, for efficiency, and because animals tend to become wary when hunted too often, men must go long distances from home and return by a different route. A route they may never have seen before. So, like birds and cats and dogs and many other animals, some sort of new sense evolved, based on dead reckoning, perhaps, or a faint perception of earth's magnetic field. They knew where they had come from. And they knew where home was. This is the reason men are reluctant to ask for directions, making them the butt of every female comic's jokes.

For though a man may not know why he is so reluctant, something inside him knows that you can not transmit a feeling for direction, even though he may have only a trace of the ability himself.

It doesn't seem to be possible to know if this ability was once far more common than now, or was still evolving when civilization made it redundant, causing it to fade back out of the gene pool. It has been observed in primitive people all over the world, though only anecdotally. I know of no scientific studies of it. But I have seen it used, and with quite amazing accuracy.

So once again, men have been short-changed in the business of life. My wife finds her way about town nonchalantly and accurately, and I find her way unnatural, and my natural one unusable. Ah, well; as has been remarked before, did you expect life to be fair?

Reader, I ask you to reserve judgement; suspend disbelief, at least until you have read what follows:

● ● ●

Hal and his brother Cliff were raised—as you may have noticed—in unusual circumstances. To be raised in isolation is not unusual, but to be raised by someone like their father certainly was. Jack Hammond was impatient with human limitations as customarily accepted. He had his own standards, and the force of personality to make his sons accept them. They in turn, weren't influenced by what society believed was or was not possible. (A good example of this effect is the "barrier" of the four-minute mile in running. Once broken, runners everywhere were soon doing it.) Among the things Jack told them was that they should never get lost while out in the woods, and it never even occurred to them to doubt him.

"A man is a fool if he gets lost," he told them. "All he needs to do is keep in his mind where home is. You don't need to know how, you just do it. After a few tries, just to prove it to yourself, you'll never need to think about it again."

When I was growing up, my friends and I used trails and streams and old logging roads in our travels through the woods, and were never far enough away from one or the other of them to need a sense of location. But when I was about thirteen, I began to go with Father to make the rounds of his trapline. Although he had trapped animals since he was six years old, he became more sensitive to their plight as he grew older, and no longer enjoyed it. But he was heavily in debt for house and land, and though he tried many ways of obtaining it, money was scarce in that year of 1942, and a good fur might bring as much as seventy-five dollars.

The most valuable fur was marten, which in that area could only be found on the upper part of the mountain behind where we lived at Wilson Creek. Trapping is only done in winter, and as Father was determined to reduce suffering as much as he could, the traps were visited as often as possible, no matter the weather. And the weather was usually foul. The best area was in the hillocks and draws on the high land between the valley of Mission Creek and where the land slopes off to Howe Sound to the east. It is an easy place to get lost in. Received wisdom is useless. Moss grows on whichever side of a tree is dampest, which may be east here, and west a hundred feet away across the draw. The winds swirl among the little hills, driving snow and rain from north right around the compass to southwest. When clouds settle over the mountain, as they almost always do from November to January, visibility is seldom more than a hundred feet. Much less if snow is falling.

We would drive as far up the logging road as the old truck would go, then walk to the end of the road and across the logging slash. From there, the way led into a forest of scrub cypress and hemlock trees, in which were ponds and miniature lakes surrounded by grass and swamp plants. Our trail led through and around these. As we went along, we would gather up the traps from stretches that hadn't proved

productive, to re-set them in new locations farther out, or off to one side. The route always changed, curving and branching, so as to cover as much fresh country as possible. We seldom—if ever—ended up in the same place twice.

On the first trip out that fall, the day was typically grey, the clouds settled solidly among the trees. We had been out for about three hours, and set all the traps we had brought.

"Well," said Father, "that's a start. Let's head for home."

I turned and started back along the tracks we had left in the snow.

"Where are you going? We don't go back the way we came. Cut straight across to where the truck is."

I looked around through the mist at the undulating ground. I could detect nothing to indicate what direction to move in. I looked at him eagerly, expecting a lesson in woodcraft. I had thought I was pretty good, but it seemed I had a lot to learn!

"How do we do that?" I asked him.

He looked at me in astonishment. "You mean you don't know where home is? I thought I told you about that a long time ago."

I tried desperately to remember. Some fragments of half-understood directions, never seriously acted on, surfaced dimly.

He said firmly, "Just let your mind go blank, but keep a picture of the truck there. Then just walk toward it. You can do it with your eyes shut."

I tried. He let me get about fifty feet, then, "I hope you have enough food in your pockets."

I turned and looked back at where he was standing. I knew well enough what he meant, but I asked anyhow.

"Well, if you keep on in a straight line, you'll hit Salmon Arm in about two days!"

I trudged back through the snow. Daringly impertinent, I said, "I don't believe you can do it either. Show me."

He did. We broke out into the edge of the slash in less than an hour of walking. It was snowing lightly by then. A quarter of a mile away, and slightly to our right, the truck could be seen.

He did the same thing the next time, and the next, and so on, starting the return journey from a different place each time, and sometimes returning to a different parking place, until I came to accept it as normal. Each time he made me try. Once I came close, and got quite excited. He let me lead, but stopped me when I began to veer off course. It had been, of course, an accident. I tried on my own behind our farm, but knew the land too well, and could never rid myself of the knowledge that the creek was over there, the old logging road back that way—nor really wanted to, I think. My purposes were better served by remembering landmarks. And I still don't know "where home is."

• • •

The years slipped by, and I went off to work for a living. But I was not convinced that there wasn't an explanation for what Father did. Perhaps he was himself unaware of what clues he used, although that itself would have been something to marvel at! Until I went to work with Uncle Henry, my mother's brother.

The middle son of three, Henry was an amiable, hard-working man. He was over six feet tall and, though he slouched along rather bonelessly, was very strong when he wanted to be. But he had watched his father Mart and concluded, "It doesn't pay to be too strong, Dicky. You get all the hard jobs, and they don't give you any more for it." But he was a tireless worker who gave full value for his wages.

I don't think it ever occurred to Henry to tell a lie. When someone did, he would shake his head in bewilderment and say helplessly, "I just can't figure it. Why would he want to say that?"

He had two weaknesses: religion and alcohol. Religion made his life miserable with guilt. Alcohol made him happy, but killed him. But for all that, he was a good man.

Shortly after I began working with him, we were talking one evening in the little shack he preferred to the bunkhouse. The talk turned to hunting, then to Father, and what an amazing "shot" he was. And then he said something that really fired my interest.

"You know," he mused, "I don't think that Paw of yours is really all human."

Facetious, I commented, "How come? I never noticed a tail on him, or fur."

"What about those fingernails of his? They're like claws. Dirty old man." (Henry's favourite exclamation.) "I never saw fingernails like that in all my life!"

I had to agree. Father did have remarkably thick fingernails.

"But that's not what I mean" he continued earnestly. "No, gosh darn it, nothing like that. But I once saw him do something that only an animal should be able to do, and very few of them."

"Tell me," I said.

He settled back more comfortably, and told me the following story. I'll let him tell it in his own words, as nearly as possible. I know the outcome is obvious from the start. That doesn't matter. The story is in the details.

• • •

"It was just about the end of November," he began. "Warren [the youngest brother] and me were working at Neemei's camp in Halfmoon Bay. We had Saturday off, so I put my old 30:30 rifle in the car and headed off to Sechelt to see if I could talk your paw into going hunting. I figured he'd probably be on his boat in Porpoise Bay, so I went there, and there he was. So I asks him, and he says 'Sure, should be a good evening for a hunt, if I can get the engine back together in time,' and he points to the floor, which has half the engine scattered around on it. So I said I'd help, and we go to work. Dirty old man! You wouldn't think a little old engine like that had so many parts. But by lunchtime, he swings over the flywheel, and away she goes, purring like a kitten, and off we go. He heads up along the west shore of the inlet. Well, I see all sorts of good places to stop and hunt, but no, he isn't having any.

"He says, 'Sure, there's deer in there all right. But on a day like this they'll be lying down listening, and sniffing that little air moving down from Salmon Arm. What we want to do is go up to the snowline, where we can pick up a nice fresh set of tracks, and we'll be moving into the wind.'

"So we go along 'til we get just by Salmon Arm a ways, and he pulls into a bit of a bay. He says, 'This is about as close as we can get to the snow, and it's a good place to tie up.'

"And I look up and I think, dirty old man! Mebbe it's the shortest, but it sure as heck is the steepest. There's more rock showing than trees! Anyhow, off we go. The snowline is pretty high, it's one of those grey days that feels like it might snow any minute, and if it does, we might come down those rock bluffs a lot faster than we went up them! But it's not so bad going as I thought. Steep, dirty old man, was it steep! That paw of yours, he must be half mountain goat. I was puffing like a walrus, and he was just breathing same as usual!

"Well, we finally gets up into the snow, and the ground flattens out a bit. We go up and to the right, and pretty soon the snow's about four inches deep. There's lots of tracks, but he doesn't like any of them. 'We'll wait for a big one,' he says. So we go up here, and down there, and across somewhere else, and finally we come across a good big track. 'This is the one we want,' he says. 'He was here just about an hour ago.' And off we go. The tracks lead back toward Halfmoon Bay, and up into the timber. The clouds have come down, and it's getting kind of dark. I'm ready to go home any time now. I says to him that it's getting a long ways from the boat if we do get a deer, but he says, 'We can't quit now, it's just getting interesting. Besides, the way back is all downhill.'

"Well, gosh darn it, that's just what I'm worried about. Some of that downhill is straight down! But there's no talking to your paw when he's on the scent.

"We go along for a little while more, when he stops and holds his hand up. He says, quiet-like, 'There's one. It's not the one we're after, but it's good enough. You take it.' He's always generous like that, your paw.

"I says, 'Take it? I can't even see it! You go ahead.' So he ups with the gun and bang. Dead deer. You know yourself, he never misses. So off we go, about a hundred and fifty feet, and it's a nice two-point buck. So he field-dresses it, and while he's doing that, I look around us. I'm getting worried now. There's a few snowflakes coming down. You can't see the tops of the trees at all, and it suddenly seems a lot darker than it was just a few minutes ago. We can't follow our trail back, it'll take too long, and we can't cut across and find it because most of it's over bare rock. And if we try to head straight back for the boat, well, we're up on the shoulder of a mountain, and if you don't aim just right, you'll end up a mile away from where you want to go. And this is a pretty fair buck. It wouldn't be that easy to carry, even on flat ground. Just then your paw says, 'Help me lift him up to this limb.' So we lifts the deer up and he toggles the legs over a big hemlock branch. Then he picks up his gun and says, 'Let's get going. It won't be long to dark now.' And he starts off down the hill. Well, gosh darn it, I just didn't know what to make of that!

"I caught up to him and said, 'Where are you going? If you're going to leave it, we could at least drag it closer to the water, maybe even give a try to get it down. We don't want to have to climb all the way back up here tomorrow.'

"He doesn't even turn around, just keeps on going. He says, 'Henry, you worry too much. We'll leave him here and go back to Halfmoon Bay. In the morning we'll just take Warren's truck, drive up the road and it should be an easy drag out.'

"Well, I thought, dirty old man! Was he trying to tell me he could go right around the peninsula, come in by a different way and from the other direction and find that deer? There weren't no landmarks, and one part of that mountainside looks just like every other part. I finally figured he'd decided it just wasn't worth packing that deer off that mountain and tomorrow he'd come up with some excuse for not trying to find it.

"So I concentrated on following him down over those rocks. I knew we didn't have a hope of coming out near the boat, and there was no way we could follow along the shore over those rock bluffs in the dark. We'd have to light a fire and stay there 'til morning. It looked like we were in for a cold, wet, hungry night.

"So I stumbled along behind him for a long while, when he speaks up, 'Well, that wasn't so bad, was it?'

"And there's the water, and there's the boat. Dirty old man, was I glad to see that boat!

"Well, the stove was still going, and the cabin was warm, and the next thing I know, the engine's slowing down and we're pulling into the wharf in Porpoise Bay, and then we're in the car and heading back to Halfmoon, and we have supper, and pretty soon it's time for bed.

"Next morning early, your paw comes around. 'Okay, let's go,' he says. I think about getting Warren to come along, help carry the deer out, but he's got a Sunday morning head, and he's grouchy as a lame grizzly bear. I think, what am I doing? No way we're going to find that deer, so I leave him be.

"So off we go in Warren's old truck. It's raining and it's a lot warmer, so we've no trouble getting up there. But when we get there the clouds are right up above our heads, the rain's coming down, and you can't see a thing in any direction. After a while, he stops and gets out, and away we go across the slash, and I'm thinking this is an awful lot of trouble to go to for nothing. It's not far from the road to the trees here, and as soon as we get in the trees, I'm lost. By now, I've had enough of this fooling around, and I'm ready to dig my heels in. And just then I look up ahead, and there's something white, and it's the deer hanging there! Dirty old man! And you say he's not part animal?"

• • •

Aren't we all! Henry's story, so detailed and told with such intensity and conviction, prompted a re-examination of my own memories. I became convinced that such a skill exists, but without some equivalent experience of their own, I don't expect others to be persuaded. I wouldn't be!

Dry Bones

Father seemed to have some sort of affinity for skeletons. Or perhaps it is simply that there were a lot of them around in those days. Some of them were of no interest as stories. A few are worth mention.

He was walking one day along the beach on one of the small islands near Sechelt, when he noticed some pieces of charred wood sticking out from under a boulder. He looked around. The beach was flat: the boulder couldn't have rolled there on its own. It was heavy, too heavy for one man to move. He searched until he found a strong pole in the driftwood, and a block of wood that would serve as a fulcrum. By prying down and then sideways, he managed to work the boulder off to one side, disclosing a circle of partially burned wood.

He was puzzled. Why would someone go to all the trouble of rolling a heavy boulder on top of a fire? He pushed some of the wood aside with his foot. Under the wood were bones. Human bones. He cleared away the wood until they were all visible. Only the feet were missing; they had probably not been covered by the boulder. The body had been made as small as possible, knees tucked up against chest. Wood had then been piled on it and set afire. But before the fire had burned very long, the boulder had been rolled on top of it.

He thought about this. It didn't make sense. Someone had died, or been killed. If it had been the first, why all the bother? A simple grave would have satisfied propriety. Perhaps cremation was desired, either by the dying person or the custom of the group. But with all the driftwood on the beach, surely they would have made a bigger fire? And why the boulder?

If a murder, why the fire? The water nearby was deep; a good-sized rock tied on with almost anything would do. Or the corpse could be dragged up into the thick brush bordering the beach. Or simply left there on a deserted island, for who would know? Nature would dispose of it soon enough.

Perhaps there was something to identify it if found, to tie it to whoever had been there. But again, the water was deep, a safe hiding place. Perhaps it *was* a cremation. A body burning in a small fire makes a lot of smoke. Had it worried someone that others might see it, and, not wanting to douse the fire and reveal what the flames had left, they had chosen to cover it with the boulder? Surely they couldn't have been so stupid as not to know the boulder would put the fire out, and the exposed wood arouse curiosity in whoever saw it. None of these speculations was satisfactory, but they were the best he could come up with. He gave up finally, and though he returned to the subject occasionally over the years, never did come up with a good answer. (Nor, I might add, have I.)

He went back to his boat and across to Sechelt, where he tied up at the dock and went to find Major Sutherland, who was much interested, both personally and in his official capacity as head of the Sechelt police. He dropped whatever he was doing, and off they went to the island and the beach. After looking around for clues and finding none, they carefully gathered up the bones in a box they had brought for the purpose.

As they were returning to Sechelt, the Major turned to Father and said, "You know, Hal, it makes a person think. You can be going about your business, while half a mile or so away, probably in broad daylight, murder is being committed and a body set on fire!"

The bones were sent to the forensic lab in Vancouver. They were pronounced to be those of a Chinese male, between thirty and forty years of age. They had been there for at least ten years, possibly quite a bit longer, for the preservative effect of fire and pressure couldn't be easily determined. There was a hole in the skull that could have been caused by a blow from a club. No more was ever learned. It is doubtful, I fear, that much effort was expended to discover what had happened to a single Chinese male! But then, it must be admitted, there was very little for the police to go on.

• • •

Another time, Father was canoeing one fall day up toward the head of Hotham Sound. Not for any particular reason. He just liked exploring in his canoe. A gas boat is noisy, and if you want to go on shore to look at something, you must find safe anchorage, not always easy in the coastal inlets of BC, where the water may be hundreds of feet deep just a short way from shore.

Rain clouds were piling up against the mountains; it was going to be a wet night. He thought he remembered seeing an old shack somewhere ahead, and quickened his strokes; it would be good to be under a roof this night, and there was not much time left before dark. Already the shadows were growing deeper among the trees. Twenty minutes passed, and he decided he could wait no longer. A few drops of rain were making circles on the dark, still water. He could see a patch of tall, dry grass marking the estuary where a small stream spilled into the sound and decided he would stop there, where there would be fresh water for tea. The shore curved out quite sharply, so he paddled around and into the bay beyond, where he would be shelterered if a wind arose during the night. And there, among the trees, he could just make out the roof of the old shack. He turned in to the shore, pulled the canoe up and, taking his little packsack with blanket and groundsheet, went to check it out.

The light was swiftly vanishing. It was now so dark that he had to choose his way carefully among the broken rock washed from the mountain by the floods. When he came to the shack he could scarcely make out any details. There were no stairs, for it was built directly on the ground. The door was shut but not locked. There was a wooden bar with a peg for a handle. It drew back easily enough, and he pushed the door open and took a step inside.

A glassless window to his left showed pale against the sky, but did little to relieve the darkness. He stood there, tense. Something was not right. He sensed a pressure there in front of him, and swung the pack out defensively. There was the sound of movement, and something big soared out of the darkness and through the patch of window. He heard it land on the ground outside, and relaxed. He knew what it was. Old places like this were often the home of dozens of mice, living under the floor or in the walls. Cougars eat mice. In fact, quite often they eat almost nothing else. They can't catch a healthy deer except under the most exceptional circumstances, and save for the occasional raccoon, porcupine or rabbit, mice form the bulk of their diet. The thing in the dark had been a cougar, looking for its dinner.

He stood there a moment more, moved to reach into his pocket for his match-case, then stopped.

He told me, "I felt that something still wasn't right about the place. It wasn't the cougar, I knew it wouldn't come back while I was there. The air smelled a bit musty, but not as bad as it might have, because of the open window. I just felt I didn't want to sleep in there."

He backed out of the door, closed it and slid the latch into place.

The rain was beginning now in earnest, heavy drops spattering noisily on the fallen maple leaves. He went to where he had noticed a big cedar tree, its thick branches almost brushing the ground. A tree like that can shed rain for a day or so, and this one would be his shelter for the night. He made a small fire from the dry twigs around him, and was soon eating a can of stew washed down by tea. He sat for a while, watching the flames, wondering who had been there before him. But before very long, the sound of rain and the flickering of the flames made him drowsy, so he rolled up in the blanket and groundsheet and went to sleep.

When you go to sleep early, you wake early, and he was awake before daylight. It was still raining, but only a few drops came through the cedar branches. He lay there listening to the sounds of life wakening around him until the morning finally dawned, grey and wet.

Relighting the fire, he breakfasted on bacon, beans and tea. The rain stopped, so rolling up his things, he put them in the bow of his canoe. Then he went back for another look at the shack in daylight.

Under grey sky and dripping trees it was still gloomy and dark, but enough light came through window and open door that details could be clearly seen. There was only the one room. A crude table and chair stood against the wall to the right. A cheap sheet metal stove red with rust filled the far corner on that side. The chimney lay around it in mounds of rust and soot. Mouldy clothes lay on the floor, and a pair of mouse-gnawed caulk boots. There was a bunk against the far wall. Something caught his eye, and he walked over for a closer look. He saw what was left of a wool blanket after generations of mice had used it for nest material. Under it, as the reader will long since have guessed, a skeleton, on its side, face to the wall, looking, in fact, quite comfortable.

"I don't mind old bones," Father told me, "but I think even I might have been put out a bit if I'd lain down on that bunk in the dark, and found I had company!"

Whether that story shows evidence for some kind of intuition or not, I leave for the reader to decide. But the next one is much less ambiguous, and has always been a puzzle to me.

• • •

This story took place at Selma Park, a small community not far from the village of Sechelt. The year—around 1930. Father was not there when it actually happened, but several people he knew were, and he had no trouble piecing out the details.

Selma Park in those days was a pleasant little community. There was a wharf where the Union Steamship line called, a store (the one Father had bought for his mother and sisters, sold by then) and a dance hall. There was a playing field for various games and sports, and a picnic grounds. When the ship came in, the wharf was often quite crowded, as it was this day.

Among the throng of people was an elderly man and his wife. He was slight of build and rather frail; she was younger than he, and neither slight nor frail. The old man wandered around and—to her mind, at least—kept getting in everyone's way as the boat was being unloaded, and passengers with their baggage were coming and going. She spoke to him rather sharply several times; not unkindly, but rather after the fashion of a mother to a fractious child. Finally, exasperated, she told him to go and find a place to sit down and keep from underfoot.

Time passed, the ship departed, and she looked around for her husband, but he was not to be seen. A bit worried now, she began to ask people if they had noticed him. Some thought that they had, others weren't sure—who takes heed of an old man wandering around when they are going about their concerns?

In those far-off days, most people went far out of their way to help each other. Soon the word spread that he was missing. They looked in the woods around the picnic grounds, along the trails and on the beaches. At last they called the police. Major Sutherland arrived with two constables and took charge with his usual efficiency.

The shore around the wharf was steep and rocky. They searched in the water below, poking about in the seaweed with long poles. Grapnels were sent for, and the bottom all around the wharf was dragged. Most people seemed to think that he had fallen in, sunk, and drifted away with the tide. They spoke wisely about how long it took a body to come to the surface, and which beach he would probably be found on.

His wife—poor woman—bitterly reproached herself. She remembered all too clearly the last words she had spoken to him. On such occasions, conscience beats us with thorns longer and sharper than grow on any bush!

The next day, the Major planned a massive hunt in the woods behind Selma Park. After consultation with the elders, he enlisted the entire adult male population of the Sechelt Indian reserve to assist in the search.

They arrived on the scene early that morning, full of enthusiasm for this novel event. But while they were waiting, one of them—an older man with a sense of mischief—began to tell ominous tales of dire creatures that lurked in the woods, waiting to snatch unwary humans from off the trails. It was probably one of these, he hinted, that had taken the old man. Now, the Sechelt people have a well-developed sense of humour. This notion caught their fancy and they proceeded to act on it. Off they went, and soon the woods echoed with shrieks of mock terror as they hunted each other through the trees. When the Major came to deploy his forces, most of them had tired of the game and gone home.

Can you blame them? What was one elderly European more or less to them? There were all too many more where he had come from! (Perhaps they didn't think this, but I would have, in their place.)

The next day dogs were brought over from Victoria, and Father arrived at the dock in Porpoise Bay, where he was told that Major Sutherland wanted him urgently. (It seems that the Major had been much impressed by his tracking ability on some occasion.) He found the Major with the dogs, and heard the story.

He set out to see what he could do. But the brush was so thick it was unlikely the old man could have pushed through it, and if he had, it would be impossible to find him in it. And the trails had been so thoroughly trampled that no footprint would have been left untouched. But at last, on an old trail going from Selma Park to Mission Creek valley, he found part of a footprint in front of a big tree that had fallen there. It was small, and had been made by a leather sole in good condition. The missing man had very small feet, and always wore black leather shoes, which he discarded as soon as they became worn. Father went back to where he heard the dogs, and found the Major, red-faced, sweaty and irritable.

Said the Major, on hearing of the track, "Let's go. I'm tired of chasing these bloody dogs through the brush. I don't think they could smell a dead fish if you rubbed their noses with it!"

The dogs crowded around, tongues lolling, tails wagging happily. They obviously didn't know they were being insulted. Their owner did, though, and grumbled sourly in their defence that "It wasn't their fault, they had nothing to go on, and if the police hadn't let everybody in Sechelt tramp up and down the trails, perhaps..."

Back at the fallen tree, the hounds were shown the bit of footprint and were once again given a shoe of the missing man to smell. Then they were unleashed and encouraged to look for scent. They ambled about happily for a bit, then one gave a loud bark and dashed off into the bushes, with the rest chasing noisily after him. Their owner went after them, and the Major sighed and prepared to follow.

Father checked him with a hand on his arm. "Don't bother. It's not the scent." He knew dogs.

They could hear the dog man calling, "Heel! Heel, sir! Heel, I say!"

They waited. There was furious barking and much cursing. Finally, dogs and owner reappeared. They had treed a raccoon. Their master felt humiliated and revenged himself on his dogs, scolding them severely. Their attitude showed that they thought they had been treated most unfairly. Hadn't they treed a raccoon? What more did he want?

They were again shown the track, but they refused to acknowledge that there was anything there, and when the old shoe was presented to them, they pretended it was a toy for them to play with.

The Major had had enough. His wit was caustic when he chose to use it. He suggested some appropriate uses for these particular dogs, ranging from cat food to employment in a tannery, "where the smell wouldn't bother them."

The dog owner stomped off in a rage, muttering not-quite-audible comments about "...Police..." (To give the dogs their due, it is doubtful that the hard leather shoe soaked with shoe polish would have left much scent on the dry ground.)

Several searchers had arrived, attracted by all the barking. They were shown the bit of track, but were dubious. The consensus was that the old man was too feeble to have climbed over the tree. If he couldn't get over it, he must still be around that area, and as that had been thoroughly searched, he obviously wasn't. They concluded that the ones who thought the man had drowned probably had the right idea, that they didn't see what else could be done and that they all had best go home.

The Major looked at Father, shrugged and spread his hands. "I'm afraid they're right, Hal. You can do as you please, of course, but I won't ask you to do any more."

The sky had clouded. It was near dusk. Father left with them, and they joined the group of searchers gathered for a last discussion at the playing field. It was decided that the search be called off. Father suggested those living nearby should watch for vultures, or a gathering of ravens. The suggestion was not well received.

That night it rained, and the next morning Father went back and far up the trail. He was certain that the print by the log was the old man's, and he knew that it is not wise to underestimate the abilities of old people if they are determined to do something. But he found no trace.

A year went by, then two, and three. Fall arrived, and one fine September day he decided to go fishing for sea-run trout. He wanted to avoid the dead and rotting spawned-out salmon in the lower part of the creek, so he took the trail from Selma Park, as it went by the pools he wanted to fish.

"I was going along, thinking of nothing much," he recalled, "until I came to where the trail comes to the steep drop into Mission valley and turns to the left along the edge of the bank. Suddenly I stopped, right at the bend. Something felt funny, and I didn't know what it was. I felt that I should turn to my right and walk along the edge a bit. So I just sort of relaxed, and let my feet go where they wanted to. About fifty feet or so along the bank was a big old fir snag, maybe six feet through at the butt. I walked along until I got to it. There was a root sticking out a bit. I stepped up onto it, grabbed onto the tree with my right hand, and leaned out so's I could look down the bank. There was quite a deep hollow between that root and the next one, and slumped in there, looking pretty comfortable, was the skeleton of the old man from Selma Park! I knew right away it was him. He had been wearing a good strong cloth coat, with patches of green leather on the sleeves and shoulders. I don't know why the mice didn't make off with the leather, maybe whatever made it green didn't taste good. Most of the rest of his clothes were gone or rotted, but the little black leather shoes were there. A bit mouldy, but looking almost good enough to be worn. The bones hadn't been disturbed by animals; there weren't many around there, and what there were, stayed down by the creek bottom. I don't know how he managed to get where he was. Hung onto the root and dropped, I guess."

He wondered what he should do. Report his find? No doubt the family would want to give the man a proper burial. But why open old wounds, healed now and safely in the past? There had never been any doubt at all that he was dead, so there was uncertainty only about the means. Better to leave him there: he looked so comfortable. The view out over the valley was wonderful. The old logging scars had healed with the soft green of alders, while along the course of the creek and in scattered patches the maples glowed in their coat of fall gold. There was no sign of human presence. It would be beautiful at any time of year. To sit there and go peacefully to sleep: a man could do worse!

He turned back to the trail. He would go fishing.

"But what beats me," he used to say, "is that I passed within fifty feet of him when I was looking for him and didn't feel a thing, but years later, when there's only a pile of old bones, I have to stop and find them!"

Beats me, too. I am certain that this story was not something Father made up. He didn't think that way. But if you, reader, are more comfortable with that as explanation, it is your privilege.

Out of the Deep

THE JELLYFISH

Seventy-five or so years ago, surprising numbers of people travelled up and down the BC coast. Both sides of Georgia Strait were well served, by the Union boats and others. People in every little hamlet and even individual farms and homesteads could count on a ship coming by. But it was different for traffic from the mainland to Vancouver Island. The number of people wanting to go from, say, Stillwater to Nanaimo was extremely small. There were no water taxis and only a few charter boats. Always alert for ways to make extra money, Father would put the word out wherever he stayed that his boat was available.

One day a group of eight people hired him to take them from Pender Harbour to Parksville, on Vancouver Island. It was late spring. The weather had been fine and sunny, but west winds down the gulf often accompany such days, usually starting to blow by about ten o'clock in the morning. Father and his passengers started early, therefore, so they would reach Parksville before the wind might rise.

It was a beautiful morning. The offshore breeze followed them for a while, and then there was nothing but calm green sea around them. One of the men wanted to steer for a bit, so Father—knowing he was reliable—let him have the wheel, and went back to chat with the others on the stern deck. They were passing the south end of Texada Island when the man at the wheel called out.

"Oh, Hal, I thought you said there were no rocks on our course?"

"There aren't," stated Father positively. "There's a thousand feet of water under the keel."

"Then what's that?" asked the wheelsman.

Father jumped up and onto the cabin for a look. There, a couple of hundred yards ahead and to the left, was the unmistakable yellow-brown hump of a reef covered with seaweed, just breaking the surface.

"I couldn't believe my eyes," he told me. "I'd been by there on the same course a dozen times or more in the last few years. I *knew* there was no reef there. But now I could see one right out there in front of me! It's a strange feeling. Something's lying to you, is it your eyes or your mind?"

He jumped down, took the wheel and steered toward the rock. But as they came near, it became less like a rock—in fact, no rock at all. He put the clutch in reverse, and stopped the boat within a few feet of the thing. It was a jellyfish! Now, as sea monsters go, this is not very impressive, I know. But what a jellyfish! The boat was thirty-four feet long. The creature's diameter lacked two feet of that, by their careful measurement. They had found a jellyfish as big as a fair-sized house! It floated there, pulsing slightly, brown-yellow tinged with purple, a bit ragged around the edge but seemingly healthy. From his knowledge of the tides, Father judged it had come in from the ocean, through Seymour Narrows. It must have been very old. How long had it been floating out there in the Pacific?

One of the men picked up the pike pole they had been using to help gauge its diameter and plunged it into the creature as far as the pole would reach. The vast mass quivered a bit.

Father snapped, "Stop that! Put the pole back where you got it!"

Thoughtless cruelty like that enraged him. The fellow hastily withdrew it and put it back on the cabin roof. He had gotten the beast's slime on his hands from the pike pole, and he knelt to rub it off on the side of the boat.

Suddenly he exclaimed, "It burns! It's burning my hands!" He rose and ran to the stern, where he leaned over the side and plunged his hands in the water, rubbing them frantically. "My skin's on fire! Do something, somebody help!"

But what could they do? Father went into the cabin and brought out some butter and a rag. The butter seemed to help a bit, but the man was obviously in great pain. Father thought it served the fellow right but didn't say so.

They all looked at the jellyfish with new respect, and clustered along the side until Father said, "I wonder what it would be like to fall in there and get that stuff all over you?" causing everyone to grab for something solid with at least one hand.

They peered into the clear green water, water in which you could see a dime on the bottom forty feet down, but they could see no end to the cloud of stinging filaments. Everyone on the boat owned a camera, including Father; some had two, but nobody had brought one along!

A jellyfish is not an active beast, however big it is. They lingered a while, then continued on their way, to the sound of moaning. The man's hands were red and swollen, his fingers like plump red sausages.

Said Father, "That must have been some poison! Maybe because the thing was so old. But just think of that creature floating around out there for Lord knows how many years, to end up as a pile of stinking jelly on a beach in Georgia Strait."

THE OCTOPUS

The octopus has always occupied a special place in people's notions of monsters. Quite unjustifiably for the most part, because it is a shy, even gentle creature. If accosted, it flees. There are far more of them on the coast than most people realize, and I don't think a swimmer has ever being attacked. Of course, there is the possibility that one would not have the opportunity to return and report such an incident, but I don't think that's the case. As to how delicate they are, I offer this example.

Father was working on a log boom in fairly shallow water, when he noticed a large octopus, about ten feet across, picking its way delicately across the bottom. On impulse he reached down with his

pole; before it could react, he pulled it to the surface, but then, feeling remorseful, he let it go. Next day, seeing a large, pale object on the bottom near the beach, about a hundred feet farther along, he went over to investigate. It was the octopus. Shock had killed it. How did he know it was the same octopus? There was a bit of a tear on one of the arms just where he remembered hooking it.

However, in nature few things can be taken for granted. A rabbit may attack you, or a butterfly! Even perhaps, an octopus.

Father was working a handlogging claim in Salmon Inlet (or "Arm," as the locals called it: I use the map name, as there is a community called Salmon Arm not so far away). He was staying at a logging camp, and he paddled the mile or so to his claim in his canoe.

The water is deep there, and stories were told of things seen in early morning or just before dark. Father paid little heed to them; there are always stories. He was about halfway back to camp one evening, the canoe sliding smoothly through the dark-shadowed water as he stroked expertly along. Without warning, and without a jolt of any sort, the canoe stopped as if he had hit a mud bank, though he knew the nearest mud was a hundred feet or more beneath him, for the mountains there plunge steeply into the sea. He tried a couple of strong pulls with the paddle, but the canoe only swung sideways a bit. As he knelt there, puzzled, the little craft seemed to quiver a bit in the water. Then a thick, ropy arm slid smoothly over the gunwale just in

front of him and hung there, writhing sinuously. Suddenly the canoe
tipped sharply. He picked up his axe from the floorboards and cut the
arm off where it lay across the gunwale. The severed piece dropped
into the canoe, flopping like a great pink leech, the suckers on the
underside opening and contracting as the nerves functioned without
direction. Abruptly, another arm slid in over the other side. He
chopped it off. One after another, never two at a time, the arms came
over the side, and one after another he cut them off. Seven in all. Some
of them came up twice, and he chopped the blunt ends off. The eighth
never did come up. The beast was a slow learner, but it finally got the
message. The bottom of the canoe was now full of huge leech-like
things twisting and flopping insensately. He ignored them until one
wrapped itself about his ankle, then he flipped them all into the bow
with the paddle. He started to resume his trip back to camp, but the
canoe was very sluggish. The creature was still holding onto the
bottom. He reached over, got the paddle under it and pried. But there
is no prying a large octopus off a smooth surface if it wishes to stay
there. The paddle would break first, and he might have to swim back
to camp. Somehow the thought held no appeal. He looked ashore, but
there was no place to beach the canoe and turn it over.

In the end, it didn't prove to be so difficult. With a good part of the
passenger in the boat instead of under it, and with the right stroke, he
could make way as long as he didn't try to go fast. He made camp well
before dark, with the hitchhiker still riding along.

He had been visible from the camp for quite a while, and the sight
of him working hard but going so slowly attracted attention: there
was a small crowd on the beach when he arrived. He jumped out, and
when he explained the problem, four men waded in and carried the
canoe up the beach, the octopus hanging from it like some huge sea
anemone, with one long arm trailing behind, twisting and twitching.

They turned the canoe over, and two men held it firm while Father
and three others got sticks and tried to pry off what was left of the
octopus, for no one wanted to actually touch it. Its black eyes rolled
and blinked wildly, but dislodge it they could not. One of the men got
a piece of driftwood and pounded at it, but the blows seemed to have

no effect on the pulpy flesh. A cod fisherman came over from where his boat was tied up to the log booms, to see what was going on. He took one look, reached in his pocket, pulled out a big clasp knife, and made a quick, expert cut. The creature went limp, and though the suckers still opened and shut, there was no coordination, and it slid off with no difficulty.

They carried it up the beach, put it right side up and spread out the pieces. Someone said, "Let's see how big it is."

So they gathered up the arms and fitted them together as well as they could. Then they all stood around in awe. A big octopus is about twelve feet across, from armtip to armtip. This one measured a few inches over twenty-two feet! I don't know what the largest one caught measured, but I think it was no more than that. As they were standing there talking, each one with his own story to tell about the creatures, the cod fisherman asked, "What are you going to do with it?"

"Do with it? What *could* I do with it?" asked Father.

"You could eat it, for one thing. Better than any fish you've ever tried, I'll bet."

"I'll pass on that." Distastefully, "Nothing that looks like that is going to sit well in *my* stomach."

"Do you eat oysters?" Affirmative. "A chunk of devil-fish looks a lot better in the pan than an oyster."

But Father was not to be swayed. "As soon as I took the first bite, I'd remember what it looked like on the beach!"

"Aside from that," said the fisherman, "it makes the best cod bait in the world." Casually, "Do you mind if I take it, if you don't want it?"

He overdid the casual; Father sensed subterfuge. "What's it worth to you? I should get something for all that hard paddling."

"How does five dollars sound?" reaching into his pocket.

"Sounds pretty good to me. He's all yours," pocketing the money.

The other grinned. "You should have haggled. I'd have paid you ten."

Father grinned back. "*You* should have haggled, I'd have given it to you for nothing!"

The Monster

Father liked to say that there were only two things he'd needed to run from: a charging grizzly and a swarm of angry hornets. But he neglected to mention a couple of exceptions. One was his flight from whatever malign presence it was that haunted the "serpent's lair," a story he told rarely, if ever. The other was the enigmatic creature out of the depths in this account. This story also he told seldom, for he valued the truthfulness of his stories—if not always in their exact details—and was very sensitive to anything that might cause listeners to doubt them. Since this sort of tale used to be quite common, and almost always depended on either poor observations or good imaginations, he generally preferred to leave it untold.

He'd been working for some while at a camp near Stillwater, living on his boat, but often eating at a boarding house nearby. The landlady's husband worked in a camp at Gordon Pasha lakes and was seldom home, but she was industrious and competent, and coped admirably. She was known locally as something of a virago, but Father's courtesy and sincere admiration soon won her over. So he wasn't surprised when one day she said abruptly, "Hal, there's something I'd like you to do for me, if you wouldn't mind." And when he assured her of his desire to be of service, "I'm having a sort of banquet for fourteen people a week Sunday and I've promised them a fish dinner. And I thought, what would make it special would be to bake them a codfish in the big outdoor oven, glaze it and serve it up whole, head and all. So do you think you could catch me a big lingcod? A really big one?" This, was just the sort of task Father liked to be set, and with much enthusiasm he agreed to undertake it.

Now, Charlie, "the Old Indian," had been by not long before, and in the course of their conversation had mentioned that he intended to stay for a time at Pender Harbour. Though his hair was silver and his cheeks more wrinkled, he still moved with spring in his step, He was as keen as ever to fish or hunt, and this would be a fine excuse to spend some time with his old friend.

As it happened, Father was unusually well equipped to catch big fish. He had intended to go out to one of the halibut banks to try his luck, so he had bought a spool of the strongest fishing line he could obtain and a couple of big halibut hooks. Though he'd never found occasion to use them for halibut, they'd serve admirably now.

Well before the day appointed for the banquet—for big codfish aren't always co-operative—he rose early and headed for Pender Harbour. The early September weather was calm and clear; there could have been no better day for the purpose.

As the dock came into view, he saw that Charlie's boat was obviously where he'd said it would be, for he'd obtained from somewhere a gallon of red lead and had painted his craft with it, stem to stern, mast and all. Shining there in the morning sun like some gaudy ship of legend, it was a thing of beauty, for at that distance you couldn't see the marks of age and misuse.

Leaning back against the cabin, basking in the sun's warmth, Charlie watched impassively as Father eased his boat to a stop and secured it to the other with an end of line. (Charlie wasn't the sort to insult a man by implying that he needed help to dock his boat.)

The first pleasantries over, he offered a piece of the smoked salmon that lay on the deck beside him. It was accepted with pleasure, for Charlie's smoked salmon was a rare delicacy even to Father's fastidious taste.

They spoke a while of matters of mutual interest, than Father offered, "I hoped I'd find you here. There's something I thought you might be able to help me with."

Charlie raised an eyebrow.

"You know Mrs. Cormack, that runs the boarding house over near Stillwater...?"

"Yah. Good woman, works hard. You ever notice how her man never gets jobs near home?"

Father grinned. He'd suspected that being husband to such a woman would be no easy task. "You know her," he chuckled. "I've promised her a cod for a 'do' she's putting on next Sunday. A big cod. And I thought that you'd probably be the man to tell me where to find one."

Pleased at the compliment, Charlie beamed, then sobered as he assumed the responsibility. Big codfish weren't to be found easily, for commercial fishing had thinned their ranks, and at best they are a shy and suspicious breed. Finally decided, he offered, "There's a place up near Hotham Sound I've always wondered about." (When the brothers had become adults, Charlie had somehow lost his "old Indian" accent.) "I've seen rock paintings there made by the old ones who were before us. They said, if I remember right, 'big fish here.' I've never seen those signs anywhere else, so it must be something special, but I've never tried there. Little cod taste better anyhow."

"Sounds good to me. Let's go."

Once underway up Agamemnon Channel, Father brought out the line and hooks. Charlie's eyes widened in surprise. "What were you going to do with these? Catch whales?" But he tied on one of the hooks and rigged a drop sinker below it.

At a suitable reef they stopped for a few minutes by a kelp patch, and with smaller rigging jigged a couple of small lingcod about a foot and a half long, for bait. (Cod are cannibals and one of the best baits for a big cod is a little cod.) Charlie poured a few buckets of water into a small galvanized tub he kept for such purposes, and dropped the little cod into it, where they settled, watching warily.

When they reached Captain Island, Charlie pointed to the area between Hotham Sound and Goliath Bay. "Head for there."

As they neared those steep bluffs that drop off into water nearly half a mile deep, he studied them intently. At last, making up his mind, he pointed off to the left. "Near that leaning tree, we'll try there. A lot of years have gone by since I was here. Go closer to shore, maybe we can still see the marks."

Father eased the clutch in, and they drifted along beneath the looming cliffs.

"Hold here," said the old man. "I'm pretty sure they were there, on that flat spot near the water, where the crack slopes up. But I think a slab of rock's fallen off there, below the crack." Then, pointing, "Your eyes are younger than mine. See what you can see, right about...there."

Too close, decided Father, after looking for a moment. Taking up the pike pole, he pushed the boat out a few feet. He watched the area intently, and when they'd drifted out to about thirty feet from shore, shapes suddenly appeared where there'd been none before. "You got it right. There's marks there. I think the rock's been worked some, and there's a bit of red, like rust, on some of the low spots. But they're almost worn away, and faded bad."

"What do they look like?"

"There's a line, like this…" he motioned, "and something that might be a fish, if you had a lot of imagination."

"Good," said Charlie. "We'll try here." He retrieved a fish from the tub and slid the big hook through the thin membrane below the jaw and behind the thick, tough lips. The fish must be kept alive to be of use, and there the hook would do little harm. Then he tied the shank of the hook to the fish's jaw with a couple of turns of twine so it couldn't be shaken off. He lowered fish and heavy sinker over the side, rolling the spool until about a third of the line was out. Then he sat watchfully, his leathery fingers creased slightly by the line.

"I wonder how the old ones knew what was here," mused Father. "They didn't have line like this to fish deep places."

"Don't be too sure what you think they didn't have," reproved the old man. And he began to tell stories about the accomplishments of the "old ones" (stories I'd give a lot to have heard—for Father's attention, I'm afraid, wasn't on them, and he remembered few of the details). While Charlie was talking, every few minutes he let out more line, about ten feet at a time, until nearly two-thirds of the 300-foot spool was out.

Father wondered what marvels lay below, what creatures made that underwater wall their home. He knew that these vertical faces harboured a riot of life, for at the time of clearest water, and in the right light, one could see far into the depths. Corals and sponges he had seen, crabs, anemones and fish of various sorts, many fish.

He told me, "People think that the bottom is where the life is. but it's there, on the rock faces, where it's thickest. It's funny, though, some places you'd think would be good have nothing on them at all."

He was beginning to think that this was one of those places.

Charlie let more line out but he seemed to have reached bottom, or perhaps a ledge, for it went slack. After letting it rest there a moment or so, he took up about ten feet of line in three quick pulls, as you do when jigging cod. A minute at that depth, and he began to repeat the manoeuvre, but no line came. "Huh," he grunted. "Stuck. Sinker must have caught in a crack." He jiggled it, to no effect, then pulled hard, and harder. Then, for no man could break that line with his bare hands, he stood up, wrapped it around his wrists and, seizing it with both hands, heaved on it. He held the strain for a moment, then let it go slack. He looked surprised. He tightened the line again, holding it lightly but firmly, and grunted something in another tongue.

"What's the matter?" questioned Father.

"Look," said the old man. But Father had already seen. Charlie's hands, tight-gripped as they were on the line, were rising slowly but steadily from his waist, to his shoulders, to over his head.

"There's something down there," said Father, "and it's coming up to meet us."

Charlie grasped the line again where it came over the gunwale, and watched his hands move slowly upward.

"I'm not sure I want to be up here when that thing surfaces," joked Father. "It may not thank us for putting a hook in its lunch!"

But Charlie appeared not to hear him. He seemed to be thinking deeply. Then he spoke softly, but his voice was tense. "Old Indian a fool," he whispered. "I knew the marks weren't quite right for 'big fish here.' But if you put a mark like this . . . " he motioned, "then you get 'don't fish here. Big thing, very bad'." He dropped the line he had been holding, now quite slack. "Hal, I think we should go. Start your engine, get away from this place."

"But," protested Father, "we can't go before we see what it is."

"Hal," came the answer, "if it's what I think it is, it will be the last thing we ever see. Go from here!"

"There was something in his voice I'd never heard," said Father. "It was fear, and that scared me. At the rate the thing was coming up

I thought we had lots of time. But then Charlie pulled in some line and there was more of it than I thought there should be. So I started the engine."

He swung the boat until it was headed for Nelson Island, and slid the throttle forward until they were moving along fairly briskly. It wasn't fast enough for Charlie. He stepped up and shoved the lever until it was on full ahead, something that quite startled Father. For, as he said, "You have to understand that it was against Charlie's religion to do a thing like that in another man's boat without his permission!"

They'd forgotten about the line, and when Father noticed it trailing behind them, he retrieved it. "It seemed to have been cut," Father told me, "and I think that bothered me as much as anything. I couldn't imagine what could have done that."

He set the wheel on course, and they stood there staring back at the place where they had been.

"Look," said Charlie, but Father had seen. The water surface near the shore seemed to bulge upward a foot or two, in a circle that Father estimated to be twenty or thirty feet across. He though he saw an indistinct darkness, but nothing broke the surface.

The trip home was uneventful. Charlie seemed disturbed, and he would answer no questions about what had happened. On his suggestion they swung over toward the entrance of the Skookumchuck. There they hooked up the other little cod and caught a thirty-eight-pound ling, more than big enough for the banquet.

"I have to admit," laughed Father, as he told the story, "that it gave me a bit of a turn when the line came tight."

Much to Father's annoyance, Charlie not only refused to discuss their experience, but declined to give his reasons for refusing. This only made Father all the more determined to seek revenge for being forced to flee.

He said, "I decided I'd go back there with a few sticks of dynamite and the rifle, and we'd see then who came off best. So I got a half dozen sticks of rock powder—sixty percent. I figured that would stop anything dead in the water. But then I got to thinking, what harm had it done? It was minding its own business when we sank a halibut hook in its mouth. What if it was one of the last pair alive, and I killed it? And anyhow, it would probably sink, and I'd have nothing to show for it."

So he never did go back, but he wondered about it all of the rest of his life.

Postscript

After writing this story, I decided that I should refresh my memory as to water depth, place names, etc. But I'd misplaced my chart of Jervis Inlet and had to borrow one from a neighbour. It was much newer than mine and all the measurements were in metric, a system I detest. But I looked at it anyhow. A glance at the figures showed me something that I found amusingly appropriate, and I mention it for the delectation of those who find such things to be of interest.

That part of Jervis Inlet contains the deepest water on the coast, about two-fifths of a mile deep. The greatest depth is in a triangular area about a mile on a side. The three apices are marked 666, the Biblical "number of the Beast"! A nice coincidence, don't you think? But I advise you not to read too much into it. It is, after all, in metric.

I've often wondered what it might have been that so disturbed old Charlie that he wouldn't talk of it, and only one thing seems to me to fit the facts. My guess is that the creature was a giant octopus. There have been a few rare reports of sightings not all that distant from the area, one claiming that the tentacles were a hundred feet long! If you think this unlikely, consider that a chunk of flesh weighing several tons was found on a beach in California in 1896. Samples taken were—sixty years later—verified as being from an octopus. Even one much smaller than that would be a fearsome creature indeed, and may well have stirred a religious response in the old man that he preferred not to speak of.

However, if some sort of strange beasts once preyed on the life that browses the vertical sea-meadows of Jervis Inlet, it's unlikely that they do so yet. A more vicious predator now stalks the coast, driving all else before it like army ants in the Brazilian jungle. The lair of "the Beast" is now a naval reserve.

The Turkey Shoot

In those days when almost every country man and most women owned a gun and knew how to use it, the turkey shoot was a popular event. Thanksgiving and Christmas were the most usual times, although they were also sometimes held on no special occasion. The first ones were rather cruel affairs. The bird was put into a box, with just its head and neck sticking out, and the moving head was the target. You killed your own turkey or you didn't take one home. But even the best shot couldn't be certain of a sure kill at such a target, and mutilations were common.

Eventually a bull's eye or paper target was substituted, with the turkey as a prize.

Father enjoyed these events and would travel miles to attend one. Not because he particularly needed a turkey, but for the opportunity to compete with other marksmen. Thus, when word went around that there was to be a big shoot at Courtenay one Thanksgiving Day in the early twenties, he made sure to be there. He had with him his new 38:55 Winchester and a couple of boxes of the special "marksman" cartridges that you could get for it.

There was a big crowd. People had come from all over Vancouver Island and across from the mainland, with every sort of rifle he had ever seen or heard of: deadly looking Krags and Mannlichers, buffalo guns and deer rifles, target rifles and those used by snipers in the army. The 38:55 was known as an accurate hunting rifle, but its fairly low muzzle velocity and the looping trajectory that entailed made most people dismiss it as a target rifle. The heavy slugs were called "brush-cutters" because they didn't deflect easily if they hit leaves or twigs.

They also flew very accurately if you calculated their trajectory correctly, and Father had a marvellous skill at this.

When the shoot started, he didn't enter the lists at first, preferring to circulate among the crowd, talk to people, watch the shooting. His friend Martin Warnock was there, and had tried his skill a few times but without much luck. He was an extremely good shot, one of the best, but the range was one hundred yards, and his gun wasn't good at that distance. The most skilful hunters rarely had occasion for so long a shot. You could seldom see that far in the BC woods, for one thing; for another, they were able to get close enough to make a kill certain, regardless of the gun.

Father paid his twenty-five cents and took his shot. It brought him his bird as he had expected. His gun was kept sighted in for that range, and it rarely missed. He entered again: another turkey. Three more times, and three more turkeys. He was enjoying himself hugely—like a gambler on a roll. But the sixth time there were only three men shooting against him, and on the seventh, only one man put down his money, after some hesitation, and lost. Father now had seven turkeys, and was running out of families he thought might need one. But he had no intention of quitting. He was having fun.

When the next round was announced, there was a lot of whispering and murmuring but no one entered. The organizer tried his best, but no one would put down money they seemed certain to lose. A group of men surrounded him, and there was talking. Father had paid his money, but now the man came over to him and gave it back. He was apologetic but firm.

"I'm sorry, Mr. Hammond, but if you shoot, no one else will, and I can't afford to give the birds away for a quarter apiece."

Father hadn't considered the effect his winning might have on the others until then. Feeling rather guilty, he readily agreed not to enter any more so that others could have a chance for a bird. So the turkey shoot went on, and now, once again, men lined up to compete.

Martin Warnock came over to where Father was standing. "Say, Hal, I hear you're barred!" They laughed at this, Father saying that if he'd won any more he'd have to get a truck to carry them away.

Then, "Well, if you're not using your gun, how about letting me have it for a few rounds? Mine's too light at this range against all that fancy artillery."

So Father handed his rifle over to Martin, who promptly won a turkey with it. Then he won another. But now again, only one other man started to enter the next round, and he changed his mind and took back his money. The organizer went over and spoke to Martin. Father walked to where they were talking.

His friend was grinning. "They've barred your gun, Hal." He laughed. "No one wants to shoot against it! But that's all right. Two turkeys are all I need anyway. Thanks!" and he handed the rifle back to its owner.

Father stayed on. The shoot was only half over, and it was a social occasion for most of the people there, Father included. In those days such an event was a welcome break in the rather lonely lives most of them led.

There came a change in the quality of the sound made by the voice of the crowd and heads turned in the direction of the road. Father stepped over to where he could see what was attracting so much attention. And there, slouching down the road that led from the north of the island, was a most extraordinary figure: someone who was not only of another time, but of another place. He appeared to be one of the mountain men of legend and story. True in every detail. The first thing, the one most immediately noticeable, was that he was dressed entirely in buckskin leather, belted, beaded and fringed like the pictures in old books. Two or three pouches hung from a diagonal belt. He wore a coonskin hat complete

with bushy tail hanging down his back. From under it, long, greasy
grey hair came down to drape over his shoulders. He was bearded and
moustached. On his feet were moccasins, at his waist on one side was
a big knife with a bone handle, and on the other side hung a powder
horn. Over his shoulder he was carrying a musket with a slightly
flared muzzle, and he had come to shoot! As he drew near, awed
voices could be heard in the crowd.

"Will you look at that!"

"Where do you suppose he came from?"

"I've lived here for forty years or more, and I never heard tell of
anyone like that!"

And so on. But the refrain was, "Now we'll see some shooting!"

"I've heard stories about these men and their shooting all my life.
Now we'll see something!"

He slouched straight into the crowd, looking to neither side, a
ghost from the past and as noiseless as a ghost in the soft moccasins.
He went to the table where the money was taken, said something
quiet-voiced, was answered and, digging into a pouch at his hip,
produced several coins. No one would shoot against him, and after
a few moments of waiting, he was told to go ahead. And then began
a ritual no one there had ever seen but all must have known about.

He unslung the ancient gun from his shoulder, reached into a
pouch and dropped something into the muzzle; then he took a brass
rod with a sort of button on the end from where it was mounted under
the gun; putting it in the barrel, he gave a quick tap. Then, from the
powder flask, he measured in the charge. Next, some sort of wad,
another tap of the rod, and from a small, heavy-looking pouch, a
round ball was folded carefully into a patch, placed in the flared
mouth, pushed firmly home. Finally he was ready. The crowd held its
breath. He looked off at the target, shook his head slightly, aimed and
fired. The sound was strange, unlike any that they had heard from a
gun before. There was a cloud of smoke from the barrel and some bits
of something fluttered to the ground. Everyone looked expectantly at
the "spotter" who would indicate where the ball had hit the target.
But his signal was long in coming, and when it did, it was the hand
wave that meant that the shot had missed the target entirely.

The voices in the crowd were puzzled.

"Must've something went wrong."

"Oh, he's just getting the range. Wait 'til next time."

And from one dissenter, "I don't think that thing will shoot that far!"

The figure from the past stood there, unmoving.

The man at the table called, "Have another go, old-timer. It's on the house. I just like to see you shoot."

Once again the ritual. This time, after the powder was poured, he hesitated, then added another dose. At last he was ready. He raised the gun and the barrel swung in little arcs as he aimed for a long while. Again the strange *boom*, louder this time, the cloud of smoke denser. The spotter, who had removed himself prudently from the area of the target, made a quick examination and once again gave the hand wave that meant "missed the board." The buckskinned stranger picked up his brass tamping rod from where he had leaned it, slid it into place. Then he turned and headed back up the road with his odd, slouching stride. He was muttering something as he went, and those near enough to hear said—awed—that his language was as colourful as his costume. It went something like this;

"Too #@*%!# far! @%#* gun! #@*%!"

As far as I know, he was never seen again.

For many years, among the various mementos scattered about our house was a ragged bit of yellowed newsprint torn from the local paper: "Gun bags too many birds. Barred from turkey shoot!" and a brief description of what happened. It has long since been lost.

There were Giants in Those Days

There is not much interest in the subject of strength these days. Oh, I know bodybuilding is increasingly popular, but it is a reflection of society's preoccupation with show rather than substance that these amazing bodies are judged by how they look, instead of by what they can do. In a time when every pseudo-sport has its TV exposure, world's strongest man competitions and power-lifting have few followers. Real strength is seldom symmetrical and never pretty, and now that even the largest machines can be controlled by a finger touch, there is an ever-lessening need for it. But things were not always thus.

Whenever men have gathered to tell stories, some of those stories have been about those whose physical strength was exceptional. We still read of the exploits of Hercules and Achilles, Beowulf and Cuchullain, the supermen of their day. Throughout all the ages, storytellers have told tales of strong men whom they knew or had heard of.

I have always been interested in such stories, and one of the first things I must have asked Father was, "Who was the strongest man you ever saw?"

It was Father's way to not answer such a question directly, but to sort of work around it.

"Well-l-l-l," he would begin. "There were quite a few strong men around. Lots of stories about men who had lifted this or that. His brothers said that Frank Johnstone once packed a 450-pound bear out of the woods on his shoulders. Charlie Klein was famous for his

116

strength, but I don't know any stories about him. One of the strongest I knew was old Harry Dusenberry. I don't really know how strong he was because he never showed off, but he was a very strong man, and a tough one.

"I was out deer hunting with him one day. We were just about ready to turn back when we spotted a nice buck. He said, 'Go ahead, Hal, you saw it first.'

"So I up with the gun and down it went. A nice shot, if I do say so myself. We went over and there it was, a nice fat two-pointer. Then I remembered that we were about five miles from the boat, over pretty rough ground, and I began to think we should have looked for something we wouldn't have to carry so far. I said that to Harry while we were dressing it out, but he didn't seem to know what I was talking about so I didn't say any more. When we were all ready, I toggled the deer's legs together for carrying and started to heave it up.

"'Here, Hal, I'll take that,' he said, picking it up with one hand and slinging it over his shoulder.

"Now this isn't an easy way to carry a deer. It throws you off balance, and all the weight comes on the muscle at the side of your neck. The proper way is to balance it across your two shoulders, so as to spread the pressure evenly. This was a pretty nice deer, about 120 or 130 pounds. But the weight didn't seem to bother him. He strode along as if he wasn't carrying anything.

"After we'd gone about half a mile, I said, 'I'll spell you now, Harry.'

"He grunted, 'Huh, what's that?'

"I said, 'I'll carry it awhile, give you a rest.'

"He sounded surprised. 'Oh, that's all right.'

"So I thought, okay, keep it then, I'll see how long you last. Well, I don't know how long he would have lasted. All I know is, he carried that deer the whole five miles to the boat. He never changed shoulders. He never even shifted it to a different position, that I saw, and I watched him pretty closely. Now I know that anyone who's ever carried a deer that way will tell you I'm lying, that it isn't humanly possible. But he did it!

"He did another thing too, that I wouldn't have believed possible if I hadn't seen it myself.

"We were in the cabin of my boat one day. He'd said something I thought was funny, and I was teasing him a bit. Now I should have known better, because Harry Dusenberry wasn't a man that took very well to being made fun of. I remember one time a bunch of us were on a hunting trip up Jervis Inlet. It had rained all day and nobody had got a deer. We were all sitting around the stove that evening, drying out and talking hunting. The talk got around to what was the surest way to get a deer; some had one way, others another. Finally Harry spoke up. People always paid attention when he talked. He said, 'There's a way to hunt that I like that some of you may not have tried. You go to a place where you know there's deer, and you find a nice little draw full of salal brush. Then, if it's a quiet evening, you pick a high spot about an hour before dark, and you sit and listen. After a while you'll hear a funny little sound, like something ripping. It's the sound the leaves make when the deer pull them off the bushes. You just wait and watch. Pretty soon you'll see a deer's head sticking out above the salal and even if you don't, it's kind of nice to just sit there and watch and listen in the evening.'

"There was a young fellow there, up from Vancouver. He was the nephew of one of the older men. Had quite a lot to say. After a moment he pipes up and says, 'I get it, fellows. We're doing this all wrong. All we've got to do tomorrow is to go up in the woods and make a noise like a salal bush, and the deer will all come running!'

"No one laughed. Harry looked at him with the air of a man who has found something unpleasant on his shoe. He growled, 'Maybe so, and maybe not, but I know that if someone made a sound like a recruiting sergeant, there'd be more room around the fire for the rest of us.'

"Everyone grinned. The year was 1915, and they all knew why that young fellow was staying out of town. Harry raised his voice a little. He nodded toward the corner of the room by the door. 'And anyone who doesn't dry off his gun when he comes in, and leaves it so the water runs down the barrel into the action, might better be silent when the *men* are talking hunting!'"

"Myself," Father used to say, "I would rather have been shot to death than have those words aimed at me in that tone of voice. There wasn't a peep out of that young fellow the rest of the night, and he sat so far from the fire he was still wet next morning.

"So, as I said, I should have known better than to tease him. He reached out and grabbed me by the belt, and then he picked me up with one hand and held me at arm's length with my feet dangling.

"He said slowly, 'Hal, I like you. You're all right. But you ought to watch that tongue of yours. It might get you in trouble someday!' Then he gave me a little shake and set me down again. Now, I would have said that no man could lift 150 pounds in that way and hold it at arm's length, but he did it, and I had a bruise on my belly the size of your two hands for a couple of weeks after, to prove it. You see, he didn't just have a grip of my pants and shirt, he'd got a handful of loose skin besides!"

• • •

There is another story involving Harry, although he isn't the central character. That honour goes to one of the men of the Sechelt tribe, whom I will call Reggie. It may even have been his name, at least the one the priests gave him. He was not young; probably in his forties. It was hard to be certain, for he was one of those men whom even age seems not to affect. The Sechelt Indians are a strong people; broad of shoulder and deep of chest, but among them few—if any—could match Reggie's massive power. (If justice were not such a fickle goddess, there would be stories told of the feats of strength of Reggie and others like him. These may exist, but I'm afraid that I do not know of any.)

He was old enough to have known a time before there were any Europeans on the land where he was born, and he'd never given any indication that he saw much good in the newcomers or in their activities. But he was pretty reasonable about it—most of the time. For Reggie had one weakness, one thing against which he had no defence. That thing was the alcohol brought with them by the new neighbours, a thing for which his people had had no need to develop a tolerance.

Now, there are many varieties of drunks: happy ones, crying ones, silent ones. Some, after only a couple of drinks, become about as good-natured as a grizzly bear with a bad hangover. And some others may stay good-natured, but be what is known as a fighting drunk, and Reggie was one of these.

Everyone had been warned not to give Reggie liquor. It was also— at that time— illegal. It was of course easily procured, and the local bootlegger was known to everyone. This individual—give him credit— had tried to do as he had been told. But it seems that Reggie had gone to his door one evening, money in hand, and asked very politely for a bottle. After one look at the big man standing there, and remembering his civic duty, the bootlegger slammed the door shut and locked it. Due to the nature of his part-time business, it was a heavy door, with a strong brass plate holding handles and lock. Reggie was not impressed. He seized the handle and tore plate, handles and lock out of the door, which he pushed open quite gently.

To the horrified bootlegger he said aimiably, "Guess you didn't see me, eh?" He held out the handles, broken wood hanging from bent plates. "Piece of door come off. Not very strong. Got bottle?"

He got bottle!

Now, in those far-off days, pre-TV and almost pre-radio, people were obliged to provide their own entertainments. One of the most popular of these was the Saturday night dance, but unfortunately, musicians for this ceremony were always in short supply. Father, who was known as a virtuoso on the button accordion, was always in demand at these events wherever he went. He enjoyed playing and never refused when asked. At this particular time he was employed building a house near Sechelt and, as usual, played at the weekly dance, his accordion often but not always supplemented by a violin, banjo or whatever else was available.

The dancing had been going on for about two hours. It was around ten p.m., the evening only about half gone; the dance would go on until midnight. There were about twenty couples present. Father's was the only instrument that night. He was playing a waltz.

There came the sound of loud voices from the veranda and the wide door flew open with a jarring crash. It was Reggie. He had been sober for about two months but he was not sober now. He was drunk, and he was looking for a fight.

Father kept on with the waltz, but as the dancers circled the room, each couple stopped at about the same distance from the intruder until they all stood there in a group, wondering what he was going to do next. Father stopped playing.

Reggie stood there, swaying slightly. He was grinning a bit, obviously pleased with the effect he was having.

He said, "Come on, girls. Who wants to dance with a *real* man?"

From somewhere in the back of the group, a voice—unwisely—said, "Go home, Reggie, you're drunk."

The grin vanished. His voice rumbled a challenge from his huge chest. "Drunk? Who says I'm drunk? I'm not drunk. Show me the blankety-blankety-blank that says I'm drunk. I'll tell him. I'll fight every blankety-blank here. Bunch of blankety-blank sissies. C'mon, who wants to fight?"

(Readers, please forgive the "blanks." Each person tends to swear in only one of the three main categories: religious, sexual or excretory. Father was not explicit, and I am reluctant to put words in Reggie's mouth that may not belong there. He might indeed have selected from all three categories: some do, but I would rather not chance it. At any rate, Reggie had a good ear for European profanity and took great pleasure in the use of it.)

Now, there was a quaint concept in vogue at that time, a strange relic of the Victorian age. Many people, mostly men, believed that women were somehow finer, more delicate, than men. That they would be deeply shocked by profanity, and should be protected from it at all costs. Father was one of those who believed this was true. (Strange to us, in these more forthright days, when the women speak and the men blush!)

As Reggie continued to urge them to fight, and to curse them eloquently when they didn't, the group stirred restively. The men felt that they should do something, but no one wanted to fight the big man who challenged them.

A large blond woman on the edge of the group pushed at her husband, saying loudly, "Henry, are you going to just stand there and let that man use language like that in front of me?"

Poor Henry, small and inoffensive, tunnelled back into the crowd, saying desperately, "Hush, Freda—shh."

There were chuckles. Even Reggie grinned. Then he let out another string of his choicest oaths.

Father told me, "I couldn't just sit there and let him go on like that. There were ladies there. Someone had to get up. It didn't look good, you know."

He put down his accordion and stood up. But just then, someone spoke from the doorway behind Reggie. "Come on outside, Reggie. I'll fight you."

It was Major Sutherland. The big man turned slowly toward the door. Father relaxed.

(I often wonder what would have happened if he had not been forestalled. The cat versus the bear! I'm afraid the bear's massive strength would have won out.)

Reggie looked at the trim figure in the doorway. "You want fight?"

"I must warn you, Reggie, it wouldn't be a fair fight."

Reggie grunted contemptuously.

The major continued calmly, "I was the light-heavyweight boxing champion of the Canadian Army, and you're drunk."

"Yes" said the big man doubtfully, "but can you *fight*?"

He walked heavily out the door, across the veranda and down the stairs. There was a bright moon, and light from the hall windows. People lined up two deep along the veranda rail.

The fight began. The Major struck first, a hard blow to his opponent's chin.

He told Father later, "I hoped to knock him out right away so that I wouldn't have to hurt him. But it was like hitting a tree stump. I went to the body, but it was like hitting a tree stump with a layer of leather on it. I just hurt my hands, and all the time he kept grinning at me!"

The Major was clearly an expert boxer. He evaded his opponent's clumsy grabs and ponderous blows with ease, while delivering a barrage of lefts and rights of his own. In a few minutes, Reggie's face was a mask of blood, his lips split and his brows cut. But it had been a good while since the Major had fought. He was, though fit, not in fighting trim. Before long his legs were losing their spring and he was breathing heavily, his blows ever less effective.

Then he failed to move fast enough, and one of Reggie's lunges partially connected with his shoulder. The force of it flung him backward to smash heavily into the wall. He stood there for a moment, leaning against the wall for support, then pushed off with his shoulders and staggered out to renew the fight. He didn't seem to be able to use his right arm very well.

Reggie stood there, obviously reluctant to fight a crippled opponent. He put out an open hand to fend the Major off.

Just then, a strong voice came from the shadowed stairs. "Major, don't be a fool. You've had enough."

It was Harry Dusenberry. The two fighters turned toward him.

"Stay out of this, Harry," the Major commanded. "It's my fight."

Ignoring him, Harry took a couple of long strides and pushed the smaller man gently but irresistibly toward the wall.

"You stay there," he ordered. "This has gone far enough." Turning to Reggie, "Reggie, you better go home before you get into trouble."

Reggie grinned bloodily. "Little man jump around like flea on hot stove. Can't hit'm. Rather fight you."

Suiting action to words, he launched a punch that might have felled a tree. Harry sidestepped it easily.

"Reggie," he warned, "I'm going to have to hit you if you're not careful."

For answer, Reggie stepped forward and reached out his huge hands to grapple. Harry let him close, then hit him a tremendous blow on the jaw. Reggie blinked, shook his head a bit, reached out. Harry hit him again, harder. The sound made the onlookers wince.

"You not jump all around. Good to fight," Reggie approved. He reached out once more, hands clutching. Harry looked startled for an instant, then his fist shot out so fast it seemed almost to disappear.

There was a sound like a sledgehammer hitting wood. The big man stood there for a moment, swaying gently, then slumped heavily to the ground, unconscious.

Several people came to stand around, as people will. The Major came, stood looking down at the man on the ground. "If he'd let me teach him some defence" he said admiringly, "that man could be the heavyweight champion of the world!"

Harry beckoned to one of the men. "You've got a truck. Bring it around here, we'll load him on it and take him home."

Which they did.

Some while afterward, Harry was talking to Father. "You know, Hal," he said, "I hit that first punch hard enough to knock any normal man out cold. The second one would have knocked out a horse or a steer. And the third, well," he held up a great knobby fist, looked at it, "that third punch was almost—" he shook his head in wonder, "*almost* as hard as I could hit!"

"That was quite a man, was old Harry!" Father said. "Oh yes, there were a lot of strong men around. Some of them you'd hear about, and some of them, maybe stronger, you wouldn't. There was one time at Clowhom Falls when I was up there doing some work on the mill building. I was talking with the superintendent when a man came running in from the woods. As soon as he saw us, he shouted, 'The flume is blocked! They don't know what to do about it. Can you come up quick?'

"We jumped into the old car they used around the mill. Partway up the road, we stopped and cut through the bush to the flume. There was a bunch of men standing there arguing about what should be done. We climbed up the timbers to have a look. The channel was about twenty feet off the ground. The sides were about seven feet high, sloping out, and the bottom was about five feet across. The flume took quite a bend at that spot, and there, stuck in the bend, was a big fir log. It must have scraped the sides all the way down, because it was a good six feet through. Of course, it couldn't make the bend, it was too long. A dozen or so smaller logs had backed up behind it.

"The woods boss was there. He said, 'Those crazy fools up at the lake should have known better than to let a log like that in. I'll fire the lot of them.'

"Some of the men there were from the crew at the lakehead, as he well knew. They looked uncomfortable. 'We'll have to knock out a section of wall and let it roll out.'

"The super said, 'If we do that, it'll take out the posts. The whole bend will have to be rebuilt. We'll be down a couple of days!'

"They argued back and forth for a few minutes. Finally the super said, 'We'll have to buck it.'

"Well," said Father. "I looked at it and I thought, I wouldn't want to be the man that tries to buck that.

"There wasn't any room to stand, nor any to move the saw. Less than a foot on either side, even if you picked the best spot. The woods boss said, 'You can't do that. There's no room.'

"The super said, 'We'll cut the flume wall, throw up a platform...'

"Just then, a little Japanese man who was standing there listening, spoke up. 'No cut wall,' he said. 'Can do.'

"'Well,' the super said, 'if you think it can be done, Haki, fly at it!'

"The fallers and buckers were all Japanese at that time, and the little man was their boss. He said something in Japanese to his helper, and that one went running off up the flume. They'd shut the water off, and he could trot along on the planks between the logs and the flume wall. We all stood around talking, and everyone agreed that it couldn't be done.

"Finally the helper came trotting back down the flume. There was another Japanese with him. He was about five and a half feet high, and four feet wide. He had arms on him thick as your legs. He was carrying an eight-foot bucking saw, a heavy one with a blade about a foot wide. In his other hand he had an axe and a couple of wedges. He looked at the log. Then he set the saw down on its side, took the axe and gave it a whack about two feet from the end. He turned it over and nicked the other side. Then he took the saw in his hands and broke the end off with his hands! He said something to the boss in Japanese and they both laughed. He climbed up on the log, walked along to the middle of it and sat on the edge of the flume. Then he started to saw, with one arm. He used that heavy saw like a man would cut a cedar board with a hand saw. He could only move it about six inches, but he moved it fast and he never stopped. He was like some kind of machine for sawing. A normal man would have shifted hands, stopped to rest, at least showed some sign that he was working hard. Not that one. He never stopped. And you have to remember that when your stroke is that short, you have to rock the saw up and down to work the sawdust out.

"When he was down a couple of feet, he said something and the helper put the wedges in, but he never did stop, even for a moment. He never had to change sides, because when the log jammed it was floating, so there was about a foot of room between it and the bottom of the flume. It took him just under an hour to make the cut. He was kneeling when he finished and the saw was almost straight up and down, and it was moving just as fast when the log dropped as when he started. He knocked out the wedges, picked up the saw and went trotting back up the flume. He wasn't even sweating! And that's all there was to it. When they turned the water on, the logs went on down the flume. Now I know it doesn't sound like much. You have to have done that kind of work to know what that man did. I've always wondered just what would it have taken to make him break into a sweat!"

By now, Father had finished with the preliminaries.

"But," he would continue, "when it comes to sheer size and power, there was one that had them all beat.

"I had a job to take a new dump machine up to a camp above the Yucataws, and set it up. I got up there about noon, and the boss came out with a couple of men and we started to move the machine off the log float onto the beach by the dump. There were some barrels of gas that had to be moved, and I heard one of the men say to the other, 'Too bad Big Jim isn't here eh? Just his sort of job.'

"I didn't pay much attention. Then after we got the machine ashore, we had to move a big chunk of rock out of the way. I used the bight of the line, but as we were setting the line, one of the men said again, 'Too bad Big Jim isn't here to heave that aside.' And I started to wonder about this 'Big Jim' they were talking about, so I asked them. One of them said, 'Hal, if I told you, you wouldn't believe me. You'll know who he is when you see him at supper.'

"Well, we worked until quitting time, and then we went and washed up. I was a bit late, so I was the last one into the cookhouse. I went through the door and there, facing me, was the biggest man I've ever seen. I found out afterwards that he was seven-foot-two. He claimed to weigh a pound for every day in the year. Three hundred and sixty-five pounds! And it was all muscle. He would have been a powerful man even if he'd been normal size. All sinew. Of course, I didn't realize then just how strong he was, but I did see that he ate enough for four men.

"That evening I went out to do a little more work, because they were in a rush to get the new machine set up. The boss sent a man out to help. We had to put a drum of gas up on a platform. The machine was gravity fed, that is, the fuel tank had to be up high, so it sat on a stand about six feet off the ground. We were trying to roll the full drum up a plank but the plank was too short and the drum kept sliding back down. Suddenly someone behind us said, 'Let me give you a hand with that, boys.' It was Big Jim, who had walked up to have a look at the new machine.

"We stood aside, thinking that he would take one side while we took the other, but he walked up to the drum, flipped it onto its end with one hand, then picked it up by the two rims and set it upright on the platform!

"Now that was one of the old heavy drums. Full, they weighed over five hundred pounds. Old Mart could have 'bellied' it up there, I think, but Big Jim lifted it up away from his body, so that the mud wouldn't get on his clothes, almost at arm's length. It doesn't seem possible when you think about it.

"Now you would think, with a man like that, that there'd be all sorts of stories about him. But there weren't, and I think the boss of the camp had the right idea when I asked him about it. He said, 'Well, Hal, I think it's like this. You take the average strong man. He may weigh a bit more than we do, but he's about our size. He does something we can't do, we're surprised. We think ''Hey, that's really something." We remember it, we talk about it. But you take a man like Big Jim. He isn't like us. You expect him to be able to do something outrageous. He walks up the road with a drum of gas on his shoulder, who's going to make a big deal of it? You expect him to do that sort of thing.'"

"'Well, maybe,' Father said, 'but I think that at least part of the reason was that Big Jim liked to stay where there weren't many people to stare at him, to treat him like a freak. He was comfortable with just a few men around who were used to him. But if he'd worked the big camps, he would have been famous.'"

But the camp boss did tell Father a couple of stories.

"It seems that the crew were going to work one morning in the crummy. Seven men and Big Jim. Suddenly the truck gave a lurch and stopped. The driver got out, looked and said, 'She's gone through a hole in the punching. We're stuck. Everyone better get out and give a push.'

"The men peered out reluctantly. It was pouring rain. They'd be working in it shortly, but they weren't eager to get wet and mud-splattered any sooner than they had to. Big Jim jumped out, took a look. 'It's all right, boys,' he announced. 'Pete here [the driver] can throw some chunks in the hole while I lift her up. Just stay where you are. No need to get out in the rain.' He grabbed the bumper, braced himself and heaved, and he picked up the truck and the seven men with such force that all seven fell over in a heap in the corner!

"Now the next story is really hard to believe, and I thought he was stringing me along at first. But I asked some of the men, and they all said that it happened, and each one added a few details of his own. So here it is.

"It seems that when Big Jim first came to camp, the men didn't know what to make of him, but pretty soon they found out how good-natured he was, and the next thing you know, they were playing practical jokes on him. Little things at first. Tobacco in his coffee, and a dead mouse in his caulk boots. That sort of thing. But when Jim just grinned at them, they began to get a bit mean. I guess it was a bit like teasing a bear. You just had to see how far you could go! Anyhow, things went along like this, until one night, they went too far. Big Jim got into his bunk, same as usual. This time, though, he started tossing and turning. There were a couple of snickers from more than one man as the sounds got louder. Finally, he got up and lit the lamp—every man had a lamp by his bunk, of course. He pulled the covers off his bed. Someone had put a couple of handfuls of bark slivers in his blankets. They're like a million little needles, and once they get into wool, you can never get them all out—and Jim, like everyone else, wore long wool underwear to bed.

"He looked around at the men, and he wasn't smiling. He said, 'Now, boys, that wasn't a very nice thing to do.' No one spoke. He put on a new pair of underwear and threw the old ones in the corner. Then he pulled off his bedclothes and threw them in the corner. He went to the nearest bunk, pulled off first one man's covers, then the other's. They pretended not to notice. The snickers had come from that direction. He said, 'Thanks, boys,' spread them neatly over his eight-foot-long bed, climbed in, blew out the lamp and went to sleep.

"That was on a Thursday. Friday came, then Saturday. The men were uneasy. Every once in a while they would catch Big Jim eyeing them with an expression that made them wish they hadn't been so free and easy with their jokes. But Saturday passed and nothing happened. Big Jim was his usual cheerful self. They began to feel a bit safer. Then came a real surprise. They're all sitting around on their bunks waiting for the dinner bell, when Big Jim reaches under his bunk and hauls out a quart of rum. He tosses it to one of the men, saying, 'Here, fellows. The drinks are on me. Just to show there's no hard feelings, eh?'

"Now in those days Saturday night at a camp like that meant a time to relax, and that meant drinking. On this Saturday night, quite a bit more than usual, what with the free rum and a bit of guilt riding them. So they went to bed that night pretty well loaded, and they probably slept a bit sounder than usual. Just as he'd planned it."

This next part Father pieced together from what the boss told him, and the stories of the men, who were more than willing to talk about it.

"It seems that about three o'clock next morning, one of the men had to get up to go outside. It was pretty dark, but they could find their way to the outhouse with their eyes closed. So he opened the door and went down the steps. Next thing the men heard him yelling, 'Help! I'm stuck! Something's got hold of me!' The fear in his voice brought most of them awake in a moment. 'Hang on, we're coming!' one of his friends called. He jumped out of bed and down the steps. Next thing *he's* yelling, 'The path's gone! How the Hell did all this brush get here? Hey, this stuff's got thorns on it! I'm all stuck up. Hey!' By now, the others were all wide awake. They couldn't find their lamps, so they all crowded out the door, pushing each other down the steps. Each man *knew* there was clear ground there, right down to the water, and that as soon as *he* got out there, *he* would sort things out for those drunken incompetents who obviously couldn't hold their liquor.

"In seconds, there were seven men floundering around in the dark, tangling their wool underwear in a ferocious mixture of wild rose bushes and wild crabapple, which has inch-long thorns. The cursing and swearing must have been frightful. If you've never heard a bunch of old-time loggers in full cry, half drunk and frightened, don't expect me to describe it to you!

"Their drink-fuddled brains were taken by a sort of panic as they trampled and tore at each other to get out of this impossible situation, and back to the safety of the bunkhouse. But once there, someone screamed, 'The bay's in the wrong place! Someone's moved the bay!' His voice was shrill with real terror. They all crowded to the windows. There was the water, shining in the starlight where the hill behind the camp should be, and there was a lantern approaching from the office where the boss slept. He was coming to see what all the noise was about.

"They started to think again. Someone lit a match. There were all the lamps, all in a row, over by the stove. They lit one, talking excitedly all the time. Then there came the boss's voice, loud and harsh. 'What the hell—how did the bunkhouse get wrong way around?'

"Of course; how could they have been so stupid? But how...?

They all thought the same thing at about the same time. One of them shouted, 'Big Jim!'

"From the back of the room, a deep, slow voice said, 'Someone calling me? What's the matter, boys—get turned around a bit? Try not to make so much noise about it, will you? I'd like to get some sleep.'

"Well," grinned Father, "I don't suppose those men slept much the rest of that night. One thing sure, they were out there at daylight next morning. They couldn't believe it. The bunkhouse—thirty feet by twelve—built on log skids neither of which two men could have moved, had been swung around until the side that had faced the water was right in against the bushes. It must have been done in the three hours after midnight, and not one of them had felt a thing! Of course the liquor would have helped along there, but how had he done it? I don't know. Pried it up on greased poles, I suppose, and slid it along with a hand spike.

"The next day it took seven men—hungover and sweating—six hours to put it back, using logging jacks. Big Jim sat on a stump and watched the whole time, offering unhelpful suggestions.

"There were no more practical jokes after that. I guess they thought, 'What would he do if he got *really* annoyed?'

"I saw him do one other thing," said Father, "and it was just a little thing. But it brought home to me what incredible power that man had.

"We were in the bunkhouse one night. It was cold, and the fire wasn't burning very well. The bull cook was drunk again and there was no small kindling in the woodbox. One of the men was trying to get the big wood to catch. He complained, 'This fire is never going to go unless someone gets an axe and splits some kindling.'

"Big Jim walks over, and he picks up a piece of wood as thick as your arm. He took an end in each hand and gave it a sudden twist. With a loud crack it split apart into a whole bunch of slivers. 'Here,' he said. 'Try this.'

"Well, I was curious. The next day I got a piece about the same size from the box, and I squared off the ends. Then I put an eighteen-inch Stillson wrench on each end and twisted. I couldn't do it, and if I hadn't seen it, nobody could make me believe that it really happened!"

Father left the camp soon after that. He never saw or heard of Big Jim again. I often wonder what happened to him. Here was our own west coast Angus MacGaskill. He should have been a folk hero, with enough stories about him to make a book. Why didn't it happen? If anyone knows what happened to him, or anything at all about him, I would be much interested.

"After Big Jim," Father went on, "old Mart is the strongest man I've ever known. He may not look like much, but I've seen him do some things that would amaze you."

This came as a big thrill to me, because "old Mart" was Martin Gulbranson, my mother's father, who at that time was living with us in a little shack in the backyard.

I had always known that he was regarded as being exceptionally strong, but had not experience enough to know just how strong he really was. I knew he could bend fifty- and twenty-five-cent pieces with his fingers, but I didn't know then how difficult that was. He told me the twenty-five-cent ones were harder to bend, as his fingers were too big to get a proper grip on them. I kept one of each for a year or two, but decided that they proved nothing; anyone could have put them in a vise and bent them double. So I straightened them out and spent them. I wish now I had kept them.

It was true that he didn't look like one's image of a strong man. He stood a little over five feet six inches, and weighed around 255 pounds. Much of this weight was in his hips and bulging stomach. His shoulders looked narrow because of the slope of muscle from his arms to his ears. With his almost totally bald head, he looked like nothing so much as a benign old Santa Claus! But after getting a book on strong men, I measured his upper arms with my mother's tape. They measured—cold—$21^3/_8$ inches. World class by any standard. And the bulging stomach was muscle, not fat. His arms were quite short, the wrists so thick that his work shirts wouldn't button, so he kept the sleeves rolled back. His hands were twice as broad as mine, and his fingers...no, you wouldn't believe it if I told you.

"I first met old Mart when he was working at the Britannia copper mine," Father reminisced. (Everyone called Grandfather "old" Mart, probably because of his premature baldness and chubby cheeks.) "And it was there that I first realized how strong he was, although I'd known him by then for half a year or more. It was late December. I had to go into Vancouver, and I timed it so that I could pick him up at the mine and take him back to Sechelt for Christmas. So on the way home I turned up Howe Sound and followed along the shore to Britannia. I tied the boat up to the dock. The mine was shut down, but I knew they were doing some exploration work, so I walked up to the mine office, where they told me how to get to where Mart was working. I'd never been in a mine before, and I didn't much like it. There was a smell of dynamite in the air, and funny echoes, and I could feel the weight of the mountain over my head. The lights were dim, there weren't many of them and I came very near to getting lost. But I turned a corner, heard the sound of hammers and then voices, and there I was.

"The foreman spotted me right away, and he came over and wanted to know what I was doing there. He was pretty mad when I told him, and he cursed the office for letting a stranger wander around in the mine without a guide. But he appeared to feel better after blowing off a bit of steam, and he seemed to be a pretty good sort. He said, 'So you came to get old Mart, eh? Well, just go straight ahead, then turn right and follow the sound of the hammer. Tell him it's quitting time.'

"I said, 'What do you mean, follow the sound of the hammer? There's hammers everywhere in here.'

"He laughed. 'Oh, you'll know Mart's hammer when you hear it!'

"So away I went. I turned right, into another tunnel, with smaller ones leading off it. The noise of hammers on steel echoed all around me. Then I noticed that one sounded heavier than the others, so I walked along in the direction the sound seemed to come from. It got louder, until suddenly, as I went by one of the side tunnels, the sound came blasting out at me, so I turned into that one. It was just about wide enough for two men to pass each other and there were no lights in it, but I could see a faint glow up ahead. I could feel the walls squeezing in on me and wished I was somewhere else, but I kept on going. The hammer sound got louder, until the air seemed to quiver with each blow. I turned a bit of corner, and saw what looked to be a ghost hammerman, lit up by the light from a lamp on a ledge just beside him. He was all white—face, hands, clothes—white as chalk from the dust the drill made. He was drilling up over his head, at about a forty-five-degree angle. He'd let the hammer drop almost to the floor, twist the drill a quarter turn with his left hand, then slam the hammer against it. And every time he did it, a spurt of rock dust flew out and onto his face and bare head. The sound made my ears hurt. White dust marks showed where he had drilled a line of holes across the top of the tunnel. His back was to me, so I called out, 'Oh, Mart! Quitting time!'

"He let the drill slide out of the hole and leaned it against the wall. Then he turned around, and the light shone full on his face. It was quite a sight! Some of it was white, some places the sweat had turned the dust grey, and there were runnels where it had formed channels in the rock dust. He looked like some demon out of a storybook. He said, 'What are you doing down here? Don't you know this is halfway to Hell? The Devil might have his eye on you!' He laughed and tossed his hammer to me playfully. I caught it but almost lost it again. It was a full-sized eight-pound sledgehammer, with the handle cut short so he could use it one-handed. I looked over at the drill. It was about six feet long, an inch thick. It must have weighed fifteen or twenty pounds. He'd held that up there, turning and hitting it, for a full eight-hour day. Just think about that. If you've ever used a carpenter's hammer to nail something up over your head, remember how soon your arm got tired? You use your whole body to hammer the way he was doing, but most of all, you use your arms and belly. And I realized then that what I'd always thought was a beer belly was solid muscle.

"He picked up a canteen of water, rinsed his mouth and spat it out. It came out grey! He poured the rest of it over his head, sloshed it

around with his hands and took the lamp from the ledge. 'Okay,' he
says, 'let's go home.'

"I couldn't believe that a man would work under those conditions.
As we were walking along, I said, 'I thought they had machines to do
that sort of thing?'

"'Machines! You can't use a machine in a place like that. There's
lots of places a man works better.'

"'But a machine doesn't mind if it gets covered in rock dust.'

"'Ho, neither do I. Besides, I like working alone, no one to bother me. And I get a bonus for places like that.'

"I found out later that the 'bonus' was an extra dollar a day, for eating and breathing rock dust for eight hours!"

Grandfather Martin was the kindest, best-natured of men, fond of amimals and good with children. I must admit he teased the cat—but the cat always came back for more. In spite of this, people were uneasy around him. I know now it was because there was a quality of barely concealed savagery about him, of not quite restrained violence. In him, the niceties of civilization had found no lodging. You could imagine him hurling himself into battle, war-axe swinging, just as he hurled his hammer against the resisting steel. He attacked a job as he would an enemy—with everything he could bring to bear. It was, I think, the secret of his strength; with such savage will to drive it, his body must fail, or grow unnaturally strong. His didn't fail him. In today's society, he would be as out of place as a pit bull at a cat show.

He loved beer (or anything alcoholic) and he exulted in his strength. He used one to obtain the other, as I learned from his sons— my uncles.

They would go to one of the beer parlours on the Vancouver waterfront. Mart would go in first. If it was well crowded with loggers in for a good time, he would buy a beer and wait. In a minute or so, one or more of his sons would follow. They looked nothing at all like their father; all were over six feet tall, lean-hipped and heavy-shouldered. They would move next to the short fat man; there would be an argument, raised voices. When enough men were looking, Mart would step toward his son, fists on hips, soft-looking belly bulging invitingly. The son would deliver a mighty punch against it. A real punch, no faking here.

Mart would jeer, his voice loud. "Come on, sonny. You'll have to do better than that!"

Whereupon his son would announce to the room indignantly, "This old man says no one here's man enough to hurt him by hitting him in the stomach!"

Now it is extremely doubtful that any logger in the place would admit—especially with a few beers in him—that there was any man living that could take the sort of punch he could throw. And so the fun would begin. The price of admission, a couple of bottles of beer if their blow didn't produce any effect on Mart, such as an expression of pain, or a grunt. Which it never did. Sometimes someone would get mean, try to take him by surprise, hit low or to one side, only to be met with a sudden thrust and tightening of that mass of muscle: only a fraction of an inch, perhaps, but enough to break knuckles or wrists.

At length, a time would come when no one could be persuaded to try, no matter how they were goaded. But there would be someone who would arm wrestle, or finger pull. Sometimes an opponent would lock his finger with his thumb. No matter; it would straighten, though the joint might gave way first! His sons said that he was never beaten at either of these contests, although he often let his opponents use two fingers to his one, and I believe them. Thus they could, with luck, get a whole evening of drinking, for the price of one bottle of beer. They weren't in town often enough that they became recognised, and it always worked, without fail.

Violent and primitive, no doubt, it was. But save your sneers if you have any. They would keep their word if it killed them, give their last dollar to a beggar, and no matter what your age or sex, you would be safe with them in the darkest alley.

When I was about nineteen, I worked in a logging camp where Grandfather was the blacksmith. As I was competent with a hammer, one of my duties was to help him if help was needed. Although approaching seventy, he was still enormously strong and could do most jobs alone, wielding a short-handled ten-pound hammer with one hand. But some work requires the smith to hold tongs in one hand, shaping tool in the other. These jobs need a "striker."

With an electric fan on the forge, the striker often has nothing to do while the blacksmith tends the iron. Instead of spending the time usefully, I decided it would be fun to throw a hammer up in the air and catch it again. This is not very difficult, and before long I was able to take his eight-pound sledge in one hand, the ten-pound in the other, spin them twice and catch them by the handle. At the cost of only bruised hands and a bit of pain when working at the anvil, I thus acquired a skill which, though useless, I was quite proud of.

When I was confident that I could perform without failure, I asked Grandfather to come outside for a moment. The exhibition went flawlessly. When I had finished, he approved, "Not bad, sonny. Not bad at all. But what good is it? Now I'll give you something to try, you want to be hammerman." (Grandfather never lost his heavy Norwegian accent.)

He took the hammers from me, hefted them, said disparagingly, "Sissy hammers."

He went into the shop and brought out the twelve- and fourteen-pound hammers. (A man of average strength cannnot swing a fourteen-pound hammer to any effect.) From the iron stock he picked out an inch-thick piece of round bar about two feet long, cut square on both ends, and went over to the stump we used as a work block. He tapped the bar in until it stayed there. Then he stood back, and with a hammer in each hand began to drive it into the stump. The air rang with the one-beat-a-second of two men driving steel. The iron bar sank into the tough stump as if it were made of rotten wood, and in seconds one last tremendous blow drove it below the surface. Then, turning so that he faced me, he suddenly sent the big hammer spinning skyward. He stood relaxed, watching as it hurtled back at him; at the last moment he braced himself and snatched it out of the air.

"There," he said, grinning. "Call me when you can do it," as he turned back to tend the forge. (No, I never called him out again.)

He was proud of his strength, but once, when I spoke of it, he laughed. "You think that's something? You should have seen Uncle, back in Norway. He could pick up a full barrel of beer and drink from the bung!"

● ● ●

"Two things I saw old Mart do," said Father, "that I'll never forget. They happened in the same place and at about the same time.

"We were both working in a camp up in Salmon Arm. There was a timekeeper there that nobody liked. Now, the timekeeper is usually the most unpopular man in camp anyhow. He keeps track of all the little things the men buy from the office store during the month, and takes it off their cheques when they get paid. And of course no one ever believes they spent that much money, so they blame the time-keeper. But this one would have been misliked whatever job he had. He was always nosing in where he had no business, and if the boss wasn't around, he figured that he was the next best thing. He hated old Mart. I think he was a little afraid of him. Mart joked pretty roughly with him at times. He was a biggish man and fancied his strength. Not that he was strong; he just liked people to think he was.

"This particular day, the supply boat had just come in and everyone was down at the float to get their mail and to help unload. The timekeeper was there of course, and old Mart. There were about a dozen hundred-pound sacks of flour piled on the dock. Mart had tucked one under each arm and turned to go when the timekeeper spoke in that sarcastic way he had.

"'Mart's so strong, we should just pile all these sacks of flour on him, make one trip of it.'

"Old Mart turned around and grinned at him. 'I guess I could pack all you could load on me.'

"'Oh, yes? You could, could you? Want to bet on that?'

"'A case of beer says I can,' says Mart.

"The timekeeper looked around him. He was grinning. He thought he had caught Mart this time. He said, 'Did everyone hear that? As much as I can load on him.'

"The boss spoke up. He didn't much like the timekeeper either. 'We heard it, and I'll be the referee, so there'll be no arguments. Okay?'

"'Sure,' said Mart. And the timekeeper said, 'Sure,' but he didn't sound too happy about it.

"He picked up a sack of flour and tried to get it under Mart's arm, but anyone could see that his arms weren't long enough to hold two, so he heaved it up on his shoulder. Then he put one on the other shoulder. Next, he got another on top of each of these. It made him puff a bit, but they sat there nicely, completely covering Mart's head. Now he brought another one over and tried to put it on top of those two, but a hundred pounds of flour is pretty hard to hold up over your head while you place it. Mart stood there patiently, not saying anything. Finally, the timekeeper managed to sling it up so's it sat crossways on the others. He stepped back to look, then he said to one of the men standing there, 'Get me a ladder.'

"Of course there had been bets placed, and the ones that had bet on Mart shouted, 'Not fair—No ladder!' Everyone looked at the boss. He shook his head. 'No ladder.'

"The timekeeper looked around. The only thing there that would hold him and a sack of flour were the other sacks of flour. He dragged two of them to where he wanted them, and put one flat and the other on top of it. Then he carried another one over and, using the first two as a platform, tried to throw it on top of the load. But it slipped off, fell onto the deck and split a hole in the side of it. Flour puffed out all over the place. That was enough for the boss.

"'All right, that's enough. I don't buy flour to feed birds, and I don't want your feet all over it either. You've loaded all you can load. Now let's see if Mart can carry it. Away you go, Mart.'

"And away Mart went, over to the foot of the ramp. Luckily it was evening and the tide was up, so he didn't have much of a climb to the dock. But the ramp was on a roller, and you had to step up about a foot or so to get on to it. And he couldn't use his hands to help him. He put one foot up, hesitated, gave a tremendous heave and was on the ramp. Someone whispered, 'Christ, I hope it doesn't break!'

"It held him all right, though it did sag a lot when he got into the middle of it. It was made of new fir poles, though, and strong. He went up it—step, pause, step, pause—and then he was off it and onto the end of the dock. He stopped for a moment, shifted the sacks under his arms, and off he went. It was at least a hundred yards to the cookhouse, and he made it without a stop. The Chinese cook was standing in the door, watching and grinning. Everyone in the camp was tailing along, hollering and cheering Mart on. There were four stairs leading up to a little platform in front of the door, and he stopped when he got to them. The timekeeper's face looked as if he had bitten into something rotten. He said, 'He can't stop there, he's got to put them in the cookhouse, or at least up the stairs.'

"Everyone could see that the stairs wouldn't hold that weight. The boss said, 'The stairs won't hold him—he's won. You're out a case of beer.'

"'But that's not fair, he hasn't carried them all the way.'

"Mart spoke up then. 'You want them up there, you've got it.'

"He dropped the sack under his right arm, caught it by the corner as it fell, and heaved it onto the porch. He did the same with the other one. Then he sort of ducked forward, and as the load tipped, he put his hands up and hurled the full five hundred pounds of it onto the other two. The cook screeched something in Chinese, everyone yelled, and the porch collapsed in a cloud of flour and a heap of broken wood!

"The timekeeper looked at the boss, who was standing there grinning. He said defensively, 'I didn't tell him to do that.'

"'Maybe not,' said the boss unsympathetically. 'But the cost of a new stairs is coming out of your paycheque, and any spilled flour too!'

"So," said Father, "that was one thing. A seven-hundred-pound load, up a ramp, along a dock and up a hundred yards of road. We got a good laugh out of that one. The other thing wasn't so funny, although I guess it was in a way, maybe."

• • •

About two months after the bet, a new man came to join the rigging crew. The boat arrived at the dock during working hours, so only Father and the bull cook were there to meet it. As it slid in alongside the float, a husky young man with a packsack in one hand jumped onto the dock. He made no attempt to help tie up the boat, but stood there with the expression of one who had found about what he expected and wasn't impressed with it. He was tall and thick-shouldered; handsome in a rather coarse-featured way, with a sulky mouth, too much jaw and nose, and just enough forehead to keep his curly black hair out of his eyes. His face was that shade of red that often indicates a man who works outdoors and drinks indoors.

He dismissed the bull cook as obviously menial, but Father's air of competence seemed to have an effect on him. He strode over, shoved out his hand and said, "Hi there. I'm Stomper. Pleased ta meetcha."

Father gave his name politely and took the hand. "Stomper" gripped it strongly, and after one shake, bore down on it with all his force, grinning a bit as he did so. But Father's rather slight build was deceptive. He had thick fingers, and forearms like Popeye's. He not only didn't flinch, but even increased the pressure a bit. Stomper looked startled, and the grin vanished as he pulled his hand away. "Where's the bunkhouse?"

Indicating the bull cook, Father said, "Mac there'll show you." Dismissing the newcomer from his thoughts, he went back to business. He hadn't been impressed.

Stomper had been put in the biggest bunkhouse with the crew he would be working with. It held twelve men, most of them young. There were two older men, one of whom Father knew quite well and liked. They met that evening in the combined store and office, which was presided over by the timekeeper. They had chatted for a few minutes about nothing in particular, when the old logger said, "Say, Hal, have you met the new fellow that come in today?"

"Yeah, I was down on the float when the boat came in. Fancies himself a bit much, I suspect. Gave me a kind of odd name."

"That's right. Calls himself Stomper. A troublemaker if ever I saw one. You should have heard him."

It seems Stomper had been lying in his bunk reading when the men returned. After the bustle of changing clothes was over, he put his magazine down, stood up and took a few paces out into the room. They had all been stealing covert looks at the newcomer, but now they stared openly.

"Hi," he greeted them. He looked around, judging the quality of his audience. Then he announced in his rather high but powerful voice, "I'm Stomper. That's what they call me. I'm known by that name from Oregon to Alaska."

He stood there arrogantly, judging their response. "And you know why they call me Stomper? I'll tell you why. When I go to a camp, I look around for the biggest, toughest man there. When I find him I call him out, and then I knock him down and stomp on his face with my caulks. That's why they call me Stomper."

Now, this certainly was done, at various times and places. Logger's boots have sharp conical spikes set into the soles, to give a grip on hard and slippery wood, and the marks they made were called logger's smallpox. But this pleasant custom had faded away by that time, on the lower BC coast, at any rate.

"You've got to admit he's got some gall," said the old logger, "sounding off like that to a crew of men he's never met before. But he talked mean, and he looked mean, and they took it."

Father agreed that he certainly did seem to "have a lot of gall," and the old man continued, "He can sure talk. He talked until supper, and he talked after supper until bedtime. I must say he had some pretty good stories. A lot of them about fighting, with him the centrepiece, always winning, of course. Some of the young fellas think he's really something already."

They speculated for a while as to who of the forty or so men in camp might be the toughest, but came to no conclusion. There were several whom no prudent man would choose to offend. Neither of them thought—even for a moment—of old Mart.

Stomper lost no time. The next morning at the breakfast table was when he chose to assert himself. Unfortunately for his pride, the man he chose was quite possibly the worst one he could have picked.

Stomper and half a dozen admirers came noisily into the cookhouse, the young men already speaking noticeably louder and more violently than usual. They all settled into a line on one side of the first table. Among those on the other side, and almost directly across from Stomper, was a big Finn bucker. He had arrived in camp the previous spring, as part of a crew consisting of two fallers with him as bucker, and was regarded with awe. Some hand-falling crews had two buckers, but there was no need of that if the Finn was one of them.

Bucking was one of the hardest jobs in the woods in the days of hand tools. A faller can be tough and wiry, for his saw lies flat on the stump and he controls how hard it pulls, but a bucker's saw is much heavier and the teeth press into the wood with no respite. So buckers were always big men, and for some reason they were usually Norwegians, Swedes, Finns or Russians. After the fallers cut a tree down, the bucker trimmed and cut it into lengths. As the fallers have only to make one cut to perhaps four for the bucker, it can be seen that it isn't an easy job. (There are other factors involved, of course.) The bucking saw was the biggest and heaviest saw used in the woods: eight feet long, on average, and a full foot in depth. When it was sharp and well into a cut, the average man probably couldn't move it. Most buckers used two hands, but some—and the Finn was one—hurled the big saw back and forth with one hand, while a cascade of sawdust streamed out at every stroke. His was the top crew in the camp, turning out more logs than anyone else.

After his first day at work, he brought his two saws back to the saw filer, telling him, "Not right, make like this," as he showed how he wanted them filed.

But saw filers are specialists; each has his own way of filing and is proud of it. They do not change it willingly. Next day the Finn was back. He said darkly, "Not right. Not way I say."

He took one of the big saws in his calloused hands, holding them about three feet apart, then brought them suddenly together. The tough steel bent double, then broke with the sound of a hammer hitting iron. He shook his finger in the face of the terrified filer.

"This time," he said sternly. "Saw. Next time, you!"

He got them filed the way he wanted them.

This was the man Stomper chose to make fun of. Now, to work like he did takes an enormous amount of fuel. I've been in camps with big men like the Finn. They take in about four thousand calories at breakfast, the same for lunch, and then at supper they tuck in! But the Finn may have outdone them all.

Instead of the usual round plate, he had one of the big serving platters. On this he spread first a double row of hotcakes. On these, three steaks. On top of them went eight fried eggs, over which he poured about a cupful of thick syrup. He looked down at it, considering for a moment. Then he held out his hand and grunted "Bacon." He swept all the bacon off the plate, arranging it neatly across his, and covered the whole thing with half a bottle of ketchup.

Stomper had been watching this with amazement and obvious disgust. Now he said, in a loud stage whisper, "Will you look at that? A dog wouldn't eat that mess. What that fellow needs is a trough, not a plate!"

The big Finn put both hands on the edge of the table. His arms and shoulders bulged hugely in a work shirt that would be loose on most men. Slowly he raised his head and looked across the table. He was a wild-looking sight. Straight black hair fell raggedly almost to his shoulders. When it grew long enough to bother him, he sawed it off with a knife. His face was dark and strong, but it was his eyes that held you, eyes like ice, of so pale a blue as to be almost colourless.

Father said, "I looked straight into his eyes once and it gave me the creeps. It was like something was hiding in there, something that you wouldn't want to see come out."

When those eyes looked at him, Stomper froze.

The Finn said in his cavernous voice, "Something bother you, mister?"

It took Stomper a moment to find his voice, and when he did he was polite. "No, no—nothing bothering me, thanks. Just teasing one of the boys here."

The Finn held his gaze for a moment, then relaxed and began to eat.

Stomper was somewhat subdued during breakfast, but in the yard afterwards, he was his usual obnoxious self. His followers crowded around him eagerly. This, they proposed, was the man for him to fight. "Everyone's afraid of him."

But Stomper was having none of that. "That man's crazy," he blustered. "Didn't you see his eyes? I don't fight crazy men. You can't stop them, you got to kill them. I found that out, believe me. I don't want no trouble like that again."

Whether he had actually killed anyone or not, it worked, and even increased his prestige somewhat. But there was still the matter of whom he would "call out." That night in the bunkhouse, he questioned the others closely. Just who was the strongest man in the camp?

Inevitably, Mart's name was mentioned. Stomper was interested.

"Seven hundred pounds, eh? That's quite a load. I don't know if even I could carry that."

And when the strong man was pointed out to him, he knew he had found his victim. With those short arms and heavy body, he would be slow. Stomper, with his greater reach, could pound away until his opponent collapsed, and the rest would be easy.

Stomper was eager to begin. He doubtless felt he had "lost face" in the confrontation with the Finn, and wanted to make a strong move as soon as possible. The next evening after supper he and his followers hung about the stairs to the cookhouse. When Mart appeared, Stomper moved in front of the stairs, blocking the way. Mart pushed by him, none too gently, and Stomper made his move.

"Hey there, you dumb squarehead, who do you think you're shoving?" he said belligerently.

But it didn't produce the effect he wanted. In fact, it didn't produce any effect at all. Mart ignored him as if he didn't exist.

"Hey you, are you deaf as well as stupid?" asked Stomper in a loud voice. But the would-be victim proceeded on his way, neither faster nor slower.

Stomper was so surprised that he waited a little too long, so that it would be undignified to try to catch up. "That's all right, he'll fight next time. I'll see to that."

But the affair didn't go according to plan. First, the boss got wind of what was going on and made it known that anyone who started a fight would be on the next boat out. And second, Mart would not fight. Try as Stomper would with insult and ridicule, Mart wouldn't respond—seemed, in fact, unable to see or hear him. It was very frustrating.

There was a reason for Mart's response, and Father knew what it was, for Mart's eldest son had told him about it. He told of how his father had once worked on the railroad. The crew he was in was the top one on the line. Tough men, and hard. There had been a bit of a scuffle. Mart, irritated, had slapped the man on the side of the head. The other had been taken away on a stretcher, never to be seen again.

It was whispered he had died. The foreman forbade talk of it. He had lost one man; he was certainly not going to lose two. Besides, in 1918 what happened to a railway worker was of little interest to anyone. Who counted? But there were murmurs, and perhaps a try at blackmail—it was hard to be certain. Whatever the reason, Mart quit and went to work in the mine at Britannia, vowing that fighting was a fool's game and there would be no tempting him again, whatever the reason.

And so the thing stood, for a week or more, until Thanksgiving day arrived. There would be an extra day off. Dinner—turkey and pumpkin pie, and a dance afterwards, for there were a few women in camp.

Came the night of the dance. The tables had been stacked against one wall of the big dining room in the cookhouse. Father and his accordion provided the music. The boss had donated a dozen cases of beer before going down-inlet to Sechelt. Some of the crew had gone also, and of course there were some, like the Finn, who were not the convivial sort. But there were a couple of dozen people there, Mart among them, and they were having a good time.

An hour went by, then there came the sound of loud voices at the door and Stomper strode in, followed by a half dozen or so of his admirers. His face was flushed from drink, but his walk was steady. He had his caulk boots on. He went over to where Mart was standing and stood there, looking him up and down, slowly and insultingly. The dancers stopped circulating and Father, perforce, stopped playing.

"I knew we'd find you here where there's free beer." He looked around at his audience. "You know how to tell a squarehead from a human? Well, I'll tell you. You cut them, and if beer comes out 'stead of blood, you know."

He looked around again to see what effect he was having.

Father told me, "The young fellows were grinning like fools. So was the timekeeper. He looked like someone that's just found a hundred-dollar bill in the street. All the decent people looked mad, or helpless, sort of. They didn't know what to do about it. Didn't want to get involved. Of course, they all knew what Stomper said he was going to do. I was worried for old Mart. He wasn't built for a fighter. For one thing, his arms were too short. He might be able to take care of himself, but I didn't know. I did know that I wasn't going to let anyone stomp on his face with caulk boots, if I had to use the cook's meat cleaver to stop it. But I couldn't step in yet."

Stomper continued, grinning widely. "And, ya know why you never see squareheads with their shirts off? I'll tell ya why. There's a big yellow stripe goes up the middle of their backs, that's why. But there's one thing I don't know, and that thing is, what does it take to get a Svenski squarehead to fight?"

Mart just stood there. His face was set like stone. Squarehead was still a fighting word to call a Swede or Norwegian. And to call a Norwegian Svenski, or Swede, was a mortal insult. But Mart's resolve was proof against even these insults.

He said gruffly, "What do you want to fight for? Fighting is a fool's game. Have a bottle of beer, make you feel better."

Stomper pretended to be insulted. "I don't need no squarehead to tell me I can have a beer, I'll take one when I want one. And I want one now."

He went over to where the beer was, took a bottle, came back, put it to his mouth and pried the cap off with his teeth; then stood there holding the bottle, still grinning. "And you just called me a fool, as I remember, and I'm gonna make you wish you hadn't. But I still want to see what it takes to get a squarehead to fight. Maybe this'll do it."

He reached out and poured the beer onto Mart's belly where it bulged out from below his ribs. Mart stood watching for a moment as it ran down and onto the floor. A man can only take so much and still think of himself as a man, and Mart had reached that limit. Or perhaps it was the waste of good beer! I never thought to ask him.

His hand shot out, snake-quick, knocking the bottle across the room. His tormentor took a step back, in surprise. He said in mock wonder, "Well, so there is life under the fat after all!"

Mart said slowly, "All right, I will fight you. But first we must shake hands."

Stomper looked around in wonder. "Why," he asked reasonably, "should I shake his hand when I'm going to stomp on his face?"

"No shake, no fight," was the answer, in a tone that would not be argued with.

Stomper thought for a moment. He was not exactly bright, but he knew well enough there would be little glory in beating up a man who would not fight back. And then there was the boss. He made up his mind. "If that's what it takes, then that's what I'll do. Shake first, then stomp." His grin returned. "Sounds good to me!"

He stuck out his hand. Mart reached for it with that surprising hand speed. Stomper, perhaps warned by the look of satisfaction on Mart's face, tried to snatch it back. He was too late.

Remembered Father, "There was a sound like you'd wrapped some dry sticks in a towel and then broke them. Knowing what caused it made me feel sick to my stomach."

Stomper screamed and fell to his knees, then over onto his side, still screaming. Mart looked down at him. His face was calm, appearing only slightly interested, as if he were watching the struggle of some odd bug or suchlike. It showed no satisfaction—and no mercy. Stomper went limp, as if he had fainted. Mart turned and headed for the kitchen, dragging the big man behind him with one hand, like a sack of potatoes. Everyone followed. From the kitchen, a door led onto a railed veranda built out partway over a deep pool, where the creek curved before entering the sea.

Stomper was beginning to roll around and moan. Mart dragged him to the rail and, ignoring his struggles, seized him by the upper arm and thigh, raised him chest-high and flung him into the dark water. There was a mighty splash, followed by choked yells.

In the light from the window and open door, Mart's face had the satisfied look of a man who feels he has accomplished something worthwhile.

He said to Father, "There. I guess he'll cool off in that."

Father answered him doubtfully, "I don't think you should have done that, Mart. Maybe he can't swim."

Mart considered this for a moment. The thought had obviously not occurred to him. Suddenly he brightened. "Maybe not," he answered brightly, "but he's in a great place to learn!"

And he stomped past Father into the kitchen, roaring jovially,

"C'mon, what's everybody glooming around for? The night's young yet. Where's the beer?"

The next morning, Stomper was sent down the inlet on the camp boat, his hand swollen to twice its normal size. The first-aid man refused to touch it. He told Father, "I never saw anything like it. It looked like it had been run over by a truck. I think just about every bone in it was broken!"

None of the young men were there to see him off, nor was he ever seen or heard of in that area again.

Epilogue

We live in a society obsessed with safety. Compulsory seat belts, extra brake lights, daytime headlights, life jackets and all that. Buildings are evacuated because asbestos has been found somewhere in them. My son's mechanics teacher wears a mask when working on car brake drums because of possible asbestos fibres, and used engine oil is classified as a "hazardous material"!

And I remember Grandfather Martin. Standing in the blacksmith's shop, surrounded by a cloud of asbestos dust, mixing it in his hands with oil to make a dam for molten metal. Peering at the work through the fumes of molten zinc. Chewing tobacco, smoking it, drinking anything with alcohol in it. He didn't spread butter, he cut off slices like cheese, and after cutting the fat meat off for his portion, cleaned the set-apart fat from everybody else's plate and ate that. He lived to the age of eighty-four, and died of a heart attack.

How he would have laughed at us, he who enjoyed driving iron on a trestle high above tumbled boulders! Oh, I know, not everyone has that sort of constitution, but isn't it just possible the dangers of life have been slightly exaggerated?

I would be the last to say that everything about the old days was good. But I look back at Grandfather and his kind with regret. With all its hazards, they enjoyed life, I think, much more than we do.

Who Were They?

As everyone knows, the history of Europeans on the coast of British Columbia isn't a long one. A hundred-year-old house is considered ancient. Even the lower coast had almost no whites living on it before 1850 or so, and the more desolate areas still had few settlers when Father, as a young man, was roaming around them. People have been here and gone, and their presence hasn't always left its imprint on history. The Spaniards were the first Europeans to visit these shores.

Father told me of how one time in Jervis Inlet, he had fallen a tree on the back of his handlogging claim. It slid about halfway down the slope when—just as he was sure nothing could stop it—the broken top plowed into a flat spot and buried itself in gravel, one of the few things that *can* stop a tree once it gets up speed on a mountainside. He carried his tools down to it, got his logging jacks from where he had last used them and went to work.

The first thing to be done was to clear a space in which to set the jacks in order to take the weight while he cut the top off just above the ground. The tree had overturned a pile of rocks at the edge of the flat ground and he decided to use them as a base on which to set the jacks. As he was trying to select ones of the right size, he noticed the mark of a rock drill in one of them. Immediately curious, he looked around more carefully and realized that the flat area was actually part of an old road angling up the hill. He followed it, though that wasn't easy to do. Trees big enough to log grew in the middle of it. If there had been stumps, they had long since rotted away. He thought a fallen cedar tree showed a cut end, but even that long-lasting wood had rotted too much for him to be certain. Then he found a few more drill holes where they had cut through a small ridge of rock. The road seemed to be heading to where he knew there was a sheer rock face about a quarter of a mile away. He thought that there must have been a mine up there to be worth that much trouble. He would explore it another time. He didn't want to leave the tree, as it was late in the spring and the slippery spots where the bark had come off would soon grow dry and sticky with exuded pitch, and the tree wouldn't slide well. He went back to work. The days went by and the months. He never did follow the road to the end.

There was one tree growing in the middle of the road that he thought worth taking. When he had felled it, he counted the growth rings on the stump. (This was a few years after World War I—the early twenties.) There were 112 of them. Trees reseed very quickly on a bare spot, so the road was probably only a few years older.

"After all," he said in self-defence when I reproached him for not following it up, "it was probably just another worked-out mine, though I always intended to go back there for a look."

I would have gone there for a look myself, but he is dead, and I neglected to get a fix on the map while he could still give one. Ah well, as he said, probably just another worked-out mine.

Another occasion produced something a bit more definite. Father was buying supplies at the Union store in Sechelt when he heard someone call his name.

"Hal, am I glad to see you. You're just the man I've been looking for." It was Art Bromly, who worked as a forest ranger in the area, a good friend of Father's. "I've got a great proposition for you, just the sort of thing you'll like."

Father was immediately wary, for Bromly was a man of sudden enthusiasms not necessarily based on firm foundations. He led Father over to an unoccupied corner of the store, and after checking all around to make sure no one was close enough to overhear, he said, his voice pitched low, "How would you like to go on a little hike? Take about two days, maybe three. Head of Salmon Arm. Top of the mountain straight back from the head." He lowered his voice even further. "I came across this old report. One of the first surveys, unofficial. Been lost in the files for more than fifty years."

"Another gold mine, I suppose," remarked Father, remembering similar occasions.

"No, no, not gold. I think it might be copper. Report says ore outcroppings all over the top of the mountain. We should be able to find it easy. How about it? Do you want to have a go at it?"

Father considered. He doubted that they would find anything. On the other hand, he had nothing urgent to do and the weather was fine. It would be a pleasant diversion, and Art Bromly was a good man to hike with; his enthusiasm never waned over a little thing like lack of success, and he never seemed to be aware of discomforts such as wet clothes or hard going.

"All right. I'm game. When do you want to go?"

"Tomorrow early. Or what about today? I can be ready in an hour."

"Tomorrow morning at six o'clock. I'll see you at the boat." Father didn't like to be rushed.

By about noon the next day, they were at the head of Salmon Arm. With the boat safely anchored and skiff pulled up into the bushes, they were soon on their way up the mountain.

Bromly had a copy of the report and a map of the area, but he wasn't at all certain of just where they were going. The author of the report had broken his compass and had been unable to get a celestial fix because of cloudy weather, so he was obliged to use lines of sight for points of reference, and the map of the area was not very reliable. In those days, maps were not the models of accuracy we take so much for granted. Where an official survey had been done, it could be very reliable, assuming the surveyor didn't make a habit of drinking his lunch—an assumption one couldn't take for granted. The larger part of some coast maps were made from sketches taken from a high point not necessarily nearby, drawn by a surveyor whose estimate of distances often began to get vague at more than a few thousand yards.

However, they settled on a course and headed up the mountain at an angle they hoped would put them in the right place. By evening, after five or six hours of not very difficult climbing, they made camp.

Bromly's calculations indicated that they were in the correct area, so early next morning they set out in search of the outcroppings of ore. They searched all that day, camped, and set out once more in the early morning. They found nothing of value. This was not surprising, because as it turned out they were on the wrong mountain. There is a copper deposit in that area, but it lies a couple of mountains over from where they were looking. Or perhaps there is another one and they just didn't find it.

However, as they were searching among some ridges and tumbled rocks where the mountain they were on extended toward the next range, they found the opening of a cave. They were eager to explore it, for caves are rare in the coast mountains and are always of interest. Father made a torch out of a bundle of sticks and twigs, and by its light they investigated their find. They were disappointed. It wasn't very deep, nor were the rocks interesting. They were leaving when Father noticed something high up on the wall near the entrance.

"Look, Art!" he exclaimed. "Someone's been here ahead of us!"

He took down a bundle of candles from a small ledge of rock. Thus encouraged, they looked around for anything else they might have missed but found nothing more. They went back outside to examine their find by daylight.

"They were strange-looking candles," said Father. "Not like anything I'd seen before. They were a deep golden yellow, quite thick, about fourteen inches long. The wax was tough, not brittle. It gave off a strange, rather nice smell when you scratched or rubbed it. We thought it was mostly beeswax but with something else in it. They had been tied together with some sort of cord. You could still see the marks on the wax. Over the years they had stuck together quite tightly. Bromly pried two of them out of the bundle and put the rest back where we'd found them."

They decided to go home. The top of the mountain didn't match the description of the one they'd been looking for. The map was useless, the lines of sight ambiguous. They resolved to give it another try someday. They never did.

Some months later, Father met his friend at a dance in Sechelt.

"Say, Hal," Bromly said. "You remember those candles we found? Well, I gave them to a fellow I know at the museum. He was interested enough that he sent them to the British Museum. Seems they have a man there who is an authority on candles. Studied them all his life. He wrote back that they were Spanish, and that they were a kind that they'd stopped making about three hundred years ago. He said that the navy had used them."

"But," Father said to me, "I doubt that they'd been there for anything near three hundred years. The navy probably had enough stockpiled to last a hundred years or so. It shows, though, that the Spanish did more than just cruise around a bit. I guess they were looking for gold. From what I've read, they were always looking for gold. I can't figure why they'd leave a bundle of candles in a cave up on a mountain, or why the mice didn't eat them all up the first year they were put up there. Maybe it's too high and cold for mice, or maybe they put something in the wax when they made them. I'd like to go back there with a good light some day and have a better look around."

He never did go back. I imagine the candles are still there on that ledge. I'd like to go looking myself someday, though I'd probably climb the wrong mountain. Perhaps my son will give it a try!

Perpetual Motion

is, of course, not possible. In earlier centuries, before the laws of energy and motion were codified, it was a quite legitimate matter for investigation. Even Da Vinci tried his hand at it, and many were the attempts to get something for nothing. One of the most famous was that of Johannus Bessler, who made a wheel some dozen feet in diameter that was said to have run for eight weeks in a sealed room. That was c. 1730. He destroyed it, probably to protect a trick of some sort.

The idea is still around in one form or another, although since the discovery of the laws of thermodynamics, the notion isn't taken seriously by science, and patent offices won't accept applications on that subject. Yet still inventors try, and still one of the favourites is one of the oldest: the over-balancing wheel, where the idea is to make moving weights apply slightly more leverage on one side of the wheel than the other.

Let me re-emphasize, for those who may have no interest in science: you cannot create energy. You cannot take more out of a system than you put in it, nor can you break even; friction must always take its toll. Without an input of some sort, every system must run down. And yet...

Father was working one fall at a camp near the head of Salmon Inlet. Sunday came, and he and two others, went up the mountain behind camp to see if they could get a mountain goat. It was a dismal sort of day and as he said, "We should have known better."

The goats—if there—were staying above the cloud line: they saw none, nor signs of any. But a hunt is often only an excuse for a jaunt, and they were well enough content. Their course had taken them quite a ways along the shoreline from camp; flurries of wet snow began to fall, and they faced a slippery and dangerous trip back to camp along the rocky cliffs. Then Father remembered that someone was living not very far away from where they were, at least he had seen wood smoke coming from among the trees there on several occasions. There would surely be a boat of some sort that could be borrowed. They decided to try it. No one liked the alternative.

Father had a good picture of the area in his mind. They angled down toward the water, and soon the smell of wood smoke came to them in the faint breeze blowing up the inlet. They found the place without much difficulty, a neat little cabin on a level rock ledge a couple of hundred feet above the water, almost hidden by trees. At their knock the door opened promptly, and a rather odd-looking man stood peering at them from eyes so blue they seemed to sparkle. He was slight of build, perhaps taller than average, but so stooped as to seem shorter. In fact, he looked almost hunchbacked. His hair was totally white and there was a lot of it, long and silky, so fine and light that it seemed to float in the air as he moved. He had a strange mouth, V-shaped, so that his lips seemed set in a permanent sardonic grin. He didn't appear particularly surprised to see three men with guns on his doorstep, but said pleasantly, soft-voiced, "Well, gentlemen. I didn't expect visitors. To what do I owe the pleasure?"

They explained their presence, and he answered them that he did indeed have a boat, and they would be welcome to borrow it.

"But you look wet, and must be cold. Let me make you a cup of tea before you go. I see few people. Your company will be welcome."

Father was a dedicated tea drinker and needed no excuse to indulge. The others were equally willing, and in moments they were standing with steaming clothes around a warm little stove of curious design, on which was a kettle already hot. During the usual small talk of strangers who have just met, modified by the rather unusual circumstances, Father looked around him with much interest. There was only the one room. A bed, neatly made up, stood against the far wall. A few clothes hung from pegs. There were three sturdy chairs and a table, obviously homemade. But what caught his attention were the clocks.

It appeared that their host was a clockmaker. There were clocks everywhere, on the table, on shelves, on the walls. Clocks of strange shapes and unusual faces. There was a workbench under a large window with a partly assembled clock on it, with little gleaming bits of shafts and gears placed carefully about it. Against the wall at one end of the bench was a very small lathe, driven by a foot pedal. Father thought it might be homemade, not because it was crude but because it seemed too finely constructed to be something bought. There were two or three big oil lamps with reflectors.

He had been conscious of a very slight sound, as of metal on metal, so faint that he hadn't really noticed it through the sound of the clocks—muted though that was, for none of them were loud. But then he noticed motion in the far corner of the room, and realizing the sound came from there, went over to investigate.

He saw a moving wheel with curved spokes inside a metal rim. About two feet in diameter, it was mounted in a strong-looking frame that in turn sat on a stand or shelf that stuck out from the wall, seeming to be carved out of the solid rock against which the cabin was built. The surface of it had been ground to the smoothness of glass. A strange metal instrument, to whose purpose he had no clue, stood near the turning wheel. He had started to go closer when his host spoke.

"I must ask you not to touch the wheel, nor indeed go too near it. Your warmth and moisture may affect it. But to arm's length will do no harm."

Father went no closer, but examined it carefully. He saw that the axle of the wheel, about as thick as his index finger, met the frame at what appeared to be a fine jewelled point. The curved spokes ran from a thick hub to the rim, and what appeared to be polished ball bearings about an inch in diameter rolled along grooves in the spokes, making the almost inaudible sound. The balls didn't move smoothly but seemed to hesitate, and he got the idea that the spokes were somehow vibrating, and that there was more to them than first appeared. He also had the feeling that the balls on one side were slightly farther from the hub than those on the other, which disturbed his sense of the fitness of things.

Fascinated, he asked, "What is it?"

"Perpetual motion." said their host calmly, as if commenting on the weather.

One of the other men walked halfway across the room, looked, asked, "What's it for?"

"To upset some people with closed minds."

Father was somewhat familiar with the subject, for Jack Hammond, his father, had found it of interest and had lectured them on it.

He said, "You can't get something from nothing, friction will stop it. What keeps it going?"

The blue eyes peered at him in sudden interest, their intensity unnerving. "What do you know about it?" he asked, the V-lips quirking, more sardonic than ever, making the question sound derisive.

"I know you can't get more out than you put in, or even as much as you put in," retorted Father stubbornly. "You can't cheat nature."

"Never would I try to cheat her," chuckled the other, in mock horror, "but there may be ways around the rules."

He poured the tea into thin cups without handles. It was good; they drank appreciatively and accepted more. Their host returned to the subject that was obviously his passion. "So," he asked, speaking directly to Father, "what do you think makes the wheel go, then? It has been turning like that for a month."

Father was at a loss for an answer, a rare condition for him. He was certain that perpetual motion was impossible. Either he was wrong or the man was a fraud and a liar. But nothing could drag even a suggestion of that from him, and he strove desperately for a way out. He was saved the trouble. The bright eyes bored into his and divined his thoughts. Their owner laughed merrily, showing a great many very small teeth.

"You think I lurk up here, in my oh-so-visible little house, so that when visitors come I can impress them with my fake machine!" He laughed again at the thought, making Father blush. "I assure you, young man, I am not so desperate for applause as that. But I accept your challenge." He beckoned. "Come," he invited, and went to the turning wheel. Father followed. The clockmaker took a match from a box on a shelf and lit the lamp that hung from a bracket on the wall, for shadows were beginning to form in the corners.

He made a gesture of invitation, saying, "For you I will terminate the experiment I was doing. See what you can find. Wires, magnets, currents of air, whatever your imagination suggests. You may slide the wheel, but I would rather you not pick it up. It was the other device that I meant your presence might derange, but that doesn't matter now."

"What is it?"

"A counter, a very delicate one," responded the other.

(This intrigues me, perhaps as much as the wheel: I don't think the technology existed at that time to make a counter that had no contact with what it counted.)

Father examined the wheel and its surroundings very carefully. He was much impressed by the exquisite precision that had gone into its making. It was like the movement of a very expensive watch made large. He failed to find anything in the least suspicious. He slid the wheel and its stand along the smooth surface until the area it had stood on was exposed. Nothing. He stepped back, baffled. A thought surfaced.

"If it is what you claim it is, it should start by itself if it's stopped. Will it?"

"Very good, young man. Very good. So it should indeed. Let us try it." He placed his finger lightly on the rim of the wheel, stopping its motion. Then he released it. For a moment, nothing happened, but then it began to move again. A ball rolled along its groove, the wheel turned, another followed, and gradually the wheel came up to its former speed.

"Well, it beats me," confessed Father. "What makes it go?"

"Momentum," explained the inventor. "Momentum. The balls roll out a bit farther on the one side and are held there for a moment longer than normal. They spend a little bit more time a little farther from the centre than they do on the other side as the wheel rises. But there is something else also, and I must admit that I do not know yet what it is, though I suspect the motion of the earth has a hand in it."

The other two had been sitting by the stove, talking quietly. Now one of them spoke up. "But what good is it? What will it do? Could it run one of your clocks, instead of using a spring?"

Gloomily the old man shook his head. "For anything practical, it is no good at all. It makes just enough power to overcome friction and air resistance and there is almost no friction. The bearings are diamond on diamond. And air resistance at that speed is nearly nothing. Perhaps there is enough power left over to run a clock. But it is no good for that; the speed is not constant. I thought to astonish the world of science, but scientists have no time for impossible mechanisms. No, it is a hobby only, and through it I seek to learn."

Father told me, "I began to believe him. He seemed so sincere. And the thing did turn."

"Did you cut the shelf just for a solid place to put it?"

"No, the shelf was for another purpose. It is not a very good place for the machine, it moves too much. It should be on a mount that absorbs shocks."

"Moves too much!" objected one of the others. "What do you mean, moves too much—isn't that part of the mountain?"

"Why, of course it is. But the mountain moves, didn't you know? It tilts in that direction... " he pointed, "about a tenth of an inch a year. And it shakes and jiggles like a fat man's stomach all the time."

The other started to protest indignantly. Father didn't think the old man should have to defend his claims, though in truth he seemed quite capable of doing so and, if given the opportunity, would probably convince them that the mountains were moving! But he interrupted nevertheless. "It's getting dark, we should be going. Thank you for the tea. And about the wheel, I think you may have something there, but I'm darned if I know what!"

Next day he took the rowboat back, towing his canoe along for the return trip. He climbed the trail and knocked at the door. The old man opened it, and again he experienced the shock of those piercing blue eyes. The wheel was still turning on its smooth course in the corner. He refused politely the invitation to come in, for the other seemed preoccupied. After a few more polite words, he left. Shortly after that he went to work at Fredericks Arm. He never saw or heard of the old clockmaker again. And I have no idea if the old man had tapped a source of energy of some sort or other. I know I'd like to examine that wheel!

The Serpent's Lair

This story is strange, frustrating and inconclusive. I don't know where it happened. Father wasn't comfortable with it, and I doubt he told it to anyone but me, in that last year of his life.

• • •

"I was waiting for the weather," he said. "I had a heavy load on the deck and I didn't want to hit any seas if I could help it, and it had been blowing southeast pretty hard. I finally pulled in behind a point for shelter as the next stretch would be rough in that wind. The month was October. It was about noon, and the rain had stopped, so I set out to do a bit of exploring. It was a part of the country I'd never stopped at and I thought this would be a good chance to look around.

"The land climbed pretty steeply for a few hundred feet, then levelled off into what looked to be quite a flat basin. There was a creek not far away, so I thought that I might as well fill up my water tank. I got a couple of buckets and paddled over to fill them. It was a poor shore to land on—all bluff and boulders—but I found a spot near the mouth of the creek where I could pull the skiff up. I decided to walk up the hill to see what that little valley looked like. It might even make a good handlogging claim. It was the sort of place where you could find good trees that didn't show up well from the water, and it had a good slope with deep water below.

"As soon as I got ashore and started looking around, I noticed a rusty spot on the flat of the rock. When I looked closer, it turned out to be what was left of a bolt of some sort set into the rock with lead.

It had been about half an inch thick, but there was nothing left of the part that stuck out but rust. It takes a long time to do that, even that close to salt water. Now I was really interested. Why an iron bolt here? There wasn't any sign of logging. The timber on the slope was just shore fir and scrub cedar, and there were no cut stumps that I could see.

"I headed up the hill, following what might possibly have been a trail, and I wasn't long getting up to where the slope levelled off. Sure enough, there were some nice trees there, but they were mostly cedar instead of the stand of big fir I'd been hoping for. The ground was nice and open, no underbrush to speak of, and as I was walking along I saw a deer horn on the ground. I picked it up and looked at it. I'd never seen one like that before. It was sort of like a hand with the fingers sticking out. I put it down where I could spot it easily, meaning to pick it up on the way back and take it home for a curio. Then I spotted another one, and pretty soon one more. All the same kind of horns, flat as the palm of your hand with these little finger-like horns sticking out from the edge. And as I walked along I saw three or four more of them. I never saw so many horns shed in one place in all my life. But I never did see one of the deer, although there must have been a lot of them. I was sorry the hunting season was over. It would have been nice to get one and have the head mounted. It would be something different."

(This is a pretty good description of palmated antlers. They don't occur on deer in coastal BC.)

He strolled up the valley, enjoying—as always—exploring a bit of new country. The area was exceptionally open and pleasant, though a bit gloomy as old-growth cedar forests tend to be; and still he followed what could once have been a trail. Then, higher up on the sloping valley side, he saw it.

"You could have knocked me down with a feather. Of all the places to see a house, that was about the last one I would have guessed."

He hurried up for a look, curiosity now thoroughly aroused. The first thing he noticed was that it looked old, very old, and unoccupied.

It wasn't just a cabin but a proper house with glass windows, a porch with steps and a rock and clay chimney wide enough at the base to contain a fireplace, though now it was half collapsed. The house itself was constructed of cedar logs about eighteen inches thick, hewn flat on two sides so that the walls were solid wood a foot and a half thick! This type of construction wasn't unknown to Father but it was quite uncommon, as it meant a great deal of axe-work, and much skill to hew the logs accurately enough to fit well. The roof was made of split cedar at least two inches thick, covered with a deep layer of moss. The windows were small, the panes of the kind that are diamond-shaped and set in lead.

When he drew near he stopped, feeling there was something wrong with the picture he was seeing—aside from the total incongruity of a house in such a place. Then he realized what was bothering him. There was nothing there but a house. There were no outbuildings. There had been no garden, flower or vegetable. The ground around had never been dug. The owner had kept no chickens nor any other domestic animals as far as could be seen. A tiny stream off to one side would have provided water, but had no pool dug out in it. He began to feel that sense of wrongness more strongly.

Going by the near corner, he put his hand on the wood. It was soft on the edges. Cedar up in the air like that lasts for many years without rotting. He looked at the corner. The joints were the simple ones allowed by square timbers but were made with incredible accuracy. He continued around the back. There were no windows there; nothing of note at all except a rusty double-bitted axe leaning against the wall. He picked it up to look at it and the handle broke in his hands. He left it and went around the house and back to the veranda again. He hadn't looked closely at it before, being preoccupied with other details. He now saw what hadn't registered in his mind at first: that the posts supporting the roof were oddly lumpy and uneven. Suddenly he realized with a shock of disgust that they were carved— and all too realistically—with twining snakes!

As I have written earlier, Father was afraid of nothing, as far as I know, alive or dead, big or small, with one exception—and that was snakes. Due to the childhood experience that I have described, for these harmless creatures—harmless in this land—he had a wholly irrational and uncontrollable revulsion.

He shuddered, and averting his eyes from the posts, went along to the steps. They were made from split cedar about four inches thick. The ends had rotted where they rested on the notched supports. He vaulted onto the porch rather than chance using them. The deck was somewhat spongy, and in some places, where it was covered with damp piles of cedar needles, had rotted almost through, but it held him. He picked his way carefully over to one of the windows, but the thick diamond-shaped panes were too dirty and the glass too distorted to see through. The door—ah yes, the door. Father had some difficulty describing that door. He had noticed that it was carved but until now had not really seen it. I wish that I had seen that door. Carved in intricate high relief, and in so much detail that it took him a moment to sort it out, was the head of a Medusa. Out of a mass of coiling, writhing serpents peered the face of a beautiful woman. The eyes had been inset with some translucent grey gem, and she appeared to be watching him malevolently. Father took a quick step backward.

"That was the worst thing I ever saw in the way of pictures. The snakes, all growing out of her head like that, I couldn't have imagined it in my worst dreams. It looked so real I almost thought I could see the snakes slowly moving. Years afterwards, I sometimes had nightmares where that face was alive and was coming after me!"

But it was, after all, just a carven door, and he wasn't going to let it put him in a panic. Then he saw the door latch. Made of bronze, it was in the form of a snake's neck and head, mouth agape, fangs menacing. To open the door, you had to put your thumb in the snake's mouth to press the latch down. Even the hinges were in the form of snakes' heads gripping the edge of the door in their mouths.

He realized that he was reluctant to open the door—doubtless due to the snake motif—but determined that he wasn't going to let this affect his actions. He was pretty sure that he would find the owner of the house inside, but bones, human or otherwise, held no terrors for him. More practically, there was no way he was going to put his thumb in that snake's mouth. He picked up a bit of branch from the

debris on the deck and pushed down on the latch in the lower jaw. With a vicious snap, the upper jaw buried its sharp fangs in the end of the stick! Father recoiled, profoundly shocked. He pried the stick out of the fangs and bent down to examine the device more closely, and to his horror saw a drop of yellow, oily liquid ooze from one of the fangs. He had a strong feeling that it wasn't lubricating oil.

"What kind of mind would think up a gadget like that for a door latch?" he said. "He must have been stark crazy. The snake had been bad enough, but now I was glad he was dead. I wouldn't have wanted to meet that man while he was alive!"

Ready for anything—or so he thought—he put his hand against the door and, alert for more traps, slowly pushed it open. It moved freely on its bronze hinges without those eerie noises that would have been so appropriate. He looked into the room.

What happened next is not easy to make clear, partly because Father couldn't find suitable words. He tried, but it wouldn't come out quite right and he gave up in frustration. It must have gone something like this:

He pushed the door open, feeling a bit nervous because of the snakes and the sense that something wasn't right, but quite prepared to enter and look around. And then...

"I felt a wave of some sort pushing out at me. It wasn't anything real like moving air, but something actually pushing me from the room. There wasn't a sound. The air smelled musty. Not bad, but strange. But there was this feeling that I wasn't wanted here. No, that's too tame.

"It was more like something in there hated me, and was willing me to go away. I didn't just not want to go in, and it wasn't that I was afraid to go in. It was more that I just couldn't take that first step through that door. Something in there wouldn't let me. You can say what you like about imagination, but I know what I felt. I couldn't go through that door."

He looked across the room, lit dimly but well enough by the open door and the two little windows. There were shelves of books on the far wall. Old-looking books, bound in leather. There was a large painting on the wall, dark-toned and difficult to make out, but he saw enough to make him obscurely uneasy. To his right, the end of a table showed. On it was a horn gramophone for cylinder records, with a few brown wax cylinders standing beside it. To the left was a small table ornately carved from some rich wood, with gracefully curving legs. On it was a bronze of what from Father's description was the Laocoön group (representing a father and his two young sons being strangled by serpents), plain to be seen in the light from the left side window. All this he absorbed in the first quick glance. There was a shadow on the wall by the bookcase. There was a shadow on the wall...Well, what of that? There are always shadows.

"But not like that," he said.

"What was it like?" I asked. "Did it move?"

"I don't know what it was like, " he answered with some irritation. "I just know I suddenly didn't want to be there any more."

He summoned up the last of his resolve and, shifting his hand to the hinge side of the door, well away from the Medusa, he pushed it slowly open.

This story is frustrating to write. Here, at its most interesting point, it stops.

Oh, there is a bit more to it, but not what I want to know! It seems that the next thing he knew, Father was about a hundred feet from the house and running. He had actually had some sort of blackout, or loss of memory.

He stopped, and spun around to see what he was running from. There was nothing there. He saw that the door was closed. He couldn't remember closing it. He watched it for a moment, then turned away and began to trot quickly back toward the boat. The evening shadows were drawing in and he wasn't looking forward to going through the darkened woods.

"I'm not too proud to admit that I looked behind me more than once," he said.

But he reached the boat uneventfully and lost no time in hauling anchor and heading down-inlet, for the wind had dropped and the swells had lessened.

Not long after this, he met some friends who had lived in the area for generations. He asked them casually who had lived in that valley. They quizzed him minutely about which valley he meant.

Then one said, "Whoever told you that someone lived up there is crazy. If anyone had built there we'd have known about it, and we don't. Why, even the Indians never go ashore there. Nothing to go ashore for."

A few years later, Father was going that way in his boat. Martin Warnock was on board with him. He decided to go back to the house. He felt ashamed of having fled so ignominiously, and decided it was time to go back and confront whatever lurked in wait there for him. Besides, as he put it, "With Martin to back me up, I was ready not only for snakes, but for the Devil himself if he was waiting there to say hello!"

But as they swung around the point, he could see that the valley had changed. Something, probably lightning, had set it on fire. The side where the house had stood showed only burned snags. A cedar forest burns hot. The house and whatever it contained was no more.

I hate this story. You see, I have the soul of an antiquarian, and old things hold a fascination for me. I long for the ancient books that I can never afford. I thrill to the sound of long-dead voices as they can be heard on antique records and cylinders. And here had been a treasure trove for the taking! Not just old books, but doubtless books weird and esoteric as their dead owner. What was on those cylinders he had chosen to accompany him to his strange and final dwelling? What pictures would that twisted, anti-social eccentric choose to have with him in that house? To never know is almost unbearable frustration. I think of it as seldom as possible, for it is profoundly disturbing to me.

Father, you who feared nothing, why, oh why, didn't you ignore your "intuition" and go through that door? Even one armful of books ... but no. They are ashes.

And so, I hate this story. But I wonder sometimes what Father saw there that spooked him so. For I am sure there was something there. He was no man to run from shadows. When asked, he would shrug and change the subject. He wasn't very fond of this story himself, though for entirely different reasons. I'm sure he thought that he should have faced what was in there. If the carvings had not been snakes! ...

I have two theories. I don't believe in malign spirits, at least not in this matter. It would take more than a feeling to panic Father. But there may have actually been a snake. A pet boa, perhaps. The leather bindings of the books had attracted Father's eye. They weren't nibbled by the mice that such a place would normally shelter. What could have kept them away? Perhaps such a serpent, grown monstrous with age, glimpsed sliding sinuously, horribly, toward him had roused all Father's loathing toward its kind.

Somehow I doubt it. Father would have killed a snake, however big—not run from it. Still...

The other possibility is even less pleasant to consider. Father liked eccentrics, but a truly warped mind disturbed him profoundly. Did the owner still lurk there in the house he had built? Not dead, but now totally insane, all skin and bones and malice. Was this what Father saw writhing snake-like across the floor toward him, mad eyes glittering in a face perhaps no longer fully human; come from his lair to deal with an intruder?

I think *I* would have run from *that*!

Fire!

There is a common assumption that people were better in the days of our ancestors. More generous, kinder, more honest. There is, I believe, some truth in this, but there were a great many exceptions. Fortunately, not many of them were as thoroughly repulsive as those in the following story.

In the late twenties, or thereabouts, until sometime in the mid-fifties, Father served as a volunteer fire marshal. As far as I am aware, there was no salary involved except when he was actually engaged in fighting fires, when—in the absence of other authority—he was required to hire men and direct operations.

It was a bad year for fires that fall. (Just which year I am not sure, perhaps around 1930). The number of men in the Forestry was not sufficient to cover all of the blazes, many of which were threatening the rich timber areas of Vancouver Island. When a fire was discovered in the hills behind Pender Harbour (or Halfmoon Bay?) a harassed official asked Father to take charge.

The local store was usually headquarters for this sort of thing: the storekeeper took the names of volunteers and relayed messages. Father's presence there wasn't necessary—no one who offered his services was rejected —but he was there that first morning, arranging for supplies and waiting until enough men were gathered to form a crew. Martin Warnock was there, chatting with acquaintances, having been one of the first to volunteer. Though yet well before noon, the heat of the sun was already enough to make the waiting men take to the shade as they loafed about the yard or in the store.

They were talking mostly about fire, its tricks and treacheries, how big this one would get and in what direction it might spread. For a summer fire is a fearsome neighbour; it veers as the wind shifts, and there was no promise of rain.

Just then the thud of heavy boots indicated the arrival of newcomers and a loud voice called out, "Well, boys, you might as well go home. We'se here, and thet ol' fire jes' don't stand a chance nohow!"

A raucous "Haw haw haw" from two or three other voices echoed this sally.

Martin Warnock looked out of the window. He turned and grunted, "There's trouble come. You don't need them."

"How can I turn them down?" asked Father. "I've no reason I can give for it."

"Yeah, I guess. They'd probably make you more trouble than if you signed them up."

There was a commotion at the door as four men pushed noisily through it. Martin Warnock eyed them sourly and turned his back in obvious disdain.

Father looked curiously at the group. They were not as impressive in person as the noise they made had caused him to expect. They were oddly alike and might well have been brothers, though he learned afterwards that only two of them were related.

They all wore slouch hats of black felt, brown wool pants and checked shirts. They were tall, lean and narrow-shouldered, each with the beginning of the pot belly that comes from too much alcohol and too little work. Three of them wore scraggly little beards stained brown at the corners with tobacco juice. The fourth, who appeared to be the leader, sported a fuzz of moustache in addition to the beard. Lank hair straggled over necks that hadn't felt water since the last rains. There was a mean look to them, some sort of aura that suggested it wouldn't be well to have them behind you if you chanced to be alone with them. They didn't belong there. They seemed intruders from another place, another era, the Ozark mountains, perhaps. They had names like Zeke and Luke and Willy and Lew. Perhaps not those, but similar.

"Waal, ware do we sign on?" demanded the moustached one loudly.

"Yeah, and ware do we get paid? I got a mean thirst on me!" from another.

"Me too," from a look-alike. "And we don't mean a water-thirst. Got to save the water for the fire."

"Yeah. Haw haw haw. You said it, Luke!"

Father went over to where Martin was looking pointedly out of the window. "Where did they crawl out of?" he asked his friend quietly.

"There's a trail goes back into the brush a few miles up the road. There's two or three shacks up there, and a bunch of kids and women. They probably set the fire," he continued matter-of-factly. "Beats working, the way they think."

Father was incredulous. He couldn't believe that anyone, however mean, would set a forest fire to get work. Especially for the wages paid for firefighting in those days.

He said as much to Martin, who laughed. "You don't think they mean to do any work, do you? The only time you'll see them is when the pay is being handed out."

Father wasn't fully convinced, but he made a mental note to watch the four and to make sure that they earned their money.

But if firefighting is anything, it is confusion. With no air reconnaissance and no radios, there was little information about the size or shape of the fire. Coordinating the efforts of forty or fifty men in that broken, rocky terrain covered with smoke required all the attention a man could give, and the efforts of even that many, armed only with shovels, saws and axes, had little effect.

The old adage "Fight fire with fire" is more accurate than most of its kind. The main weapon against fires in those days was carefully set backfires, meant to block the path of the fire by giving it only ashes to feed on. But much skill was needed to predict the wind's effect and to choose the terrain properly. One mistake and you would have two or more fires to fight.

And so, Father forgot about the straggle volunteers.

He and his crew had been there in the burning hills for a week or so. It was around midday and he was scouting ahead of the path of travel of the flames. They had been lucky with the wind, but still the fire was advancing, as yet only over scrub timber and a few of the more heavily treed valleys and draws, where they had managed to contain it with backfires.

He must have been an odd sight, clothing scorched, full of holes caused from sparks, eyes red from the acrid fumes of the burning evergreen trees and lack of sleep. But he was young, tough and wiry, and still very alert. He was standing on a rock ridge just where the land began its steep slope to the lowlands and the sea, when he heard that regular cracking of brush that no animal but a human makes. Curious, he hunched down to watch. In a few moments, to his surprise, a young girl of twelve or fifteen years appeared in the draw beneath him. She was carrying a gallon jug and was forcing her way through the short, thick salal brush as quickly as she could go. He climbed down to the bottom of the draw and was standing there as she came around a shoulder of rock. Her gaze was on the ground before her and she never saw him until she was only a few paces away. When she finally noticed him standing there, she stopped short and half turned, as ready to flee as any wild thing. She was thin, but looked strong and active. There was a bruise on her cheek and she was panting.

He said quietly, soothingly, "Aren't you a long way from home? This is no place to be, there's a fire not very far away." Noting her wild eyes, he added, "Don't be afraid, I won't hurt you."

She glared at him with a mixture of fear and desperation that touched him deeply. He wanted to help her.

"Please, mister, don't stop me. I'm late, I got lost, and Paw and Uncle Luke will be mad at me for not bringing the jug sooner, and their breakfast." She spoke quickly, urgently.

He had noticed a shabby parcel slung over one shoulder. "I'm not going to stop you," he reassured her, and stepped a couple of paces aside.

She darted past him and disappeared up the draw. He slouched back against the dry moss, waiting. He wasn't quite sure why. In a little while, he heard her coming back again, and seconds later she came running and stumbling down the draw. She was crying, there was a red welt on the other cheek, and a slight trickle of blood came from the corner of her mouth.

He stood up, blocked her way, and she stopped, sobbing fitfully. He felt a cold rage at the sight. "Who hit you?" he asked gently.

She looked at him warily, putting a hand to her cheek, considering. Finally she said, "No one hit me, I fell."

He looked steadily at her, and she blushed. She didn't seem to be used to lying, and he liked that.

"Are you sure you can find your way home?"

"Oh yes," she said positively.

He thought deeply as she watched him, more relaxed now and reassured by his obvious concern. Finally he told her, "Go home, and don't worry about them. You won't have to come back here."

"But, Paw—"

"Your paw and the others will be back home today. I promise you."

"Well-l-l, all right then."

He stepped aside and she hurried past him. When she had taken a dozen steps or so, she stopped and turned to look back at him. "Thanks, mister." A quick smile lit up her face, and she was gone.

He listened as the sound of her passage grew faint, feeling a great wonder that she should have found her way up here, after only being shown once, as she must have been.

He turned at last and walked silently up the draw. The way led into a patch of scrub cedar, and the brush thinned so that it was no effort to move quietly. Before long, he heard the coarse "Haw haw haw" that he associated with the unpleasant strangers, and then the sound of voices. He began to pick out words.

" ...gurl of yours ...good-lookin' ...mebbe should stay a bit... "

Clearer now, "Yeah? Suppose she does. What's in it for me?"

He stepped around a room-sized boulder and there they were, sprawled about on the soft dead cedar twigs littering the ground, food in their hands and the jug within reach. One was facing toward him and glanced up in surprise. "Waal, looky here what the cat's done drug in!"

The one the others called Zeke, he of the moustache, put what he was eating down carefully on a rock, then rose to his feet. "Why, if it ain't the young fireman fella." Mockingly, "Ain't you a long way from your fire, young fella?"

"Yeah, what're yew sneakin' round 'ere for, spyin' on folk what's mindin' their own bizness?"

Father looked at them in disbelief.

When telling me about it he said, "I didn't think anyone like that existed outside of storybooks. They were as out of place there as a walrus in a corn patch."

He answered, matching them tone for tone, mocking them. "You fellows are quite a ways from the fire you're supposed to be fighting, aren't you? Is that a jug of water you're going to pour on it? Looks kind of small."

Zeke flushed darkly. "Don't you get lippy, fella, or you might find it harder walkin' out than walkin' in."

"Don't you worry about thet fire," put in one of the others. "We'll put 'er out when we get good and ready. We started 'er, and we can put 'er out."

Zeke glared at him, snarling viciously. "You shut your dang mouth, Willie, or I'll lay a stick acrost it!"

Luke spoke, yellow teeth gleaming through scraggle beard. "Hell, gimme a few more pulls from that jug, ah'll pee on 'er. That'll put 'er out. Ain't no fire can stan' that!"

"Haw haw haw," came appreciatively from his clones.

Even Zeke was grinning. But his voice was mean as he said, "Now you be off with you, young fella. And don't come sneakin' around here no more, or..."

Father looked at him contemptuously, then, without speaking, turned and made his way back down the draw. When he reached the little flat where the rock ridges ended, he stood there thinking.

In his mind he saw the girl with the bruised cheek and bleeding lip. He felt rage; he must do something, but what?

He looked around him, considering.

The ground was tinder-dry. It was a long way from the fire to set a backfire. On the other hand, should the wind turn and the fire reach this draw, sparks and burning leaves and branches would drift down onto the flats below, starting even more fires. At the moment, the wind was blowing up the draw, pulled by the updraft from the big blaze. A backfire here now could do no harm, and it might prove very helpful. Mind made up, he got out his waterproof match container, unscrewed the cap, took out one match, closed the container and replaced it in his pocket.

Lighting the match on a rock, he touched it to one of the dead salal leaves at his feet. It caught instantly, crackling and sending up a wisp of smoke. The flame was almost invisible at first, but the crackling grew louder quickly, and in seconds the fire was on its way. He lit the tip of a dry branch and walked across the mouth of the draw, setting two or three more blazes going. In half a minute or so, the flames were ten feet high, and advancing up the draw as fast as a man could walk.

He retreated a few paces and sat on a fallen tree, waiting. In spite of his experience with fire, he was impressed by what he was watching, for a fire in dry woods, even if you are using it, is a fearsome thing.

He hadn't long to wait. Above the noise and crackle of the fire came the sound of shouts and curses as first two, then one more, followed by a final straggler, emerged from the pungent smoke of burning moss. Hopping, leaping, sliding and stumbling, they came out into the clear air and stood coughing and slapping at burned spots on their clothes. The one called Willy was the straggler, and he joined the others with a small plume of smoke trailing from his felt hat.

They watched him silently for a moment, grinning. Finally, one said, "Willy, ye dam fool, yer hat's on fire."

He snatched it from his head and slapped it against his leg, but the greasy felt only smouldered more brightly as the air fanned it. It seemed not to occur to him to put his foot on it to smother it, but after a moment of regarding it helplessly, he hawked and spat a great gob of tobacco-stained saliva on it, which he rubbed in thoroughly with thumb and fingers. With great satisfaction, as if he had done something worthy of admiration, he announced, "There. I guess thet'll fix 'er!" As he looked up, his gaze lit directly on Father, sitting there with a grin on his face.

At his change of expression, the others swung around to look in that direction.

Zeke's face was vicious as he snarled out, "Yew think it's funny to burn us out, eh? Well, let me tell yew, young fella, we kin find out where yew live, and fires can start in funny places, d'ye hear me?"

As Father didn't live in a house at that time, the threat didn't worry him, but he thought it might be as well to stand up as they moved toward him menacingly. Someone said, "Yew tell 'im, Zeke," and they spread out until they were standing in a rough semicircle a few paces in front of the young man who stood there regarding them so insolently.

Before they could speak, he told them coolly, "Might as well go home, boys. No room left here now. Might be a lot of backfires around here, next little while. Oh, and I wouldn't bother to go down and pick up your wages, there won't be any. No work, no pay, you know."

Father told me, "They were certainly a mean-looking bunch, but they were nothing to be afraid of. I knew I could outrun them through that brush and over those rocks if I had only one leg to do it on! But I hoped it wouldn't come to that. I didn't care for the idea of running from that sort."

Zeke went on, showing yellow fangs in a mirthless grin. "Well, young fella, yew've had your fun, and now it's our turn."

He reached in a pocket and pulled out a big black-handled clasp knife, which he opened, drawing the blade slowly over his thumb. Willy had been looking around and now picked up a piece of branch about three feet long and as thick as his wrist.

Luke drew a knife the twin to Zeke's, and Lew picked up a fist-sized piece of granite.

Said Father, "The rock worried me a bit, I must admit. It's a nasty weapon."

As he stood there poised to run, or to fight if he must, he heard what he had been hoping for—the sound of two men crashing through the brush, careless of the noise they made.

When the four started to move in on him, Father called, "Just in time, as usual, Martin!" For through a fringe growth of young trees off to the right came Martin Warnock. Father had guessed he would come when he saw the smoke, for he had been on that edge of the main fire.

Behind him came one of Martin's friends, a relative of some sort, I think, named something like Bo.

Martin Warnock was a husky man, but beside Bo he looked almost frail. Bo was built something like a gorilla, but with longer legs. His strength was prodigious. (It was said of him that he had once carried a full-grown cow across his shoulders, but unfortunately I know of no other stories about him.) Bo had a curious habit. Unlike most excessively strong men, he loved to fight. He found few opportunities, it is true, which is not difficult to understand: in addition to his strength, he was known to be completely oblivious to pain, and it is most discouraging to fight someone you know you can't hurt. As a result, even individuals known for their belligerence tended to be very polite to Bo.

He was otherwise extremely good-natured, and Father liked him. As the two approached, Martin said, "Funny place for a backfire isn't it, Hal?" Then, after a comprehensive glance at the tableau before him, the course of the fire and where it had started, he grinned widely, for he had a quick mind that didn't miss much. Sounding amused, he said, "Been burning out a nest of skunks, have you, Hal?"

Bo had been looking at the four men—now bunched together—holding weapons. He said hopefully, "Fight?" (Bo never wasted much time on words.)

Zeke scowled. "You stay out of this, Warnock. It ain't none of your business!"

Willy spoke up. "Yeah, and keep your tame ape on a leash!"

Only a very stupid man would have made that remark. Willy—give him some credit—realized what he had done, and turned pale under the dirt, but it was too late.

Bo said questioningly, "Tame ape?" His face lit up, and he grinned hugely, exposing lots of big square teeth. He said again, but this time positively, "Fight!"

He took three long steps toward the men grouped there before him. If he noticed their weapons at all, it wasn't evident to the others.

His opponents stood frozen for a horrified moment. Willy broke first. He squawked, and dropping his club, he fled the oncoming destruction. Fast as he was, the others were right on his heels, leaping over obstacles with an agility that Father would not have believed had he not seen it. For it is true, fear indeed lends wings!

Bo had stopped when they ran from him. It was beneath his dignity to chase after them. He wore an expression of hurt disappointment. He took a few more steps, picked up a chunk of wood, hefted it once or twice, then hurled it after the fleeing men. It spun end over end and, whether by luck or skill, struck one of them square between the shoulders. Father thought it was probably Luke. Luckily the piece of wood was rotten and burst on impact, or it might have killed him. As it was, the force of the blow sent him sprawling head first into the brush. He let out a strangled sort of yell, but his friends never even looked back to see what was the matter. If possible, they ran a bit faster. The one who had been hit, seemingly undamaged, rose and followed the others over the edge of the flat. For a few moments the sounds of their flight came back to the listeners, then silence.

Martin Warnock remarked, "Good throw. Too bad it didn't hit him in the head."

"Nah," said Bo. "Can't hurt those sort, not by hittin' 'em in the head!"

Days passed, and they held the fire at bay until it eventually ran out of fuel, partly due to the backfires. At last the rain came, and they all went home.

A month or two later, on happening to meet Martin Warnock at a dance, Father asked him, "Say, Martin, did you ever see any more of that bunch of misfits that Bo put the run to?"

"Who? Oh, them. Well, we paid them a visit, Bo and me and a couple of others. They weren't very friendly. Fact is, they decided this wasn't such a good place to live, and they all pulled out for someplace else."

"Good riddance," judged Father approvingly.

Dam Sauvages!

"Eh, Hal, I want to talk to you. You're just the man I'm looking for."

Father was just coming out of the little log cabin in Wilson Creek, where Ole Olverstadt, the old Norwegian shoemaker had his shop. He looked dourly at the speaker, the owner of a small logging camp in the vicinity, known locally as "the Frenchman." He didn't much like the man, but was far too polite to let him know it. Seeing what he was carrying, he chose to ignore the man's words, countering, "I don't think even Ole can do much with those old scraps of leather, John."

"What do you mean? These here are perfectly good caulk boots. A leetle bit worn on the sole maybe." The remains of the boot soles were hanging precariously from their uppers.

"Well," said Father solemnly, "maybe if you get new soles, and you put new uppers on them, you'll have a pair of boots. But I think you'll need new laces." The ones on the boots were a patchwork of knots; the man was notoriously frugal. But the Frenchman wasn't to be distracted so easily. He dismissed the boots with a contemptuous gesture.

"I do not want to talk about boots. Curse the boots!" he burst out passionately. More calmly, he began once more. "I have a job for you. You'll be good at it."

"What kind of a job?" suspiciously.

"It's those dam sauvages," passionate again. "You know what they've done now?"

"Can't say I do. What have they been up to?"

Father knew that the Frenchman hated the Sechelt Indians. He also

182

knew why. The logger had used land belonging to the band without their permission. Part of his road was built on it. Not only that, but he had cut down several good-sized trees when he had built the road, and taken the logs. When all this was discovered, and the suggestion made that he owed the band some money for using their property, he had flown into a rage. But it had done him no good. Pay he must, or be denied use of the land, and finally, pay he did. But he neither forgot nor forgave, and from then on, they were "those dam sauvages."

Father concealed his grin and waited expectantly.

"I'll tell you what they've done. They've gone up the valley and cut down one fine cedar tree. My cedar tree. And they're making a canoe out of it. One of those long canoes they race in."

"Well, it is only one tree," said Father reasonably. He considered mentioning the trees the Frenchman had cut on the road and not paid for, but thought better of it.

"One tree! What do you mean, only one tree? It's my tree, on my claim, and they're not going to get away with it!"

"But you know, they were here first." Mischievously, hoping to provoke an outburst, "Surely it wouldn't hurt to give them one cedar tree for a canoe?" He wasn't disappointed.

"God damn. I don't give no dam sauvages no God damn tree!" So loudly that Ole opened his door and peered out to see what all the shouting was about. Seeing the Frenchman, he hastily shut it again.

"You just wait," darkly. "Those dam sauvages will learn who they are dealing with. They will find soon enough that he is no fool. No sir!" and confidentially, with lowered voice, "I have a plan, and you will help me with it. Those long canoes must be worth a lot of money. So this is what I will do. I will watch them every day, and when the canoe is all finish just about, I will be there with the police. It is my tree, the canoe is mine. That is the law." Magnanimously, "I will not prosecute them for cutting my cedar log into little chips. But I will take the canoe. But I must watch all the time, and there is only one of me." He shook his head sadly at this evidence of poor planning by the Creator (while Father was at the same time thinking that things could have been worse).

Then he brightened somewhat. "But this is where you come in.

I will pay you to watch for me when I am gone, and we will teach those dam sauvages a thing or two, eh?"

"I thought then," commented Father, "that there wasn't a single one amongst those 'dam sauvages' that I wouldn't rather know than that mean little weasel there in front of me."

"You mean," he said incredulously, "that you want me to sneak around up there in the bushes, spying on those people while they work, so that you can take their canoe from them when they get it finished?"

"Exactly! I knew you'd understand. I ask you. Is it not a good plan." Generously, "And I will pay you five dollars each day, even though you are not really doing work."

Father shook his head decisively. "I'm afraid you'll have to find someone else. I can't spare the time just now. I'm sorry." (Father was sometimes too polite, I think!)

He brushed by the logger, who stood there speechless, unable to believe that anyone could refuse to participate in such a wonderful plan. Finally, as Father was going out the gate, the Frenchman managed, "Well, just so you don't say to anybody what I tell you, eh?"

Father made no reply. He had every intention of passing on the information given to him so freely. He hadn't asked for it, nor had he agreed to keep it secret.

On his way back to Sechelt, he took—as always—the shortcut from Selma Park through the Indian village. He soon spotted someone he knew, repairing an old skiff pulled up on the grass near the beach. They exchanged greetings. He admired the repair work, made a suggestion. They discussed boats, fishing, mutual acquaintances. Then, "I met the Frenchman who's logging up the valley. He's pretty mad."

"Huh, he's always mad. Maddest man I ever saw. I think he must've been born mad. What's he all fired up about now?"

"Well, it seems he thinks he owns every cedar tree up in the valley, and one of them's missing or something."

Nothing changed in the other's manner, but he was now alert. "A cedar tree?"

"Yeah. He's sitting up there behind a stump, waiting for it to turn into a canoe. Then he's going to get the law to go up there and make him a present of it. Thought you might be interested. Be a shame if all that work went to waste."

"That sneaky bastard! We knew he was poking around out there in the brush. We were all laughing about it last night. But we didn't know he had something like that up his sleeve."

"Oh, he's a sly one, all right. I kind of thought he owed you people a tree or two, but he doesn't seem to feel that way about it."

They spoke of other things for a few more minutes, then Father walked on toward the store. He had taken only a few steps when, "Oh, Hal." He glanced back. "Thanks."

"I wondered what would come of it," he said to me, "but I didn't see anyone to ask. A week or so went by, and one day I met Major Sutherland at the store. I liked the Major, and we always got on pretty well, so I went over to say hello.

"After we'd talked for a few minutes, he says, 'Say, Hal, here's something that should give you a laugh. Happened just the other day. You know that mean Frenchman that's logging in the valley? Well, he came to see me. Bloody mad he was, too. Said that "those dam sauvages" had stolen one of his trees and were cutting it up. Insisted I go up there and send them packing. I didn't want to have anything to do with him, but you know I have to investigate when anyone lays a charge of theft. So next morning he picks me up in that old truck of his and away we go. I thought we'd never make it up that road of his— that mud would bog down any ordinary car—but those Model Ts are really something. Finally we get to where he's aiming for and he has a big mean grin on his face. He keeps saying, "that's my tree, and anything that's made out of it is mine. Be sure you tell those dam sauvages that." So we're chugging along, and all of a sudden he gives out with a great yell, and he stops the truck and jumps out waving his arms. There's a clearing by the side of the road, and there's the butt end of a big cedar log, and about sixty feet away the top of it. In between there's piles of cedar chips. Nothing else. Frenchie's running around like a wild man, yelling at the top of his voice, all in French. Now, I can speak French fairly well, but I can only get a word or two of what he's yelling. The only thing that comes through clearly is "dam sauvages." Finally he stamps over and shouts at me, "My property has been thieved and you just sit there. I demand that you do something! It was here last night at dark." And I thought, you really have to admire those fellows. They carried that great long canoe through the brush, across the creek and up the bank to the trail, then out through Selma Park to the village, and did it in the dark! I asked him, "Well, what do you expect me to do about it? Can you identify it if we do find it?' He shouts "Identify it? Of course I can identify it. Don't I know my own tree when I see it? And I know where it will be. They will have taken it to their boat shed, and that is where we will go. I will show those dam sauvages." So off we go back down the road, if you could call it that. He drove like a madman, and I want to tell you, I'll never make jokes about Model Ts again. I don't know how that old truck stayed in one piece. And I don't know how I managed to stay in it! But we made it out to the road, and charged up to Sechelt as hard as he could go. Of course the whole village heard us coming, and the Chief was sitting on the steps of his house when we got there. And it seemed like half the village was standing around watching. I told Frenchie, "Let me handle this." So I went over to the Chief, and after we'd said hello, I said to him, "Say, Chief, there's a fellow here who thinks you might have something of his." He looks over to where Frenchie is standing by the truck, and he grunts that deep sound they make in those big chests of theirs: "Huh. What?"

"""Well, he says you have a canoe that belongs to him."

"""Huh. He knows how to make a canoe? He couldn't make a paddle for a canoe!" Everybody laughs, and Frenchie looks like he's got something nasty in his mouth and can't spit it out. So I suggest that perhaps we should go and look at the canoes.

"'The Chief grins and says, "Sure, why not? Canoes good to look at. All painted up nice and fresh." And right then I knew what they'd done, and I couldn't help grinning a bit too. So off we all went to the big shed on the beach where they kept the racing canoes. There they were, all three of them, and you know as well as I do there were only two there last week. All three of them have a nice new coat of paint.

Well, you should have seen Frenchie. I thought he'd explode. The sight of everyone standing there with big grins on their faces just about drove him mad! He headed for his truck, cursing all the way, and the last words I heard were "dam sauvages!" And away he went, with that old Ford just smoking, leaving me to get back any way I could, which was all right with me. I'd had enough of his driving anyhow.

"'If he hadn't been so mad, he might have figured that if you rubbed a bit of paint off, only two of them would have old paint underneath. But I didn't think it was my duty to suggest it. Besides, it wouldn't have proved he owned the other one anyhow.'

"And that's the story of how the Frenchman lost a tree, and the band gained a canoe."

Trotsky

There have been until now no dog stories in these collections of Father's stories. He had been raised with a dog, old Sam, and had owned a dog for most of his life. He liked dogs even more, perhaps, than he liked cats, so there *should* have been dog stories. But such tales tend to be little more than anecdotes, and none that I remember seemed noteworthy enough to chronicle. However, the story of Trotsky is an exception.

Father, at the urging of Martin Gulbranson (old Mart) was going to a farm in west Sechelt to pick out a cow and deliver her to Mart's homestead, for Mart knew little about cattle. He was in good spirits, because he knew that while there he'd contrive to find some time alone with Mart's daughter Lily, his future wife and my mother.

As he neared the farm he heard a dog barking, which surprised him, because he knew the owner was no dog lover. Then he heard a man shouting in anger and he surmised that some stray dog had gotten in and was chasing the livestock. But by the time he turned the corner and vaulted over the fence, all was quiet.

Some cattle were grouped across the field, looking edgy, and their owner, having seen him coming, was hurrying across the field to meet him. Red-faced and sweating, he looked even more irritable than usual, which was no easy feat. He was an ex-remittance man, very evident from his way of speaking.

After the brief formalities of the greeting, Father commented, "I heard barking. Did you finally decide to get a dog?"

"That I did, that I did, sir. Worst decision I could have made.

I thought I'd get a dog to keep the coons away from my chickens. but that demned dog's *worse* than a coon. I'll be working, and suddenly I'll hear chickens squawking, and up that demned brute will come with a chicken in its mouth and give it to me. My own chicken! Never hurts them, I'll say that for him. Has a way of getting them by the wing without ever leaving a tooth mark. Demned if I know how he does it. But the chickens don't like it; puts them right off laying. And the cattle! Whenever a cow wanders off by herself, he's got to get her back to the bunch, and you know how cows are, they won't be herded by any demn dog, and he chases them—that was the barking you heard. A wonder their milk doesn't turn to butter in their bags!

"And I can't make the demned fool stay here and look after the place. Won't stay. I chained him to a stake, but he chewed the stake off—thick as your arm, would you believe it? And when I was coming back home, there he was, halfway to Sechelt, dragging his chain and a chunk of post behind him!"

Father hadn't tried to hide his grin as the words poured over him. The farmer, seeing that he was getting no sympathy, stopped short, then brightened. "Say, Hal. You don't want a good dog, do you?"

Now it happened that Father's dog had died a year or so before, and he hadn't got another. This was the longest period in his life that he'd been without a dog, and the thought had occasionally surfaced that it was something to be remedied. "I just might, if it's the right dog. How old is he?"

"Oh, about a year, maybe two. He'd be great for a man like you, with no cattle." Casually, "I'll let you have him cheap because I know you'll give him a good home."

But Father answered just as casually, "Oh, I wouldn't buy a dog. I know someone's got a couple of good pups . . . It's better to get a dog when it's young. But where is he? Call him out, I might as well take a look at him."

"Well-l-l," reluctantly, "you see, I took a switch to him and he's sulking. But he'll come . . . Here boy. Come on boy . . . Come here, you demned rascal you!"

Sure enough, out of a dip in the ground from where he'd been watching them came a very peculiar-looking dog indeed.

Father would reminisce, "He was brown and black in patches. Mostly beagle, I guess. Enough jaw for a dog twice his size, but just barely enough leg to reach the ground properly. His hull didn't quite scrape bottom, but there wasn't much water under it. But his gait. I'd never seen anything like the way he trotted. His front and back legs moved at a different pace—the back ones always seemed to be going a little faster than the front ones—so he always went a little crabwise! I couldn't help laughing when I first saw him trotting toward me."

This odd creature came to within half a dozen steps, then stopped and eyed them suspiciously. "Here, sir," commanded its owner in a tone of approval manifestly falsified. "Good dog, good boy, come on now," as he patted his thigh with one hand. But "good boy" moved no closer. "Demn the brute; never pays a mind to what I say. You can have him. Take him away if you think you can use him."

Father knelt on one knee, held out a hand, palm up. "Hello there," he said, soft-voiced. " Do you want to come home with me?"

The dog was listening intently, its flop-ears slightly lifted. Then it walked slowly over and sniffed at the proffered fingers. Brown eyes looked into Father's grey ones, and the long, heavy tail began to wag the dog. It was love at first sight.

Father patted and talked, and talked and scratched, and when the dog rolled over and presented his belly, he rubbed that too. Until the exasperated farmer jeered, "Demn me, why don't you pick the brute up and kiss him?"

To which Father, unfazed, returned, "We're not good friends enough yet!"

He rose to his feet, and the dog, excited beyond restraint, began to run in tight circles around the two men, faster, recalled Father, "than you'd have thought those short legs could have moved him."

But when they went to get the cow, he fell in behind without being told.

After quite a bit of discussion, Father chose a cow, and tied the piece of rope he'd brought around her neck. With much coaxing, and a bit of help from his new friend, Father led her to the gate, but there the dog stopped. Suddenly droop-tailed and forlorn, he looked sadly up at Father and whined a small appeal.

"Come on, boy, let's go," coaxed Father. No further urging was needed: the tail began to vigorously exercise the hindquarters.

Remembered Father, "He gave one bark and took up what would always be his favourite place, a step to my right and a step ahead. He never looked back."

The mile or so to Mart's place was covered without incident, but once there, I'm afraid the cow got scant attention. The new dog was the star of the show as Mart's numerous children made much of him. There was one thing that could have meant trouble, but it passed almost without notice. A clucking chicken ran by, pursued by its imagination. The dog's ears perked up and he took two quick steps, but then he stopped and looked back at Father. "I said, 'No, don't touch the chicken,' and I guess the tone of my voice was enough for him. He was one smart dog. Good thing too, because Mart's wife was death on anything that bothered her chickens."

Thus it was that Father found his dog, and a dog found his man. "I called him Trotsky; you know, after the Russian. Because of the funny way he trotted. Not the Russian—I don't know if he walked funny. But it seemed to fit, and he came to it as if he'd been born with it. I didn't know then what a bargain I'd got, but I soon found out."

They were inseparable. Trotsky stayed nearby when Father worked, out of the way but ready to come the instant he was called. He loved fishing, spending as much time swimming in the creek as on land. He was a good swimmer, which was just as well, for his short legs rarely touched bottom in pools of even modest size.

He was afraid of nothing, and he'd stand up to dogs much bigger than himself. Father feared for him at first, but soon found there was no need. Trotsky could take care of himself. He had only one method of defence, but that was so effective that few dogs, however fierce, undertook to challenge him twice.

His method was simple. When the fight started, he wasted no time on lunging or snapping, but would dart in and seize his opponent's leg in those powerful jaws. There he would stick, while his massive neck muscles shook and twisted the limb until it was broken, while the leg's hapless owner could only snap and worry at the tough, folded skin on the back of Trotsky's neck. "Oh," said Father, "his ears got chewed up some, but he never seemed to mind much, and the way he kept shaking his head kept the other dog from getting a good grip. When it started to howl from the pain, Trotsky would let go, or he'd let me pry his jaws loose, which most dogs won't do when they get a good grip."

One day when they were trout fishing up Gray Creek, they came upon a black bear on a gravel bar. Trotsky charged, barking furiously. This time Father was really concerned, for a bear is strong and fast almost beyond belief, and can kill a dog with a single blow. But there was nothing he could do, for Trotsky paid no heed to his shouts.

As this peculiar-looking creature approached, the bear reared up a bit to get a good look. The barking annoyed it, but it wasn't much alarmed; what could something that small do?

Trotsky dived under the reaching paws and, somehow knowing not to take a grip, nipped the tender underside of a hind leg. The bear spun and slapped, but too late: Trotsky nipped the back of the other leg. It was bite and bark, bark and bite, and Trotsky's bark, remarkable in a dog that size, was as formidable in its way as Father's.

"I couldn't believe it," he marvelled. "A bear can toss a ten-pound salmon out of the rapids and onto the bank with one slap. But then, the salmon is either not moving, or swimming in a straight line. Not Trotsky. He never took two steps in the same direction, and he moved so fast, sometimes he looked to be about six feet long! That bear was always at least one move behind him. Finally the bear had enough and took off up the bank. Trotsky didn't try to follow him. At a dead run like that, a bear can do about forty miles an hour. Trotsky trotted back to me, head and tail held high, with half a foot of tongue hanging out. You never saw a dog so proud in all your life!"

But there was one time that Trotsky—and Father—found more than they bargained on. For some time he'd been working in the Salmon Arm–Narrows Arm area, mostly hauling freight and towing shingle bolts. During this time he lived with his older brother Cliff in a shack in the woods west of the wharf head.

Cliff had little time for animals, but he and Trotsky were good friends. As he put it, he "admired Trotsky's give-no-quarter attitude."

Late one early fall evening, getting on for bedtime, Cliff was reading a western and Father a week-old newspaper—not easy in the dim yellow light from the oil lamp. Trotsky went to the door and asked to be let out. He liked to take a last patrol around the perimeter before settling for the night. Cliff obliged him, then went back to his book.

About half an hour later, they heard a few barks and then a whole volley of barking.

"Must have treed a coon," guessed Cliff. But the first deep tones quickly became high-pitched and closer spaced.

"More than a coon, I think," opined his brother.

The barking reached a hysteric pitch, then stopped abruptly. Seconds later they heard the patter of running feet, then scratching at the door, and whining. Father opened it, and Trotsky dashed through and went—not to his accustomed place, but under the bed!

"I think I'll go have a look," decided Father. He took Cliff's rifle, which was smaller than his and made less noise. He checked the clip and jacked a shell into the breech, then picked up the flashlight he'd bought but never used. "Good time to see how well this picks up eyes."

"Have fun," said Cliff, turning back to his book.

"C'mon Trotsky, let's go hunting." But Trotsky paid no heed to this favourite summons. "That's odd," mused Father. "Oh well, I won't need him." He closed the door gently, and soft-footed up the trail toward where they'd heard the barking. There was a bit of moon, enough that he didn't need the light to show him the familiar trail, but at brief intervals he shone it in short arcs to pick out eyes. He heard the rustle of salal leaves and directed the light there, raising the rifle as he did so. Eyes, cougar eyes, close! He swung the light, saw the big cat clearly in its bright beam, and brought the gun to bear on it. But it's not easy to align a flashlight beam and a rifle sight if you've never done it. Father had always used a lantern; he fumbled for a second or two.

Without warning, something heavy slammed into his back, hurling him violently into the brush. The impact sent gun and flashlight flying from his grip; the light, when it hit the ground, went out. Momentarily stunned, he didn't hear where they fell. He was cornered there, alone in the dark, between two cougars. Recovering quickly, he crouched, ready to fight for his life.

"Cliff!" he shouted. "Come here, bring a light." Then, putting all his force into it, "Cliff! A light, bring a light!"

But no sound came from the shack. Groping about, he found a fist-sized rock. "I felt better then," he told me. "There's nothing like having a good rock in your hand if something's after you."

Alert for the slightest sound, he paced softly back, stopping frequently to listen, but he reached the door without incident.

Cliff looked up from his book. "What was all the noise about?"

"You fool!" raged his brother. "Didn't you hear me shout for you to bring the light? The woods are full of cougars!"

"Was full," corrected Cliff. "No cougars are going to stick around in that racket. And hear you? They must have heard you over in Sechelt. And why should I bring a light? Couldn't you find your way home in the dark? Besides, I'm not going out on those rocks in my sock feet. By the time I got my boots laced up, whatever was going to happen would be all over. Why bother? It'd be easier to find you in the morning."

Against Cliff's logic, Father was, as always, defenceless. Cliff was a master at verbal evasive manoeuvring: to argue with him was to court frustration.

Father lit the lantern. "Come on," he ordered, "you can keep a lookout while I find the gun and the light."

"You're dripping blood over everything," Cliff observed. "Take your shirt off. Let's see what you look like." And when it was off, "My, that's a nice set of cat scratches," he approved. "Hold still while I plug them up. You're so stringy you can't afford to lose much juice!"

Ripping some strips from the blood-sodden shirt, he took the scissors and clipped off some ragged bits of flesh, ignoring his brother's yells of anguish, except to bid him "Hold still."

Father had very sensitive skin and, though he never complained, felt pain very keenly. Cliff, on the other hand, was contemptuous of it, oblivious to his own or others' suffering. Once while Father was working with him, Cliff, wearing his usual worn-out canvas running shoes, stubbed his big toe so badly that the toenail tore half off. The torn bit kept catching in his sock until he would stand for it no longer. Taking a pair of pliers from the tool box, he removed shoe and sock, and pulled out the offending nail with the pliers. Holding them up with the torn-out nail still gripped in the jaws, he observed to his horrified brother with considerable satisfaction, "There, that'll put a stop to that."

Without washing the blood off, he pressed the strips of shirt firmly against Father's wounds, then stuck them there with liberal applications of adhesive tape.

"Take it easy with that stuff," cautioned Father, for the adhesive tape of those days adhered with matchless tenacity.

"Quit squirming," ordered his brother. "I want to hear you yell when I pull them off!"

They found the gun and the light, which had a broken bulb, and the tracks of two cougars, one much larger than the other. It was the big male that had jumped on Father, sending him sprawling across the clearing and into the brush.

Next day Cliff borrowed a pair of hounds and they spent the day tracking the cougars up into the mountains behind Halfmoon Bay.

"They're heading for Pender Harbour in as straight a line as they can," observed Father. "I wonder why they want to get away from Porpoise Bay so bad?"

"I don't blame them," said Cliff, "after the noise you made at them last night."

Father's back healed promptly, and according to his brother, he yelled quite satisfactorily when the tape was pulled. For the rest of his life he bore three long, ragged scars below his left shoulder blade that fascinated me when I was young. When I was old enough to understand, he told me about a deeper scar that had left no mark. "Up until then," he said, "the woods were my home. Night or day, it didn't matter, I belonged there. After that, especially at night, the least little noise made me feel a bit uneasy. Or even when there wasn't enough noise. Ever after, on a dark trail, the skin at the back of my neck would prickle. From that day on, the woods was home for me no more."

Mid-November, and Father agreed to go with a couple of friends to hunt goats in Narrows Arm. But there was a problem, and its name was Trotsky. For he had never come to accept his physical limitations. The mountains the goats preferred were difficult enough for humans, impossible for a dog with legs as short as Trotsky's. Yet he would not submit to being left on the boat.

Father had tried often enough, but it was no use. Trotsky would chew through rope or leather, and when he tried chain, the sight of Trotsky's bloody gums made him vow never to do that again.

Trotsky would consent—reluctantly—to stay at home with Cliff, who made certain that he remained there. But Cliff was away for a few days exploring the possibilities of a new trapline, and various obligations prevented the others from changing the day of the hunt.

Father went to the Union store and bought a stout lead of tight-braided linen, guaranteed by its makers to keep any dog at home. Then, on the morning of the hunt, he left Trotsky in the care of a friend who lived on his boat when he was in Porpoise Bay. He warned the man to keep Trotsky in his cabin or on the lead, telling him, "He's so stubborn, if he gets loose he'll try to swim after the boat and drown himself."

Being assured his dog would be watched carefully, they set off for

Narrows Arm, Father trying hard to put the mournful eyes and doleful whines of his dog out of his mind.

The hunt went well. Each man bagged his goat, and they were back at the wharf well before dark. As he eased the boat alongside the float and reversed the engine, Father listened for the joyful barks that would be Trotsky's greeting when he heard the familiar sound of the engine. But no sound came. Shutting off the engine, he went on deck and called, "Trotsky, here boy, I'm home." No response. Suddenly concerned, he went across the floats, leaving the others to tie up the boat.

He knocked at the door of the friend's boat and opened it without invitation. The owner, glancing up from some task, appeared surprised. "Back already? That didn't take you long. How did you make out?"

"Where's Trotsky?" demanded Father.

"Isn't he out there? I tied him to the net drum over there," pointing. "He was making so much fuss I couldn't stand it, but he stayed nice and quiet after that. Give him a shout, he's probably asleep."

But Father was already out the door. He went quickly to the net drum. Most of the dog-proof lead was there, its free end well chewed, but no Trotsky.

At the look on Father's face, the other said hastily, "He must be around somewhere. He won't have gone far. Maybe he went back home."

Father called, knowing there would be no answer. Going over to the little group of men who also lived there on their boats and who were standing admiring the catch, he asked, "Has anyone seen Trotsky?"

"I saw him standing on that end float a couple of hours ago," remembered one.

"I heard a splash," another said, "and saw him swimming. I never thought anything of it. I know how he likes to swim. What's the matter, can't you find him?"

Without answering, Father jumped onto his boat, ducked into the cabin and started the engine. Forgetting that it had been tied up, he threw the clutch into reverse, then out again as the ropes tightened and the tie-up rails creaked. A quick try showed him the knots were pulled too tight to undo easily. Grabbing his deck axe, he ran to the bow and cut the line with one quick blow, then back and did the same to the other. In seconds the boat was in full reverse, leaving a group of very startled men.

"Hey," shouted one. "Where are you going with my boat? Hey!..."

Father paid them no heed. There was still an hour or so of daylight left. He might have mistaken a distant swimming dog for a seal. Knowing Trotsky's prowess as a swimmer, he thought the stubborn dog had probably made it as far as Porpoise Island, about a mile and a half from the dock. He would find Trotsky there waiting, alerted by the sound of the engine. But he was wrong.

Dusk was rising from the calm water as he tried to decide whether to follow the near shore, or to set his course up mid-channel. He chose the last. If Trotsky was near the shore, he would be there tomorrow. Throttling back to half speed, Father strained to see into the growing dark, to no avail.

When sight would serve no further, he stopped the engine at intervals to shout into the quiet air and listen. Trotsky would hear him and reply; the sound of a barking dog will carry for miles on a quiet evening.

At last, forced to admit defeat, he returned to the dock, and to two impatient hunters.

"No sign, eh?" asked one, and at the terse reply they quietly helped each other to their trucks with their catch. Father left his in his boat. He'd deal with it in the morning.

He spent the most part of the next few days scouring the shoreline for miles in every direction, and landing on every sandy beach to look for tracks.

"I used to wake up with a start at every little night noise," he told me, "thinking it was claws at the door. You see, I hoped he might have landed on shore, and gone back home overland, through the woods."

But there would be no more scratching at the cabin door. Trotsky would never come home again.

One last hope Father would never relinquish. There was a lot of traffic on the water in those days. Someone may have seen the swimming dog and taken him on board, to spend the rest of his days, perhaps on a fish boat, somewhere up the coast. It was better than nothing.

As for the man who had betrayed his trust, Father never spoke to him again. "There's an old saying," he said to me, "With friends like this, you don't need enemies."

Cliff was as affected as Father had ever seen him, for it was his habit to keep his emotions under stern control. Said he, with total seriousness, "We'll take the fellow out to the middle of the widest spot in the inlet and let him try to walk home."

"He'd have done it too," said Father. "After his experiences in the war, he didn't think like the rest of us." He talked him out of it, though not without much difficulty.

"He's not worth it," he assured the determined Cliff. "There's too many people living at the wharf. They'll know who did it, and you never bothered to learn to lie. Do you want to spend the rest of your life cooped up in jail?"

That was enough of a clincher for Cliff; he needed freedom as an eagle needs it.

Several weeks later, while the owner was at the beer parlour one Saturday night, his boat sank where it was tied. The supposition was that a salt-water cooling hose had come off its fitting. Father was sure that Cliff had had some part in it, but decided not to ask him.

There would be other dogs, good dogs, for whom Father cared deeply, such as Teddy, the golden lab named after Teddy Roosevelt, that helped to raise me: a dog of rare quality and character. But there would never be another Trotsky.

The Devil's Hole

This is a story that I've never heard told in its entirety. I've had to piece it together from various episodes recalled by both my mother and my father, assisted somewhat by having spent some time in the Yaculta area. It is my firm impression that in spite of its obvious dramatic interest, Father disliked the story because of a feeling—never spoken—that he had not come off well in it. That he had failed in some obscure way to meet the strict standards he set himself. And as Mother lacked the skills of a storyteller, tending to concentrate entirely on the dramatic highlights, the information she held had to be pried piecemeal from her memory.

Father met Martin Gulbranson's daughter Lil when she was fourteen (he was twenty-four) and decided shortly after that she would become his wife. (Though I rather suspect—knowing Mother—that the decision had been made for him!) Standards were strict on such matters in those far-off days; he was required to wait until she was twenty-one. She was what might be called an alpha female, and took on as if it were her due the task of applying order to Mart's numerous brood, younger and older. The confidence in her abilities this gave her would stand her in good stead in years to come.

When the time was deemed proper, she married her faithful suitor, and went straightaway to live with him in a logging camp. For her this was no hardship; though she loved parties and dancing, she had been raised in the midst of a forest and delighted in fishing and hiking. And, of course, neither dancing nor parties were strangers to the camps. But when she became pregnant, even she must admit that this was no place to birth a baby, and she went to stay with her mother, who by that time had moved to Vancouver.

Life in the logging camps could be hard on women in the early years of the century. The worst was when a camp was so isolated from the paths of shipping that there was little or no contact with other people, until snow made logging impractical and everyone went home for the winter.

The camp at Frederick's Arm, as everyone called it (the chart name omits the possessive) wasn't one of those, for the Union Steamship Company included the camp in its stops, but it was isolated enough for most people. It was a lonely, gloomy place to live even if you were a logger, for there is no open prospect, and the mountains, though not high, are dark and steep, and the grim grey fortress of Mt. Gardiner's peak broods ominously overhead. Einar Ellingsen, inventor of the Ellingsen logging jack (the finest ever made), had a camp at the head of the inlet in 1929, and having known Father of old, had asked him to organize the sorting and booming grounds.

I was born that year, and as soon as I was a few weeks old, Mother sent a message informing Father that she would arrive in camp on the next-but-one sailing of the SS *Chilcotin*. (I heard, years later, that she left his messages unopened until after sailing time, as she knew he would forbid it!)

On the due date—for the Union ships usually ran on time—she arrived at camp to find an exasperated husband and a half-finished, one-room shack with a tin heater but no stove. It might have been worse. Early April has its charms, even in Frederick's Arm. She was young, healthy and adaptable, and a woman with a new baby has no time for gloom; she set about making the little shack habitable.

She found that there was another woman already in the camp, with two children, a girl of seven and a boy of about a year or so. This would have seemed at first to be a stroke of luck, for two women in such circumstances usually manage much better than one. But when you can't choose your friends, you may find yourself stuck with someone you'd prefer to be without, which proved indeed to be the case.

Mrs. B was a tallish blonde, somewhat sharp-featured and sallow-complexioned. As Mother put it, "If she'd taken better care of herself she could have been quite attractive." She hated all logging camps, especially this one. She was a social creature, loved being among people, entertaining and being entertained. Desperately lonely, she had turned to drink; what at first had been a means of coping had by now become a drug she couldn't do without. Mother hated alcoholics, having seen too many of them, and her initial sympathy soon turned to ill-concealed distaste, and then disgust. Late one afternoon there came a gentle tapping at the door; it was the girl, sent by her mother to borrow some small item. She was a shy, almost furtive child with her mother's blond hair and sharp features, to Mother's eyes painfully thin, ragged and unkempt. At her obvious interest in the odours of supper cooking, "Have you eaten yet, Florence?"

"Oh, yes, ma'am."

"What did you have? Was it nice?"

When Mother, for whom her child's nutrition was paramount, discovered that Florence's evening meal had been a bowl of cornflakes, her contempt was boundless. More than forty years later, I remember that when she spoke of Mrs. B, she made sure to add, "And would you believe? She fed her children cornflakes for supper!"

It wasn't that Mrs. B was a bad mother, but that she was inconsistent, which is much the same thing. For a few days she would overwhelm her children with love and attention, only to neglect them totally when she lapsed into one of her glooms, which could only be alleviated by alcohol. The boy was too young to notice much, I suppose, but the girl, Florence, became resentful and disobedient. As a result, her mother told anyone who'd listen that she was a "difficult child."

Mrs. B's husband Oskar knew quite well that matters in his home were going wrong, but was puzzled as to what course to take to correct them. The working season was short, the hours long, the work hard. He came home each evening, often after dark, too tired to do much but eat and fall asleep. He knew his wife was drinking, and did what he could to interdict her suppliers, but there were too many in those days when almost every bay had its still. Some were unknown to him, others unsympathetic.

He sought Father's advice as the only other married man in camp. "What can I do? She's a good woman, but she has to have people around her all the time. I couldn't find work, and when Einar offered me this job I just couldn't turn it down. I hoped it would do her good to get up here away from debts and trouble—she can't handle money, you know," he confided, "and I can't just up and leave. We need the money, and Einar depends on me. I just don't know what to do."

But this wasn't a subject on which Father had a fund of experience, and he hated comfortable platitudes. He promised to try to get his wife to be more sociable, knowing that she would not, but determined to make the attempt, for he liked Oskar and wanted to help. He felt sorry for the unfortunate man, out of his depth—as most of would be—in matters such as this.

A few days later, Florence, on some strange whim or other, drank a quantity of gasoline. When it began to burn her throat and stomach, she ran home screaming, and collapsed on the kitchen floor. Gasoline in those days was more volatile than now, and burned the mouth like acid. Her screams and those of her mother brought everyone in camp out to see what the trouble was, including the first-aid man. The odour of gas on the girl's breath made the cause obvious, but he had no idea what to do in such a case. He tried to get her to drink milk, then—unsuccessfully—to force it down her throat. He ran to get the crude stomach pump that was part of his meagre equipment, but couldn't force the tube past the tortured muscles of her throat. She died at last, after several hours of agony.

A working camp has little time to spare for tragedy. Within a few days even her father was as hard at work as usual. Mother, her sympathies strongly aroused, offered what help and consolation she could, but the woman, wracked by grief and torn by guilt, was inconsolable. If only she'd tried harder...

She stopped drinking, lavishing her attention on her remaining child almost to the exclusion of everything else, including her husband. He treated her with much patience, though, as he told Father:

"Sometimes she doesn't even seem to know I'm there. I guess she'll get over the shock in time, but it worries me."

Mother, receiving similar treatment, began to curtail her visits. "She's not right in the head," she told Father. "She talks to the girl sometimes as if she was right there in the room with us!"

During this time, Father, instead of wasting effort on the shack, had been building a floathouse, on a raft he'd constructed of ten big cedar logs specially selected from the booming grounds he supervised. Kitchen, living room, two bedrooms and a bathroom with water tank, built of lumber cut by the mill at Yukataw Bay and roofed with split cedar shakes; life in it forms part of my earliest memories.

The weeks marched on and the shadows grew longer as the sun's visits grew shorter. Then fortune, who in life as in gambling cares not what has gone before, dealt the unfortunate woman another, greater blow. One morning she found the baby who had become her life dead in his crib, victim of one of those inexplicable ailments that seem to strike young children at random. When they took the dead child away, the distraught mother had to be restrained by force, and her shrieks were dreadful.

The people of the little community were shocked. Some of them felt that such events had to be the result of more than mere chance. There was talk of the place being jinxed, and some spoke darkly of malign spirits that were said to inhabit the gloomy hills.

The loss of her second child was too much for the poor woman's mind to accept. She withdrew from reality, spending her days sitting in the corner crooning to the children she refused to admit were gone. At times she would seem almost normal as she told her desperate husband merry stories of what the children had done that day. But then she would appear not to notice he was there as she sat listening to voices he couldn't hear, and watching things that only she could see.

She ate little, growing steadily more haggard and unkempt. For some reason the dark brought her closer to sanity. She would miss her children, and standing in the doorway, call out into the night for them to come home. When they didn't, she took to wandering through the camp in search of them.

The first time this happened, her husband found her and brought her home, speaking gently to her, for her eyes were wild. But madness has its cunning. Next day she waited until he slept, then went out to search again. These attempts invariably ended by someone rousing Oskar, for her calls left a trail of wakefulness behind her.

She began to imagine that her children must be in danger, held somewhere against their will. As the young moon rose, she went out again, arming herself with a butcher knife and wearing an old white housecoat, her feet bare. It was nearly midnight and the camp was still; even the dogs were silent. In the two bunkhouses, the men had been asleep for hours. No one stirred when the door opened.

"Tommy, Florrie, are you in there? Mommy's come to take you home."

The men woke, to behold an apparition out of nightmare. Crouching in the doorway, limned by the moon's wan light, was the madwoman, nine inches of knife blade thrusting menacingly at them from her clenched fist. "Pale-faced she was, and haggard, and her glance was fey."

"Tommy dear, Florrie, Mommy's come to get you."

The men were Irish and Norsk and German. They knew well what they saw, but steeped as they were in the wild tales of wraiths and apparitions of their homelands, they had a superstitious dread of madness. To a man they piled out of the other door, leaving the bereaved mother to look for her children wherever she pleased. One of them roused Oskar, for they knew he had a calming effect on her. He came and led her home; they'd look for the children in the morning, he promised, and it seemed to satisfy her. If the men got back to sleep, or if they had nightmares when they did, isn't known to me.

They refused to go to work in the morning, and a delegation went to Einar Ellingsen to explain why. "We won't stay here in this camp while that crazy woman wanders around in the middle of the night with a knife," they told him. "If she's still here when the next boat comes in, we'll be on it."

Reluctantly, Einar went to speak with Oskar. "I'm sorry," he told his friend, "but you'll have to take her home. The men won't stay if you don't. I'll give you an extra month's wages, and welcome. But she'll have to go."

As Oskar had been trying to find a way to break the same news to Einar, the matter was easily concluded. But the means proved troublesome. His wife wouldn't be coaxed to leave on the steamer; her children might need her. At the least attempt to persuade her she sobbed bitterly.

He didn't persist long. He hadn't wanted to leave their belongings in camp, some of them treasured family heirlooms his wife had insisted on taking with her, and most especially not his boat, his most valuable possession. But the boat, meant for work, was too small for two people to live on, and certainly would carry few of their belongings.

As it happened Father had also decided to leave, for he had felt all along that this camp was no place for his young wife and infant.

To his friend Einar he said, "I'm going to take Lil closer to home. I didn't want her to come, but there's no arguing with her when she's made her mind up. And the only way she'll go is if I go. You don't need me now anyhow, the work's going smoothly."

Einar agreed readily that Frederick's Arm was no place for a woman. "I suppose you'll hook the house behind the tow that's going out next week? Might as well get a ride as far as you can." Then, "Oskar and his Mrs. have to leave. Guess you know that. But he's got no way to get his stuff out, or any place to keep her. Do you think you might have room? I know he won't ask, but it would help him out a lot. She won't take the steamer, and I don't know what she'd do if he tried to take her away from her things..."

Father told me, "I didn't want to do it, but how could I say no?"

To Einar he said that he'd talk it over with Lil. If she didn't mind, it was all right with him. (Father could lie if need be; he just didn't do it well!)

He expected Mother to refuse, but she surprised him by making no objection at all. "You don't want someone like that around," he told her, "You never know what they might do." Father had an uneasy mistrust of the mentally ill, not shared by his wife.

"Oh, she'll be all right. She doesn't mean any harm. If she knows she's going home, she'll do a lot better."

But the truth would turn out to be very different.

Fearing trouble, Oskar told his wife that they were going home to Vancouver, where he hoped they might find the children. She made no fuss. In fact, as he told Father later, she was oddly quiet, and he hoped she might be getting over it. She stayed that way while they loaded the furniture and belongings into the floathouse, though Father thought that she eyed him strangely.

On the day the tug was due to call for the tow, she went along with them quietly, to be greeted cheerily by Mother and shown the spare bedroom that would be hers while she was with them. She spoke only once. "The children have gone on ahead. Oskar's taking me to them."

"She looked at me so strangely," reported Mother later, "as if she wasn't listening to what she was saying."

Now the shore lines were cast off, the plank walkway hauled in, and Father towed out the floathouse to tuck it into the place he'd prepared for it at the tail of the booms. Oskar moored his boat close by.

The tug was late. In those days tugs were almost always late; it seldom mattered much. In this case, though, it mattered a great deal, for they were north of the Yukulta rapids chain and must pass through them. (Pronounced "Yukataws" by anyone I've heard speak of them.) They had about five miles to travel before they reached the Dent Island rapids in Cordera Channel, and must be there before slack water, and night.

The Yukataws may not be the fastest rapids on the coast, but they are awesomely powerful. At their full flow, I've sat eating lunch 800 feet above them on the solid rock of Sonora Island and watched the coffee in my companion's cup vibrate tremulously to the force of their passage. They've wrecked log booms, sunk boats and drowned many people who took them too lightly.

Three hours late, the sound of a steam whistle announced the coming of the tug as it rounded Owen's Point into Frederick's Arm. Knowing it would take only twenty minutes to reach them, Father unfastened the tow and nudged it out into the inlet with his boat. Within minutes of the tug's arrival, the towline tightened and they were on their way.

After a last check on the floathouse and a word or two to his wife, Father caught up to the almost stationary tug, tied on and jumped onto the deck, where the captain-owner greeted him cheerfully. He was a middle-aged, burly, jovial sort of man whose belly showed that he ate well, and whose ruddy complexion wasn't entirely due to sunburn. He'd spent most of his life in the area and knew the rapids, as Father put it, almost as well as he thought he did. At Father's expression of concern about the time, he scoffed scornfully. "Don't worry, Hal, I've been through there a thousand times. You'll be as safe as if you were in church!"

The air in the cabin was aromatic. Father thought he recognized the distinctive pungency of the liquid produced by a still near Fanny Bay, more expensive than most and said to be worth it. But the captain showed few signs of its effects. Abruptly his tone changed. "Say, Hal, would you mind taking the wheel for a while? I've been up since yesterday morning. Need to catch a few winks."

Father did mind. He wanted to go back and see how the women were doing. But then, he reflected, Oskar knew far better than he how to placate the sick woman, so he agreed, albeit reluctantly. Down the stairs to his sleeping quarters went the captain, saying over his shoulder, "Wake me when we're off Horn Point." A few seconds later came the unmistakable sounds of a liquid being decanted.

It was a quiet boat, and the sounds and smells of a steam engine have a peculiar allure; Father settled comfortably to his task. At the speed they were making, the five-mile trip would take about four hours. It would be dark by the time they reached the rapids.

Back at the floathouse there was a certain tension in the air. Oskar, exhausted from sleeplessness and worry, had gone to his boat to get what rest he might after assuring my mother that she need only call if it became necessary to rouse him. Alone in the floathouse, with only her baby and a madwoman for company, Mother began to wonder if she'd done the right thing, knowing it was too late now to mend it.

Mrs. B's manner had changed since morning. Instead of the vacant-eyed docility she'd shown then, her gaze was intent now and somehow calculating as she sat silent in the rocking chair across the room.

Polite attempts at conversing brought no response. Nervous, but determined not to show it, Mother found work to keep her occupied as the hour passed, very slowly.

Once out of Frederick's Arm and into Cardero Channel, Father felt their speed increasing, and as they drew near Horn Point, a familiar outline in the dusk, he called down the companionway, "Wake up, Skipper, you'd better take her now."

When no answer came, and still none to a louder hail, he secured the wheel and bounded down the steps to shake the snoring sleeper into wakefulness. As the captain stumbled clumsily up the stairs, it became obvious that his unsteadiness wasn't only the result of the remnants of sleep.

"I guess we'll tie up in Horn Bay for the night," supposed Father. "It'll be too long after slack water to go through now."

The captain wasn't exactly drunk, but he was in no mood for caution. Swinging the big brass-spoked wheel to the right, toward the Sonora Island shore, he dismissed the notion. "No, no, the back eddy off the bay'll be gone by now. Better to run it than take a chance of ending up wrapped around Dent Island. Dark makes no difference. Better to go through in the dark. Can't see down into the whirlpools." He laughed merrily at his joke, but its humour was wasted on Father.

All the while he'd been steadily swinging to the right, upstream and against the current.

"What are you doing?" Father questioned, thinking he'd changed his mind and was heading back. "We can't go back now, we'll never buck the tide."

"Don't intend to. When it's this late after slack it's better to back the tow through. When you go through too fast you can't steer."

Knowing there was some truth in this, and that it was too late now to change their course, Father made no answer. They were sweeping along rapidly, already feeling the uneasy swayings and dippings that announced the first upwellings and whirlpools. Father's thoughts turned to the floathouse and its occupants, heading into the turbulent water with no log boom ahead of them to smooth their path. Then he thought with horror of the "Devil's Hole," the infamous whirlpool so big it could—and had—swallowed boats whole. He ran to his boat, started the engine and cast off. The current had yet to reach its full force. Perhaps by pushing on the side he could steer the tow clear of it.

In the floathouse they were several hundred feet farther into the rapids. The muted thunder of the moving water seemed to make the walls quiver, and the floor moved queasily. Mother's unwelcome companion had been growing ever more agitated since the motion began, and now she seemed to have come to some decision.

She rose, and holding the sill of the window to steady herself, she said, pointing to the crib, "Give me the baby. I want to hold it," in the tones of one who will brook no refusal. At just that moment, a particularly severe lurch brought me awake, crying fretfully. "Give him to me. I want him."

Mother had not the slightest intention of complying. Snatching up her baby protectively, she took a defensive stance behind the table. "Go away, you're frightening him!"

At this, the woman's face assumed a ghastly rictus that she must have thought was an ingratiating smile. Taking a step closer and holding out her arms, she wheedled coaxingly, "Give him to me. I lost mine, and I need him. You're young, you can have more, lots more, so it's right that I should have him."

"Don't come any closer," warned Mother, "or I'll scream for Oskar."

This seemed to infuriate the other, and her face contorted frightfully as with an incoherent cry she staggered across the swaying floor into the room where her things were stored. There came the sound of clattering cutlery, and she reappeared clutching her long-bladed butcher knife.

"Give him to me," she demanded. "If you don't, I'll send him to keep my Tommy company!" Knife raised threateningly, she started to come around the table.

Taking two steps backward, her eyes locked on the other's, Mother pulled open a drawer near the sink and took from it the big carving knife she kept there. Raising it high, "Go back," she ordered. "You try to take my baby and I'll cut your hands off!"

Father had reached the end of the tow, and by the light of the rising moon could see that the current was drawing it directly over the Devil's Hole. He swung the boat—now lurching violently—against the side of the boom and shoved the throttle forward as far as it would go. As he told it, "I might as well have tried to move Sonora Island!" Inexorably the force of the current carried the tow—and of course the floathouse—over the giant pool of spinning water.

In the kitchen, by the light of the swaying ceiling lamp, the two women were performing a grotesque pavane around the table, first one way, then the other. Mother, handicapped by her baby, tried desperately to think of a way out. No cry for help would rouse Oskar, asleep in his boat on the far side of the house. She tried to speak soothingly to the menacing figure stalking her, but no change of expression softened those staring eyes and twisted lips. And then they crossed over the swirling funnel of the Devil's Hole.

The floor dipped so suddenly and steeply that the table and Mrs. B were thrown violently against the far wall. Mother, feeling the floor lurch, instinctively dropped her knife and clutched the rim of the sink for support. Thunderous concussions rocked the house, rattling the windows and knocking dishes from the shelves, as a surge of water roared over the float, swept up the steps and knocked open the door. The noise was frightening as the power of the whirlpool sucked the big logs out of the boom and spat them out again to slam against the underside of the float.

Across the room the madwoman had also dropped her knife, and was crouching there, her hair in wild swirls across her face. She began to howl like a desperate animal, great long wails that seemed not to come from a human throat. Then, as suddenly as it had come, the battering stopped, as the irresistible force of the tow behind them thrust them out of the great vortex.

Oskar, sleeping the sleep of the weary, never noticed the rocking of his boat. He was used to sleeping when the sea was rough. But when the buoyant logs began shooting to the surface, one of them struck a glancing blow to the bottom of the boat, hurling him out of his bunk to land painfully on the floor. For a moment he was dazed and bewildered by the din and darkness, but realizing where they were, he made his way unsteadily across the heaving logs to the floathouse, from where wild howls were coming. He feared what he would find.

Meanwhile, Father was having great difficulty in the tumultuous water to find a way to secure his boat and hurry to the aid of his wife. He couldn't risk drawing alongside the float, for a direct hit from a log would destroy the boat. After a few tries, he managed to get near enough to the boom to leap out and throw a quick knot in a chain ring. As the howls began, he ran cat-footed across the booms to arrive at the door at the same time as Oskar. As they crowded through it, Oskar went to his wife, who stopped her banshee wailing at the sound of his voice, and Father to his. The two big knives near the women's feet sent a message that needed no explaining.

"She was going to kill our baby, to send him where hers is. Where were you?" Mother's voice shook with fury and released tension.

Across the room, the accused woman sobbed uncontrollably. "I wouldn't have hurt him. How could you think I would hurt him?" she gasped out between sobs. But I doubt anyone believed her.

Oskar, his face a mask of repressed emotions, led his wife to their room and closed the door. He realized now what he'd refused to admit before: his wife was hopelessly insane. He'd take her off at the next settlement where a steamer called. She'd have to go to Essondale, the hospital for those like her. I believe she died there, but I'm not certain.

Next morning in safe water off Yukataw Bay, Father vented his frustration on the captain, somewhat hungover and uncomprehending.

"I don't know what you're bitching about," he complained defensively. "I got you through all right, didn't I? Only lost a few logs that'll be in Calm Channel. You can pick them up tomorrow." When no answer came, he went off shaking his head at people's ingratitude.

The rest of the trip was uneventful. Father unloaded Oskar's goods at Powell River, from where they were shipped to Vancouver. Mother, with the resiliency of youth, was soon over her fright, and came to relish having so dramatic a story to tell. And I, who was a witness to it all, remember nothing.

Cliff

I've made few references in these pages to Cliff, Father's elder brother. I wish I could have written more, because he was an interesting character and certainly had experiences worth writing about. But he spoke little of them, and none have come down to me.

Physically he was much like his brother, about five feet, ten inches tall, small-framed, but wiry and tough. He was impatient of authority and must have had a hard time in the army. But he was cited for bravery, though it seems not by his own corps.

When he returned from France, lungs ravaged by mustard gas, a wild and savage streak had surfaced, directed as much at himself as at others. He was not a man to be trifled with: there was an intensity to him that wasn't usually apparent in his more easygoing younger brother. The camp boss of an outfit where Cliff had worked for a short time told Father, "I didn't feel comfortable around him. If you gave him an order he'd look at you like he was a bomb getting ready to explode. Good man, but I wouldn't care to be the one that crossed him!"

Father once told me, "Cliff was a changed man when he came back from the war. Most men were changed, of course, but not like that. When he was discharged the army doctors told him what he'd have to do, how he'd have to take it easy, get an inside job, that sort of thing. He told them to go to hell, that he'd rather be dead than live like that. So I think he knew he hadn't long to live, and after what he'd seen he didn't much care. He was like that doctor fellow down in Texas, that everyone was afraid of because he knew he was dying, and didn't care what happened to him [Doc Holliday]. Except that Cliff didn't go around shooting people. But it wouldn't have bothered him if he'd had to."

The winter after Trotsky disappeared, Cliff went off to work the trapline he'd been investigating at the time. It was located in one of the little forked creek valleys five or six miles from the head of Salmon Inlet. He'd found plentiful signs of marten in it, and signs of fisher along the shore, and decided to spend the winter working it. The mountain was steep and rugged, but the wildness of the terrain was more of an attraction to Cliff than othewise.

Someone had tried to trap there years before, and had built a ramshackle cabin before they gave up and went elsewhere. But it suited him well and he settled in quite happily. As his only means of transportation was a rowboat, he seldom came home unless the need was urgent.

The day before Christmas, Father decided to bring his brother a few treats to mark the occasion, which Cliff was certain either to forget or to ignore. But various matters intervened, and by the time he set out from the dock, dusk was rising among the trees along the shore. The trip took about two hours, so full night had come by the time he arrived at the cabin.

There was no light showing, and no answer came to his hail. At Porpoise Bay there had been a dusting of snow. Here there was over a foot of it, a Christmas sight indeed in the searchlight's beam. Assuming his brother was sleeping and hadn't heard him arrive over the sighs of the wind, Father launched the skiff, put the provisions and his bedroll in it and rowed ashore. Cliff's boat was there, pulled up between the trees.

Father pulled his up beside it and tied it there, then shouldered his burden and made his way up the rocks to the door of the shack. In the flashlight's beam, no tracks showed in the fresh snow. He pushed open the door and entered, expecting to find Cliff snoring in his bunk. But to his surprise, the single room was empty. He tried to light the lamp, but there was no oil in it. Expecting something of the sort, he'd brought a gallon with him, and tried again. But there was no wick, and this he hadn't brought.

He was concerned about Cliff. The mountain above was steep, and the way to its upper reaches where the marten hunted lay through treacherous ravines, difficult enough to get through in daylight. But there was nothing he could do about it then. When morning came, he'd go looking for his brother.

The ashes in the ancient stove were cold. He looked around for wood to light it, but could find none. Snow had begun to fall again and the wind was rising. In the light's beam he saw a snowflake drifting, and noticed then what he'd missed before. Thicker at the walls and tapering out into the room were thin white streaks of snow, each marking a crack in the wall through which the snow had drifted, and the floor glistened with tiny crystals. After one look at the bunk and its thin, torn blankets, he spread his own out on the floor where the snow was thinnest. It was going to be a long, hard night.

Father was always a light sleeper. Some noise outside the door brought him to alertness. He seized the flashlight, slid out of his blankets, and pacing softly to the door, flung it open. There, lit by the light's glow, stood Father Christmas! Cliff, bulky in snow-covered mackinaw and windbreaker, beard and moustache caked with snow, pushed through the door as his brother stepped aside. An inch of fresh snow covered his slouch hat like icing on a chocolate cake. Over his shoulder he was carrying a bulging brown gunny sack frosted with snow.

Shaking himself like a dog, he dropped the sack, doffed his windbreaker and tossed it aside. "What's the matter with the lamp?"

"No wick in it."

"Oh yeah, I forgot." Rummaging through his pockets, "Here, I use it sometimes if I need a bit of fire when I'm out." It seems he always carried with him a flask of oil and a little oval bowl carved from stone that he'd found, which served him for light and heat.

He put the wick in the lamp and lit it; shadows leaped as the flame flickered fitfully in the draughts. He went to the rusty stove and took from it a blackened pot that Father had ignored. "You eaten?" he asked, offering it politely to the guest first, for Cliff was ever courteous, even to his brother, who took the pot and peered doubtfully at its contents. It was half full of congealed porridge, on which had formed a layer of brown scum.

"Thanks, but I'm not that hungry."

Cliff took a spoon crusted with dried porridge from a box nailed to the wall beside the stove and wolfed down chunks of porridge.

"Where's the wood?" asked Father. "I'll light a fire."

"What do you want a fire for?" Cliff seemed genuinely curious. He went to his bunk, climbed in without taking off his wet clothes and, pulling the ragged blankets over himself, curled up with his face to the wall. "If you want a fire, there's an axe outside the door. There's a downed tree about fifty feet to the left. If you need kindling, you can pull a shake off the wall. Blow the lamp out, don't waste the oil. See you in the morning."

Now Father understood why there were so many places in the walls for the wind to blow through. He returned to his blankets, but arrange them as he might, he could neither get warm nor go to sleep. After an hour of listening to his brother's snores, he gave up and rowed back to his boat.

Waking to the smell of wood smoke, he peered out through a porthole. The snow was still falling, but the wind had stopped. He rowed ashore and climbed the bank to the cabin. Cliff was skinning out a marten from the sack, and two or three carcasses lay on the floor beside him. He'd lit the stove and the air inside was slightly warmer than out. The room was full of the smell of cooking meat. The stove lid was off. Where it had been was an even blacker pot than had held the porridge.

"What's for breakfast?"

"Marten stew." Then, knowing his brother's fastidiousness about food, "Good meat. Lives on squirrels. What's that face for? I don't know why you're so squeamish. Throw in a couple of spuds, let it boil for an hour . . . Fit for a king"

"I brought some bacon. I think I'll have that. Want some?"

"Slices of fat off a pig's belly. Dirtiest animal there is. Sometimes I just can't figure you!" But he drank copiously of the tea that Father brewed in the old enamel coffee pot, and even accepted a couple of slices of bacon.

Now, in the light of day, Father examined the room more closely. All around the walls were hanging "stretchers," frames of wood on which skins, inside out, were stretched taut and rubbed with salt to preserve them. The air was ripe, even above the smell of cooking marten, with the smell of salted animal fat. He'd scarcely noted it the night before; all trappers' cabins smelled like that, including the ones he'd lived in himself. But it showed the trapping had been good.

As Cliff sucked the meat from the marten's bones, they talked desultorily. He refused to come home for Christmas. "I've got to check the traps on the other branch. You can come with me if you like." He put on the clothes, still sodden, that were warming by the fire. "No? Well, you can pick me up in a week or so if you want. I should have enough furs for a load by then."

Without further words, he stuffed his sack into the pouch of the mackinaw, took his gun from the rack by the stove and set off up the mountain, not bothering to close the door.

I once commented to Father that Cliff sounded a bit crazy, and asked why he'd tortured himself like that. He pondered for a moment, then, "We're all a bit crazy. Cliff just didn't care about showing it. As to why he did it, well, I think it was like this. For one, he wanted to be a mountain man like the Johnstone boys even more than I did. But there was more to it than that. Cliff came back from the war pretty much an invalid, and he was determined to toughen himself, to force his body to work. When it wouldn't, I think he started to feel that it was his enemy, and he was just getting even with it!"

Rosinante

Cliff survived the winter, and in the spring went to work for the shingle bolt camp at Clowhom Falls. The shingle mill was near tidewater, but most of the workers lived at the lake, in camps or on floathouses. This meant that supplies had to be transported over a trail between the salt water and the lower lake, a distance of about half a mile, fairly steep. The freight handler was a man everyone called "old Darby." His means of transportation was a horse-drawn sled, and the horse is the heroine of this story.

She obeyed old Darby's commands—he called them "requests"—with such precision and thoroughness that her sagacity was a byword. And he claimed that if he made a mistake, she would correct it. Rosinante was her name, and she fitted it to perfection. Of a strange yellow hue, Rosinante was sway-backed, sag-bellied and knob-kneed. Her hip bones thrust up under her hide like—as Father put it—a wet rag thrown over a saddle. Old Darby swore she could think better than most of the men in camp, a claim that Father wasn't inclined to debate.

She pulled a sled instead of a wagon because the track was rough and muddy, and for another reason more persuasive. For old Darby was getting ever older, and to lift bundles and boxes often weighing a hundred pounds or more into a wagon had become more than he could manage. But he was a valued employee, faithful to his duty and careful with his freight. He and Rosinante managed their business well.

But age spares none of us, or hasn't up 'til now, and old Darby was no exception. His back ached, his joints creaked and his feet hurt. Like

219

it or not, the camp superintendent must find another freight handler. And old Darby must forsake Rosinante, for where he was going to live could be no horses, and he was heartsick.

"Find her a good man," he pleaded. "She's too old to learn new ways." But good men even then, as now, are hard to find.

The new man's name was—I think—Simon Smith. He was large, red-faced, neither young nor old, with a reputation for a hot head and a quick temper, and for being something of a bully. Old Darby knew him, disliked him, would have rejected him, but was given no choice. Simon Smith worked hard—when he was sober—and knew horses. Yield Darby must, and yield he did, but when Father took him down the inlet for the last time, there were tears in Darby's eyes.

"Keep him from hurting her, Hal, if you can. He beats his horses, I know he does. If I find out he's beating Rosie, I'll come back and kill him, I swear to God I will!"

Father promised to do the best he could, but knew it was an empty promise, for he was working with his boat and spent little time in camp. So he wasn't witness to these events. But he knew the superintendent well, and others of the crew, and probably heard more of the story than if he'd been there. Especially as his brother was involved, if only slightly.

On their next meeting Cliff was contemptuous of the new man, but wouldn't say why; Father soon found out the reason. It had happened on a Sunday morning, soon after breakfast. The superintendent was reading on his veranda and the men were lounging in the sun. Someone more sharp-eared then the rest noticed a faint sound.

"What's that squawking noise?" he asked. "It seems to be coming from up there," pointing at the sky overhead.

Now they all began to hear it, and their eyes were directed skyward.

"There," said Cliff, whose eyes were sharper than most. "It's a heron, and an eagle's after it."

(Nothing I know that's of comparable size squawks as loudly as a frightened heron. It beggars belief that such a skinny neck can produce such sounds, yet breathe and fly while it's making them.)

The frightened bird never ceased its croaking; lighter than the

eagle, it couldn't fall as fast (in spite of Galileo) but it made up for that in skill and desperation. Slipping and sliding through the air, it evaded the eagle's dives and clutching talons with seemingly preternatural skill. But the watching men knew it was doomed. Hurtling toward the ground, the birds must soon swerve or be destroyed, and in level flight the heron was no match for the plunging eagle.

But the heron must have known that as well as they. The mill was built out from the hillside on pilings, the space beneath it going from about twenty feet in the front to nothing where it met the ground. With a last squawk and desperate side-slip over their heads, the heron darted under the mill and flared its wings to come to a perfect landing. Dimly visible, there it sat, ruffling its feathers and making low, hoarse, rasping sounds. The eagle flew into a nearby tree and sat watching.

Smith went toward the mill, evidently intending to go after the heron.

"Where are you going?" asked Cliff.

"I'm going to chase it out. I want to se the eagle get it. Why? What's it to you?"

"Leave the bird alone," said Cliff quietly. "It's earned a rest."

"Don't tell me what to do, little man, or you'll be sorry you tried."

Cliff walked over to him and spoke so quietly that some of the men couldn't make out his words. But the superintendent on his veranda just above had heard them clearly. "He never raised his voice, but something about it made me glad he wasn't looking in my direction."

"Go on out of here," he said, "or I'll get an axe and cut you down to size."

Smith started to say something, but he looked into Cliff's eyes. I don't know what he saw there, but that red face of his turned paste-white and the words died in his mouth. He went off to his bunkhouse, and I never saw him again that day, but next morning he had a hangover.

Cliff and old Darby had gotten on well since their first meeting, when Cliff had asked, "Did you name Rosinante after Don Quixote's horse?" Darby had never been asked that question before; he was so thrilled that this young man had read his favourite book, that in his eyes Cliff could do no wrong. He was greatly pleased when Cliff arrived there to work, but much regretted having to leave so soon after Cliff had come.

"You will keep an eye on her, won't you?" he asked anxiously, when the decision to leave had been made. "It breaks my heart to leave her, but I can't take her with me, and who else would have her? She'll be better off here than anywhere else."

"I'll do what I can," Cliff reassured him. "You know you didn't have to ask. I never saw a horse I cared about before, but she's one of a kind!"

Indeed she was that, and nothing proved it so much as a steep little hill about two-thirds of the way to the lake. Darby had built the sled so that it held about what Rosinante could pull, on average, and no more. But sometimes the cargo contained heavier goods than usual, and that was when the old horse showed judgement that astonished everyone who witnessed it. In fact, old Darby had been known to load on a bit extra when he wanted to impress someone with Rosinante's intelligence. One of these had been Father; he remembered it well.

"When we got almost to the bottom of the hill she gave it a bit of a run, until all the sled was on the start of the steep part. She stopped and caught her breath, then she leaned into the traces and took a bit of strain, then a bit more. She took half a step back, blew out a breath and shook her head. She looked back at old Darby and rolled her eyes at him. 'See, too heavy,' he said. He rolled a sack of coal off the load. Same thing again, still no go. This time, though, she didn't look back but she snorted and stamped her feet. He took a case of canned milk off the load. It couldn't have weighed more than fifty pounds, but it was enough. She leaned into it, leaned back, then she strained forward until her haunches bulged, and away she went. She didn't stop until she reached the top of the rise, blowing like a bellows. That was some horse!"

Smith had been informed of all this and had it demonstrated to him, but he was unimpressed. Back in the bunkhouse, "She'll go when I tell her to. You just have to let them know who's boss."

The first trip out and back, he was at it again. "I showed that old nag what's what. She'll take the load up the hill all right, if you ask her to the right way."

That evening when he went to curry her, Cliff found welts across her flanks. In a cold fury he sought Smith out, and to the delight of the onlookers, told him, "If I find stick marks on that horse again, I'll dress you down with a pick-handle." Whereupon he swung around and left the big man standing speechless. Seeing the censure in the eyes upon him, he said defensively, "I only laid a switch along her sides. If I don't, she won't do anything I tell her."

Matters stood like that for a week or so. What happened next only filtered down to Father when it was all over. It was told by one of the Chinese swampers who assisted Smith when the need for supplies was urgent, to his own superior. Who in turn told it to the superintendent, who related it to Father but not to Cliff. Cliff only knew that Rosinante had died, but not how. He quit the next day to go handlogging, feeling that there was no longer any reason to stay. Father never told him, because he thought his brother would go back and get into trouble if he knew the truth.

Smith, with the cunning of the foolish, cut a bunch of willow switches that would sting but leave no mark, and hid them at the bottom of the hill. He had no need for them until a load of coal arrived for the blacksmith shop at the head of the upper lake. Smith piled on the heavy sacks, then loaded the usual supplies on top of them.

Rosinante laboured mightily until she reached the hill, then stopped, and nothing Smith could do would make her budge an inch further. He shouted and cursed and raged, found his bundle of sticks and beat her until they broke, to no avail. Rosinante only hunched her back and stood there, head drooping.

Smith's rage was fuelled by the sight of the grin on the face of the Chinese swamper, obviously enjoying the show. For Smith wasn't liked by the Orientals, whom he called "chink" to their faces. But he dared do nothing to the little man, for he knew that if he did, he might be found one morning floating face down in the lake.

So he did something only a foolish man blinded with rage would do. Pulling his clasp-knife from his pocket, he strode up behind Rosinante and thrust the blade deep into the big muscle of her leg. Her reaction, swift beyond telling, was to kick him savagely, breaking three of his ribs and sending him sprawling into the rocks that lined the road.

Then she seemed to come to a decision. She shook her whole body, stamped her feet and neighed, a sound no one had ever heard her make. She lunged into the traces, got the sled halfway up the hill, and dropped dead.

Smith limped off to his bunkhouse and began to get drunk on a hidden bottle of whisky. The Chinese swamper reported what he had seen to his superior, who, after sending a crew to get the supplies, reported to the superintendent, who sent for Smith. "What are you going to do about that dead horse?" he demanded.

Smith eyed him glassily. "What horse?"

"The horse you killed, you damned fool. I want it out of there. Drag it off into the brush and bury it deep. And get the blacksmith to get a board and burn the name Rosinante on it. It's the least I can do for old Darby. And if it's not done overnight, you'll whistle for your wages."

Smith went. He could do nothing about the horse himself, with his bruises and broken ribs, and the other men just laughed at him when he asked for their help. He was forced to persuade a gang of Chinese labourers to dispose of Rosinante, and they held out for several more bottles of rice wine than they felt the job was worth, just for the pleasure of it.

The superintendent fired Smith for drunkenness, and because he loathed the man. Then he had the trail improved, bought a Model T truck and hired the cook's teenage son to run it. It served well enough—but it was no Rosinante!

Peg-leg's Pool

Father had many stories, and some of them he preferred not to recall too often. this is one seldom told, and never in its entirety. It wasn't easy to write, for its interest lies mostly in the details, and those I had to extract from him a bit at a time, when he cared to remember them, and infer those which he did not. I hope it proves to be as interesting to you as it is to me.

For most of a year, from early spring until winter, Father worked out of a small camp near Gray Creek in Porpoise Bay. Part of the time he boomed logs, betweentimes he handlogged. The land where the little cabin he and Cliff had lived in had been sold; an old fisherman now lived in it as a sort of caretaker. It didn't matter, Father would rather be nearer his work. Similar shacks and cabins dotted the shores of Porpoise Bay, and he found one to his liking conveniently close to both his jobs.

Gray Creek is a pleasant little stream that used to have fine trout in its lower reaches, and Father welcomed the opportunity to explore it. For though he'd trapped there for a season, fished it once or twice and knew well the surrounding area, he'd never really become familiar with the creek valley. But now that he was living there he lost no time in remedying that omission.

One fine spring afternoon when he'd finished his work at the camp, he decided to try his luck fishing the steep and rocky pools of the mid-part of the creek. With his telescoping steel fishing rod in his hand, and a box of raisins in his pocket, he set off up the trail beside the creek, resisting with difficulty the temptation to try the beautiful pools of that lower section.

But he soon saw that someone had gone before him, for there were fresh footprints going up, but none returning. The prints intrigued him mightily: he'd never seen their like. The marks made by the right foot were normal, made by a boot of average size, but the other puzzled him. It was the mark of a foot all right, but a bare foot, with wide-splayed toe marks distinctly showing. And plain to see in the centre where the instep should have been, was the impress of a goat's foot! There was something else wrong. No matter what the consistency of the ground, the toeprints kept their same width. It was all quite unnatural, and he couldn't wait to meet the man who'd left such cryptic traces.

He told me, "My best guess was that he had a club foot on a short leg, which he'd put a peg under to make it the same length as the other. But I wasn't satisfied with it."

And he wasn't much wiser when, a few minutes later, he saw the man who had made the prints. At that point in Gray Creek there is a falls about twenty feet high that plunges into a deep, dark pool, the largest in the entire creek. It was the best spot for fishing, as any trout that came up from the salt water could go no farther, and some of them were very big and very cunning.

But it was difficult to fish, for some peculiarity of the rock over which the water rushed produced a giant swirl, a surface whirlpool twenty or thirty feet across, under which the big fish lurked where it was difficult to place a lure.

Little trout aplenty could be found in the shallows where the water exited, and along the edges, but what angler will settle for such when large ones are near? One place alone gave opportunity to try for them. On the left side of the pool, a large fallen tree sloped down from the bank near the top of the falls, to where its top was buried in the gravel near the exit. Nearly four feet through, slippery and moss-covered, it rested at an angle shallow enough to be walked up, with care. A third of the way up that log was the spot from which the pool could best be fished. And there sat the man who'd left the strange tracks, his right leg dangling, the other, mysterious one thrown over the right thigh in a way that Father doubted he himself could have held for very long. But worse, a folded jacket with some lures spread on it covered both lap and leg.

So loud was the roar of the falls from the last of the spring melt, and so intent the fisherman on his sport, that he neither saw nor heard that he had company as Father detoured up the bank and around the pool. For out of politeness he stayed far enough away not to disturb the man or the fish he sought. But from the top of the bank, as he went back to walk the creek beyond the falls, he got a glimpse of the fisherman's face, and though it was only quarter-on, a very strange face it seemed indeed.

Hoping to get a better look at it, he stood there for a few minutes, spying on the man, if you will, as a hunter studies his quarry. But the man's head and body were immobile, his gaze intent as he tried to see through the swirling water. Only his hands moved, and they caught Father's regard, for he fished in a way Father had never seen before. His right hand held a rod of polished wood about four feet long. On its tip was a ring, half an inch or so across. His left hand held the line, which passed through the ring. As he retrieved line, he used a figure eight motion to wind it about the fingers of his hand. When the lure was in, he cast it with a flick of the short rod, and as the line spiralled easily from his fingers, he could cover most of the pool's area. (Father was much taken by his system, a precursor of the spinning reel, but found when he tried it that it wasn't as easy as it seemed.) Frustrated once more, he set off up the valley. When he returned from his explorations the man was gone, leaving more of the puzzling tracks behind him.

Back at camp he described something of what he'd seen to one of the older residents—or rather, started to. For no sooner had he begun than he was interrupted with, "Oh, you must have met old Peg-leg. You better watch out for him, young fella. Young and tender like you are, he's just apt to skin you out and eat you!" Further questions brought only grins and scurrilous innuendos. Questioning others brought similar responses, and their tenor was that Peg-leg went too

far beyond the bounds of oddity and had best be avoided. Though strangely, no one could come up with a single instance where he'd actually done something wrong!

Father was still no wiser. The name was descriptive, but he didn't see how it could fit. A peg-leg leaves no prints of bare toes! Reluctantly he decided to shelve it for the present. Rather than ask others, he'd find out for himself. But at least he'd ascertained that Peg-leg lived in a cabin of some sort midst the trees and brush near the verge of marsh grass on the other side of Gray Creek. Armed with this information and his own, he began to fish the pools before the falls, and to take strolls along the shore on the other side of the creek.

He had no fear of being skinned and eaten. Father was—without knowing it—a disciple of Isaak Walton. He was firmly of the opinion that anyone so absorbed in angling was likely, if not certain, to be a decent sort of man.

He hadn't long to wait before his efforts bore fruit. Walking up the trail to the falls one evening, rod in hand, he met Peg-leg coming down, carrying a string of smallish trout. There is (was?) a fraternity among men who fish for trout. A code, you might say: one doesn't pass another under such circumstances without a greeting.

"Caught your supper, I see. Nice little string," offered Father pleasantly, trying not to stare too openly at the man before him.

"It'll do, it'll do," returned the other, in a deep, rich voice. "But I only fished one pool. There'll be lots left for you."

Encouraged by this, Father offered, "I saw you fishing at the falls the other day. How'd you make out?"

Peg-leg looked surprised. "You must move like a shadow. I didn't know anyone was near. But I guess I was concentrating too hard on those big trout that live there. No luck, though—too smart for me, as always. I saw I was wasting my time, so I gave up and caught a few little ones like these," half holding up the string of trout.

Peg-leg seemed willing to talk. Judging from the comments of those questioned, it seemed likely that he found few opportunities to do it. Father accepted the gambit, and before long they were chatting in as friendly a fashion as he could have wished. And as they talked, Father took surreptitious stock of the man beside him.

It is the head we see first when we meet someone new, and in any case, Father deemed it impolite to let your gaze wander elsewhere on first acquaintance. But for all that, much as he would have liked to examine Peg-leg's extremities, it was the head that fixed his fascinated eyes. First, the whiskers. It was impossible to ignore the whiskers. He'd seen the like before, but not on a living head. They'd been in a picture supposed to be a faithful rendering of the prirate Blackbeard.

The hair had been allowed to grow about six inches long. Then it had been separated into eight or ten plaits, comprised of smaller strands braided together. About a half-inch from the ends, the plaits were secured by pieces of knotted blue ribbon. Above these, hanging from his upper lip, drooped long, heavy moustaches that framed the corners of his mouth and mingled with his beards. Their last few inches were also plaited and tied with blue ribbon. Bushy eyebrows jutted out below a blue bandana, skull-tight. From beneath this, long strands of hair, plaited for the last half of their length and tied with red ribbons, brushed a pair of massive shoulders. Bushy tufts of hair sprouted from ears below which hung intricately carved hoops of ivory, two inches across.

But it was the colour of Peg-leg's hair that held the eye. How can I describe it? It seems inadequate to say that it was brown, or red, or a strange shade of orange-yellow, for it was none of these things, but all of them together. And though I've done the best I could, I suspect the total effect was indescribable. All of this display ornamented skin so heavily tanned that Father thought Peg-leg may have come from some warmer clime—Spain, perhaps, or North Africa.

In spite of his resolve, Father's gaze lingered over-long.

"You seem interested in my hair. Is it perhaps the colour?" Gold-brown eyes twinkled with mirth.

"I was just thinking," hedged Father diplomatically, "that I've never seen the like of it."

"Indeed you haven't, sir. Indeed you haven't. And I will admit that I'm not entirely pleased with it. You see, the dye from the roots has warred with the stain from the bark, and I am the loser. But it's better than grey. I hate grey hair growing on me. My father had grey hair, and I hated him. I'd have cut his throat if I could, but he was a holy terror, and I was only twelve when I ran off to sea." He laughed heartily at Father's expression. "Don't look so shocked. I only said that I would like to have cut it, not that I did!"

Father had been so absorbed by all this, he'd failed to introduce himself. He hastened to amend his lapse of manners.

"Glad to meet you, Hal, glad to meet you. You can call me Peg-leg. I suspect everyone else does when they talk about me. I like it, it suits me well. They don't say it to my face, though. The fools, they fear the strange. I see fear in their eyes when first they meet me, and

I despise them for it. Sometimes when we cross paths in the woods, I give them reason." Without warning, his face assumed a grimace so fearful that Father almost backed off a step. The eyes rolled back, big teeth showed in a satyr's grin, and the swarthy cheeks creased until the face was scarcely human. Then, swift as a thought, the friendly grin was back. "I saw no fear in your eyes. What makes you different?"

"I don't call a dog bad until it bites me, and maybe not even then."

"Good answer, good answer," approved Peg-leg. "And what do they say about me down there? I'm sure you asked."

"The general idea seemed to be that if I wasn't careful, you might skin me out and eat me. They seem to think you'll eat anything that swims, flies or crawls."

Peg-leg's laughter echoed from the rocky banks. "I will, I've had to." Memory sobered him for a moment. "All's meat to a hungry man. There were times I'd rather forget..." The grin returned abruptly, not entirely mirthful. "They've learned to keep their dogs at home." Again his manner changed. "What did you think of the tracks I left?"

"Well," said Father, "I've seen a lot of prints, but I've never seen any that puzzled me as much as yours."

"Like to see what made them, would you?"

"Sure would, if it wouldn't trouble you too much."

"No trouble at all. Proud of it, in fact." Perching on a convenient rock, he swung his left leg, bulging with muscle, over his right thigh. The foot flopped oddly, but it took Father a moment to realize that the whole lower leg, from where the trouser was stagged off above the knee, was carved of wood. A grey sock, cut off at the ankle, made the calf muscle look real, and the bare wooden foot had the uppers of a shoe painted on it. Coming out of the instep was a carven goat's foot; on either side of it the hinged wooden foot and heel, spring-loaded, moved up or down.

Father's obvious delight at this strange construction dissolved such vestiges of awkwardness that might have remained between them, and before much longer they were on their way to becoming friends.

Peg-leg suggested they catch a few more trout to add to the string, so there'd be a meal for the two of them, which they did. And when they had enough, they set off down a little trail that led to Peg-leg's house.

He was an excellent cook, the meal—brook trout, fried potatoes and wild greens—quite up to Father's standards. And afterwards, as dark stole stealthily out of the trees, they sat and talked. And Father heard much of things he'd always loved to read about: wars, and naval battles, privateers and strange sea creatures, and savage lands he knew he'd never see.

But none of that has come down to me, and as I can't report on their conversing, but heard only bits and portions of it as Father remembered (for it was never one of his stories), I'll summarize what I know. Of course, not all of it was told on that first evening.

Peg-leg was older than he seemed. He'd been born in Portugal in about 1860, which would make him about sixty years old when Father met him. He'd lost his leg in the Boer War of 1898; it was amputated by an army surgeon, without anaesthetic, as usual. The blue bandana covered a scar made by a cannonball. As he said, "It's not many who can say they were hit by a four-pounder and lived to brag about it."

He'd shipped out as cook on a whaler, because with only one leg he was no longer considered to be an "able seaman." He was good with his hands, and when he tired of whaling he became a ship's carpenter on the Japan run.

Father, a good man with his hands himself, was much impresssed by Peg-leg's workmanship. His little house was built of poles and split cedar, left rough on the exterior, but planed to a glossy finish within. Put together almost entirely by dovetails and wooden pegs, it reminded Father of the sort of construction Jack Hammond liked to use.

Most of the projecting surfaces—shelf edges, cupboard doors, etc.—and all of the furniture, he'd finely carved, to Father's great admiration. On the shelves were many books he'd bound in leather, and all about the room were scrimshaw, the best Father had ever seen.

One evening he admired Peg-leg's earrings. "What kind of ivory is it?" he asked. "It takes a nice finish."

Peg-leg unhooked one, held it out with a sardonic smile. "No ivory. Part of my leg-bone. I got the surgeon to saw me off a piece. Couldn't see good bone go to waste."

Father took it gingerly and admired the carving, then handed it back, feeling vaguely squeamish and embarrassed by the feeling.

"If you like that, you should like this." Peg-leg took a pipe from a rack of five or six and passed it to Father. "It's part of the knuckle bone. I spent a lot of time on that one." The pipe was an exquisite piece of work. The bowl was made from the rounded part of the bone end, while the shaft—split, steamed and bent—formed a graceful stem. This was ringed with narrow bands of gold to hold the sections tight, and the mouthpiece was of gold. Father praised the work and handed it back, with an inward shudder he hoped didn't show.

They met often that spring and summer, sitting in rocking chairs, sipping wine made from salal and blueberries, for Father would take a glass of wine on occasion if he thought it good. Peg-leg would stroke the big feral white cat he'd half-tamed, while they discussed the world's ways and told each other stories. Peg-leg had an endless fund of stories, and by then Father had quite a few of his own. And the year grew older.

In early fall the cutthroat trout come up from the sea to feed on salmon eggs, and to lay their own. Some had grown very large, and from his perch on the sloping log, Peg-leg had spotted an exceptional one hounding the spawning salmon, and he greatly coveted it. He sat for hours casting his lures in vain. For it was gorging on salmon eggs—his lures held no appeal.

Peg-leg vowed he would catch that fish, and bent all his considerable talent to that end. After a few failed attempts he began to study motion in water, and when he was satisfied, he applied the skill he'd used to carve such marvellous scrimshaw to the construction of a lure of such fatal attraction that no trout could resist it. He showed the result to Father.

"It was a marvel," he reminisced. "He'd made a little jointed fish of bone, about three inches long. Each short section was joined to the next by thin wire, and it was flexible as a minnow. There were little angled fins that caught the least bit of current, and gave the thing a staggering, limping motion, like an injured minnow. Two hooks hung from the middle sections, and he'd painted the sides, back and belly in different patterns of red and yellow and silver. To top it all, he'd glued on some strands of white cat hair to wave and quiver as it moved. I don't think even old Charlie's lure could have topped it." He hesitated, then, "I don't know, maybe that's going a bit far. But it was a marvellous thing he'd made, just the same."

Said Peg-leg, "I'm going to take it to the pool first thing in the morning. I'll stay all day if I have to, but I'm going to get that fish! Come around when you've finished work, and I'll cook it for supper."

At five o'clock that evening, Father set off for the cabin, carrying an apple pie he'd made for dessert. But when he came out into the little clearing, the chimney showed no smoke, there was no answer to his knock, and Peg-leg's fishing pole wasn't in its accustomed place. He entered and set the pie on the table while the white cat glared at him from the sill of the open window. As he went swiftly up the trail to the falls, Father had that hollow feeling under the breastbone that we get when we're apprehensive of something bad.

He ran the last few hundred yards to the pool as the falls roared ominously in the evening stillness. He burst through the bushes bordering the creek below the pool, but there was no familiar figure perched partway up the log, nor, as swift glances showed, to be seen elsewhere. Then his heart lurched, and he felt sick inside. Projecting from the swirling water was Peg-leg's wooden foot. The pool he'd loved so much had taken him for its own.

He hesitated, wondering what to do. He didn't fancy swimming out into that grim, dark water to bring the body ashore. He'd have to get a rope to snare it. He stood watching the leg as it followed the circling water. Around it went, under the falls, to disappear and rise again. A chunk of wood thrown in didn't act that way. The body must be caught in a deeper current.

He wondered what had happened. He remembered that Peg-leg had said he couldn't swim. Most men of the sea never learn the skill. But he was a powerful man, shoulders and arms lumped with muscle.

Surely he could have clawed his way to shore somehow. But the leg, carved from light cedar, would have held his hips high while the muscled shoulders would have submerged his head. He'd have been swept under the falls before he could think what to do. The battering water would have forced him down into turbulence robbed of its buoyancy by entrapped air. Even a good swimmer could drown if caught unprepared in such a manner.

He watched the leg as round it circled, under the falls, out of sight, long pause, up again a dozen feet away. He felt a sense of loss, but little sorrow. Peg-leg wasn't a man to grow old and die in bed. He'd spoken of this contemptuously, calling it "straw death," the Viking term. He hated sickness and despised weakness, and wished he'd died in combat. He'd have been satisfied with this. Father turned to go. Peg-leg was on his last, long journey.

He trotted down the trail. Dark was still hours away. He'd better let the police know. Major Sutherland became quite irritated if he wasn't the first to be informed of an accidental death. Chiefly because, as he'd once said, it wasn't always an accident.

At the beach he went to the camp's office, from whence led a strand of wire that went to the switchboard at Sechelt. The Major was home. In his usual decisive manner he told Father, "Wait there. I'll bring a couple of men right away. You can find some rope while you're waiting."

He was as good as his word. In less then half an hour his boat drew alongside the camp float and the Major and two men, one carrying a stretcher, came ashore. Another half hour saw them at the falls, the leg still endlessly circling.

"Well, Malcolm," said the Major. "You're the swimmer. Strip off and fetch him in."

"Not me," came the emphatic answer. "You couldn't pay me enough to go in there."

"Me neither," said the other, without being asked, shaking his head vigorously.

"Someone could go up the log with the rope and snare him as he goes by," suggested Father. The man named Malcolm took on the task because he was the best swimmer (save Father, but he was having none of it). On only the second cast the leg was snared. Malcolm threw the rope end to the others, and they hauled Peg-leg's body into the shallows.

So graphic was what they saw, that the effect can't properly be described: it was the stuff of nightmares. Peg-leg, bent double, his face a mask of rage, teeth grimacing, had both hands clasped around the stump of his wooden leg, as if he'd been trying to climb it to the surface. He may have been attempting to take it off, but the straps fitted snugly and even on dry land weren't easy to undo quickly.

While they were looking at the still-submerged body, none wanting to be the first to touch it, the good leg started twitching, a curious jerky movement. Someone burst out with "My God, look, he's moving!"

It certainly appeared so, but Father looked more closely and thought he saw the reason for it, and a glimpse of flashing scales confirmed his guess. Peg-leg's rod was close beside the leg, held there by its tangled line. And on the line, securely hooked, was a big cutthroat trout, surely the one for which Peg-leg had lusted. In death, he'd won. Or had the trout won? There was no way to tell if the trout had taken the lure as the body dragged it through the water. Or if the excitement of the strike had toppled Peg-leg from the log so that the trout had caused his death.

They pulled him ashore and Father took up the line. The exhausted fish came in with scarcely a struggle. It was a magnificent sea-run cutthroat, as fine as Father had ever caught. His practised eye estimated it to be over five pounds in weight. He twisted the hook out of its jaw and let it swim away.

"What did you do that for?" protested Malcolm.

"Would you eat it?" Father asked.

A pause, then, "No-o, I don't suppose I would." (Strange how fastidious we can be when death is involved.)

"Straighten him out," ordered the Major, "so we can put him on the stretcher."

But try as they would, that they could not do. Peg-leg's considerable muscles were as rigid as his wooden leg. "Stiff as a board," as Father put it. Made that way, I suppose, by dying in the cold water.

Though Father always maintained that he'd put out such titanic efforts to survive that his mind had locked his muscles into a state that survived his death.

What were they to do? No one wanted to shoulder two hundred pounds of soaking-wet body. One suggestion was that they leave him there until the muscles relaxed. The major vetoed that; some meat-eater might find him there.

Finally it was decided that they'd tie him beneath the stretcher and take turns carrying it on their shoulders. That worked tolerably well, but the head swung and the braids flopped. It must have been the strangest sight that trail had ever seen. Said Father, "If Peg-leg was watching from somewhere, how he would have enjoyed the sight.!"

Death by accident was the verdict of the law. Peg-leg was duly buried and soon forgotten, except by Father and those others who'd been there. But the pool became known locally as "Peg-leg's pool," and as time passed it gained the reputation of being haunted.

A group of youths seeking a thrill resolved to spend the night there. They came back next morning visibly shaken, vowing that never would they do *that* again! Questioned, they spoke of noises they didn't like to talk of, or even think about. But then, anyone who's slept by a waterfall knows that they make strange noises, especially in the night.

Viking's Way

This is the last story in the last book of the trilogy about my father and his times. I left it until now because I think it brings the series to a fitting end.

Father forbade me to speak of it, for reasons that remain unclear to me, but that he thought sufficient. I've weighed his prohibition at some length and have decided not to obey it. I gave no word, nor any assurance that I would heed his stricture. I am almost as old now as he was when he died, old enough to make my own decisions and to stand by them. It is my story now, and I will tell it.

• • •

Father was working then at Vancouver Bay in Jervis Inlet. The timber was good, the trees large, the loads heavy. Well up the valley, the loggers came upon a draw that held a grove of Douglas fir of remarkable size.

These antedeluvian monsters were the oldest trees anyone had ever seen. But just how old remained a mystery, for the growth rings were so narrow in some places that they couldn't be counted. The trees were so old that their bark, usually a foot or more thick on large fir and tough as cork, had sloughed off until there was only a few inches of it, soft and scaly, and the ground was knee-deep in flakes of bark. Father had measured one tree at seventeen feet across the stump, and there were others nearly as large. Somewhere in the house there is a photo of the end of a log boom, seventy-two feet wide. In it the logs are tightly packed—all seven of them!

Loads of such weight placed great strain on the equipment. One of the first casualties was the motor of the loading machine, which, to move the logs a few feet at a time had to be revved to such speeds that in protest it sent a connecting rod through the side of the block. There was nothing to replace it with, and work came to a halt.

Father was sent on an urgent mission to procure another, for he knew of a truck engine at Pender Harbour that he thought could handle the job.

He set off immediately, but the tasks of locating the owner, buying the motor, transporting it to the dock and loading it on his boat took much time. It wasn't until the middle of the next day that he was ready to return to camp.

His friend Charlie, the old Indian, the mentor of his youth and Cliff's, was there on his boat. Father was surprised to see how frail the old man looked. From his talk it seemed that he spent more time now tied at one dock or another than wandering the coast as he'd done in the past. His boat, too, showed signs of decrepitude, though it was probably seaworthy enough.

Yet though his hair was now only wisps of silver threads, the old man was spry as a cricket, and his mind alert as ever. He was much interested in the manoeuvring of the heavy engine from the dock to Father's boat, and he entertained himself—and Father—with derogatory comments about the competence of those involved. Several times he groaned audibly at the ineptitude displayed, and covered his eyes with his hands that he might avoid the sight of it.

With the engine loaded and tied down, Father started his own, but before untying his lines, he remembered that when he'd docked, there'd been an unfamiliar sound when he'd reversed. He tried reverse, then neutral, forward and back to reverse... Something went *clunk*, and the gears made expensive grinding sounds. He shut the engine off. He'd be going nowhere with it for a while.

"That sounds bad," judged Charlie.

"Worse than you think," returned Father. "I can fix it, but every hour I'm away the camp's shut down. They're depending on me to get this engine to them. Do you know of anyone around who has a boat

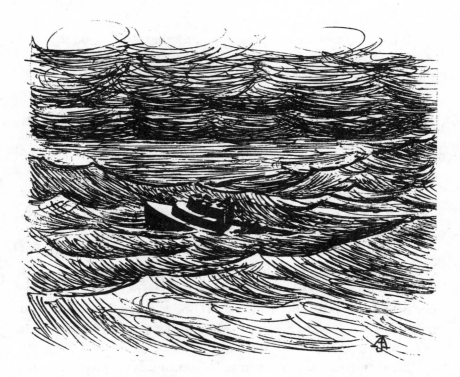

I can hire?" For the boats that usually harboured there were away fishing.

Charlie shook his head sadly. "It's bad to be old," he mourned. "Old and useless. What have I done that you should treat me like this?" And, at Father's puzzled look, "What are friends for, if not to help in times of trouble?" At Father's look of doubt and irresolution, "Put the little engine on my boat, and we will go, and you will be their hero!"

Only half persuaded, Father examined the old craft carefully. The deck was not strong, but if he put a few planks on it to hold the engine . . . He opened the hatch and lowered himself into the hold. The deck beams had some dry rot, but they'd do. The cedar planks of the sides and bottom were sound, but soft. His knife point went in the width of a fingernail, but not easily. Most of the ribs were sound. The stuffing-box was leaking, but stuffing-boxes always leaked. He climbed back on deck.

"Satisfied?" asked Charlie.

"It'll do, I guess. But why don't you fix that stuffing-box?"

"Only exercise I get, pumping out the water," came the prompt answer.

"How's the engine?"

"Start it and see for yourself."

So Father did, and it sounded reliable enough. Charlie often neglected what he considered non-essentials, but he made sure the engine ran.

"She'll do. I'll get some planks to put it on." The glow of pleasure on the old man's face gave Father a satisfaction he hadn't expected, and made him very glad he hadn't had to say no.

He went up to the store, where he found some short cedar two-by-twelves. A few ends had to be trimmed, but that made them fit more snugly. With some difficulty they pried and levered the engine from one deck to the other, but Father was good at that sort of thing, and they managed. It wasn't as easy to find secure ties on Charlie's boat as on his, but that too was managed.

Charlie's gas tank was—as usual—almost empty. That was soon remedied, but Father checked the oil and found it resembled black molasses more than lubricant. It should have been a few minutes' work to change it, but the oil-drain plug was corroded, and declined to be removed. Such is the way of boats; Father persevered, and overcame.

Throughout all this, a southwest squall had blown in from the gulf, bringing strong gusts of wind and rain. Dark was only a couple of hours away; Father looked at the racing clouds and judged, "This squall should be over by the time we leave in the morning."

"Listen to you," scoffed Charlie. "Leave in the morning. Is this a man that's in a hurry? They are waiting for you to come. The squall will be over by midnight. We will leave now. Don't you trust old Charlie to guide you through the night?"

Father considered this carefully. The trip would take about six hours, perhaps more if the tide was against them. It would be good to be there by morning, so the engine would be ready when the crew went to work. Charlie was weather-wise. If he said the wind would die, it likely would.

"We'll leave at dark," he decided. "That'll give the wind time to go down before we get to the worst stretch. I hope you're right about it."

"Old Indian always right," said Charlie smugly.

Night found them heading up Agamemnon Channel, and true to Charlie's prediction the wind went down before midnight. Or rather, it changed direction, and the rolling swells diminished. But the fitful light from a half moon obscured by roiling clouds was suddenly augmented by a lightning flash, and Father said abruptly to Charlie, who was steering, "Better head for shelter. I don't like the look of that."

"We can weather it," said Charlie serenely. "You should be more calm, if you wish to grow as old as me. Worry is bad for you."

"It's going to turn norther, do you want to buck into that? If we go along the shore where we saw the creature, it'll miss us."

So Charlie swung the wheel over and they headed for the shore just past Hotham Sound, where at need, Goliath Bay would afford them shelter.

But the weather wouldn't wait for them to get there. A savage gust of north wind made the spray scud, and from the tumbled clouds the lightning was getting brighter, while thunder rolled above them and echoed from the hills.

There had been phosphorescence in the water since they'd left the dock, but now they were in a stretch where colliding currents had brought the little creatures together in enormous numbers, and the spray threw quantities of them on every surface, including their own. And they stuck where they might, glowing like tiny blue lamps at every shock.

The wind was howling down upon them, whistling eerily as it met the stay-wires of the mast, and the boat began to plunge into the swells rolling down from Prince of Wales Reach. Father took the wheel from Charlie as sheets of water began to come over the cabin from the bow. A strong gust tore away the canvas cover protecting the engine, and it disappeared into the dark. The swells were growing by the minute and, as the old boat came off one, it crashed heavily into the next. Father knew the hull wouldn't stand such shocks for long.

He looked to where Charlie stood bracing himself in the hatchway. His hat was gone, his thin hair matted to his head. He was laughing, as the spray lashed his face.

"Charlie," he called above the wind. "Take it for a bit. I'm going to cut the engine loose. It's too much for her."

The old man smiled an elfin smile. "Foolish boy," he said, reverting to the manner of speaking he'd used when the boys were young. "Make fuss over nothing. Boy not be afraid, Charlie take good care of him. We go on long trip, see new places." But he came and took the wheel, feet wide-braced for balance on the lurching deck.

The thunderstorm was above them now. By a lightning-flash Father saw a waterspout form from the scudding spray, only to be blasted into vapour when a lightning strike found it. He wrapped one arm around a stay-wire and groped in a wet pocket for his knife. It wasn't needed. A heavy shock jolted the boat so hard that one of the eye bolts holding the engine tore out of the wood. The quarter-ton of metal rolled, tore out the other, hit the deck just forward of the hatch, and crashed through it into the hold. It landed top of the propellor shaft, which bent under the impact and jammed, stalling the labouring engine.

Father crawled to the hole and lay on his belly, trying to see if the hull was damaged. He thought he heard water running but it was hard to be certain in the noise of the storm. Abruptly he felt odd, as if his ears were buzzing. He put it to lying there with his head in the hold, so he drew himself up and crouched on his hands and knees, feeling the hair prickling on his scalp and neck. He felt a tension, a sense of foreboding, as a hazy blue light glowed from the mast top. Then the world exploded in a blaze of light.

The mast burst into splinters as the charge coursed through it, and the iron stay-wires glowed bright red for an instant before they flashed into incandescence. That was the sight, etched into his mind, that Father would remember most clearly. Half-blinded and more than half-deaf, he clambered up the heaving deck to where Charlie lay in a heap under where the wheel had been. He tugged at the huddled form, surprised at how light it was, and stretched it on its back across the deck. One cheek was gashed and bloody, but there was no other damage he could see. He checked for life, knowing it was futile. His old friend had gone on that last trip alone.

The boat had broached, but the weight of the engine on the keel kept it from capsizing. Noticing the eerie quiet, he saw that the wind had lulled, and though lightning still flashed and thunder rolled, it was a quarter-mile away, and sporadic. Already the swells were easing. As fast as it had come, the storm was over.

Water sloshed in the hold, and the deck was noticeably closer to the water. The old boat wouldn't stay afloat much longer. It too was on its last trip. Burdened with the weight of two engines, it would go down like stone.

He took Charlie's frail form in his arms and, balancing carefully, carried him to his bunk and tied him there with a few turns of line. He didn't want his friend's body to come floating ashore somewhere. The cabin was full of the smell of coal oil: the glass jug must have broken. That was good. He'd light it. His friend would have a Viking's funeral. Charlie had always liked stories about Vikings.

But he put the thought from him, attractive as it was. People lived along the Egmont shore and at Doriston, only a few miles away. A fire might be seen, the alarm raised. No one ignored a boat on fire, and he wouldn't take the chance of being responsible for a rescue effort. Besides, the boat would sink before a decent blaze could get started.

He took a last look around, then went to the stern where Charlie's little skiff was tied securely across the stern well. He'd have no trouble reaching shore. The swells were rolling smoothly now; he'd be as safe as if the sea were calm.

The stern well was nearly full of water, and the deck awash each time the boat rolled. He launched the skiff, unshipped the oars, rowed away a hundred feet or so and sat there watching in the moonlight. Little more than the cabin was showing now.

He didn't have long to wait. Stern first, Charlie's boat slipped gently under the surface. In the space of a breath, it was gone.

Father felt a sense of .peacefulness, a sort of tranquility that surprised him at first. But not for long. Charlie had been ready for the journey. His sendoff was fitting. There'd been fire and water. It was the Viking's way.